Koomera Crossing: Now and Then

At the present time, Ruth McQueen is in her seventies. Ruth's heir, her beloved grandson Kyall, has fulfilled her every hope and dream. She loves him so much he can move her to tears, when she hasn't shed a tear in all the years she's been widowed.

Kyall will succeed her. Ruth can die happy. Kyall will marry well—a young woman Ruth approves of from an "exceptional" family. Since his early teens Kyall's had all the girls falling madly in love with him. Girls from the right side of the tracks.

Only once did Kyall cross over into forbidden territory. It was about sixteen years ago…. This wasn't the first time Ruth tampered with others' lives, but it wa̲s̲ t̲h̲e̲ w̲o̲r̲s̲t̲. She retains disturbing images of that p̲a̲...

N............................in. Ruth McQueen is ....en if they come in th.............................uth won't have her b............................verything she did, she did for him.

What does it matter that Kyall and Sarah Dempsey grew up together? That they formed a bond Ruth tried hard to destroy? For a grown woman to hate a mere child is demeaning. But it happened, and that hatred will continue unabated into the future.

In the end, Sarah brought the whole unhappy business to a halt. She got pregnant….

Dear Reader,

I'm currently involved in an exciting new project: a series of five books centered on the Outback town of Koomera Crossing in the Channel Country of far southwest Queensland, my home state. It's an endlessly fascinating, unique part of Australia—a riverine desert on the fringe of the Wild Heart, which is what we call the vast 56,000 square miles of fiery red sand at the continent's center. There are no permanent waters in the great Simpson Desert, but the Channel Country—by virtue of its natural irrigation system, a mighty filigree of tree-lined watercourses, billabongs, lagoons and swamps—is home to the nation's cattle kings.

The Channel Country, even to other Australians, is as remote as the far side of the moon. This remoteness, the loneliness, the savage beauty and the overwhelming sheer empty vastness give the Never Never its glamorous mystique. Often described as one of the world's harshest environments, the "Red Center" is transformed into paradise after rain. No one who has ever seen the incredible desert gardens, mile upon mile to the horizon, could ever forget such a sight.

My KOOMERA CROSSING stories are all set in this area. They are about the people who have been born and bred in the great Outback and will never leave it, and the people somehow damaged by life who find their way there, desperate for answers in the peace and freedom of the Outback. This is the land of the dreaming. Of miracles.

My first book in the series, *Sarah's Baby*, a Superromance novel, is about a young woman raised in this Outback town who returns after many years of banishment as resident doctor at Koomera Crossing Bush Hospital. Sarah's memories of her hometown are both glorious and devastating. Her journey home to Koomera Crossing, courageously undertaken, has far-reaching effects—far beyond anything she has imagined. Not only does fate give Sarah the chance to rebuild her shattered life, it steps in to reinforce what we all surely know: lies cannot be lived forever....

Margaret Way

Sarah's Baby
Margaret Way

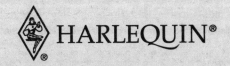

TORONTO • NEW YORK • LONDON
AMSTERDAM • PARIS • SYDNEY • HAMBURG
STOCKHOLM • ATHENS • TOKYO • MILAN • MADRID
PRAGUE • WARSAW • BUDAPEST • AUCKLAND

ISBN 0-373-71111-5

SARAH'S BABY

Copyright © 2003 by Margaret Way, Pty., Ltd.

Sarah's Baby

PROLOGUE

Koomera Crossing
Outback Queensland
Australia

THIS IS THE TOWN. About as far off the beaten track as one can get. Roughly a thousand miles from the dynamic cosmopolitan cities of the continent's seaboard, where the bulk of the population lives. This is the Australian outback. The Never Never where the power of nature prevails and love for the ancient landscape suffuses life. It's what makes the outback unique.

Here the creeks run dry or ten feet high, bursting their banks and spilling their iridescent green waters across the fiery red sands. It's either drought or flood. One follows the other without break. But when the floods recede? The drought-ravaged country is transformed into a wildflower-swept paradise.

The red plains, parched and quivering under the all-powerful sun, are overnight transformed into a blindingly beautiful undulating ocean of brilliant yellow and white as zillions of paper daisies sprout with astonishing momentum from the reenergized soil. The lonely sun-scorched desert tracks, once trod by brave explorers and their chosen men, are obscured by a mantle of pure magic. Exquisite ephemeral plants create a kaleidoscope of colors—the scarlet des-

ert peas, the felty bellflowers, woolly foxgloves, the suc-
culent pink parakeelya, the fluffy lilac mulla mullas and the
lime pussy tails, the native hibiscus and the thickets of pink
and white rain lilies, the pure white Carpet of Snow that
so gloriously embroiders the bloodred sands. These are the
miraculous sights that give the Inland its fascination. These
glimpses into heaven affect the lives of outback people like
the hand of God upon their hearts. They can live in no
other place on earth, despite all the hardships and isolation.
They will never leave and if they do, they always return.

The town of Koomera Crossing is on the desert fringe.
In the early days of settlement, it was called O'Connor's
Waterhole in memory of one of the most romantic and fool-
hardy of explorers, Sweeney O'Connor, a young Irish adventurer who once enjoyed a spell in an English jail before
being put on a boat to Botany Bay, where the good colo-
nists were shocked by his howling hotheadedness and lu-
natic ideas.

O'Connor, to no one's surprise, all but perished on the
site of the town. This was in the early 1800s when he was
well into his doomed trek to find the fabled inland sea.
Many Europeans in those days were convinced that a sea
lay at the continent's center when it really lay underground
in the Great Artesian Basin. Only O'Connor's fervent
prayers—and he later confessed he had to dig deep to remember any—and the intervention of a great thunderstorm
plucked him from the greedy arms of death. Life-giving
water filled the dry creek bed where he and his faithful
Indian sepoy, Gopal, had made camp, along with their four
camels and small herd of goats. Ironically, the lot of them
nearly drowned in the flash flood, although they emerged
on dry land, smiling and blessing their various gods.

Instead of the inland sea O'Connor had boasted he would
swim in, he found a land of savage grandeur, blazing heat,

vivid color and monstrous rock formations that had the power to undergo spectacular color changes. To O'Connor's eyes, it was "the most violent, most bizarre environment on God's earth" until it was refreshed and reborn by rain. Hell and paradise as a matter of course.

That long-ago thunderstorm saved O'Connor's life although he was to die at the age of twenty-nine, a scant two years later with an Aboriginal spear sunk deep in his belly. A tragic end, the more so since he'd left behind someone he loved with a baby kicking in her womb.

When the fledgling sheep stations started to prosper and the settlement developed into a service town, O'Connor's Waterhole, already elevated to O'Connor's Crossing, reverted to its Aboriginal name. *Koomera* refers to a stopping place with plenty of *moojungs* (birds), *nerrigundahs* (berries) and a rock pool or waterhole *(koomera)*. So Koomera Crossing became a place of safety and promise. A place where a man had the opportunity to make a new life for himself, where he could raise a family. Or hide. These were the men who broke rules. Men who rebelled against the confines of the city. These were the adventurers and the visionaries and—it has to be said—a few out-and-out villains.

At the present time, some fifteen hundred people call this outback shire home. A relative handful of people with vast, majestic, open spaces to themselves. Everyone in town knows what everyone else is doing; at least they all like to think they do. In any event, gossip whips around Koomera Crossing like the wind in a dust storm. It's always that way in a bush town, but the community is closely knit, its members unfailingly supportive of one another in time of need.

The town is located more than one thousand miles northwest of the state capital of Brisbane. It continues to serve this important sheep- and cattle-raising region as a vital transportation point.

Koomera Crossing has a mayor, a rich woman and handsome, with her thick shock of hair cut like a man's. Enid Reardon, born McQueen. Enid is a forceful, energetic, outspoken woman who's spent her life trying to live up to her mother, the matriarch Ruth, but will never make it. Enid, for instance, has never done an unthinkable thing. Ruth has.

The McQueens are one of the oldest pioneering families in this vast area, and they all but own the town. The town geographically comes under the heading of the Channel Country. This is an extraordinary part of the world—riverine desert, quintessential outback. Deeper into the southwest pocket, even more remote, is the home of the country's cattle kings, with their giant sprawling stations that carry the nation's great herds.

The Channel Country is immense. Seemingly without end. There, one cannot escape the untamability of the land or fight its powerful allure. To the Aborigines, the Channel Country is a region of magic and mystery rich in Dreamtime legend, many parts of it capable of inspiring fear. The area covers at least one-fifth of the state and is more than twice the size of Texas. The name—Channel Country— refers to the great complex network of braided, interconnecting water channels, billabongs, lagoons and creeks, through which the Three-Great-River system, the Diamantina, Georgina and Cooper's Creek, make their way to what remains of that fabled lake of prehistory, Lake Eyre. Known as Katitanda to the Arabana, Tirari and Kujani desert tribes who won't go near it. The lake fills rarely, to the wonderment of man, beast and bird. Only twice in the twentieth century, in 1950 and 1974. Its surface, all four thousand square miles of it, is mostly covered by a glittering pinky-white ''polar'' salt crust, some fifteen feet deep.

It's as incongruous as the pack ice it resembles in the red heart of the desert.

Ruth McQueen, already halfway to being a law unto herself, saw the lake fill in 1950 when, as a young woman, she and her husband, Ewan, took a joyride over it in their private plane. Ewan was destined to die in a plane crash years later, when his Cessna came down in very turbulent conditions just outside Alice Springs in the Red Centre. Flying is a tricky business in the outback. The air is so hot there's little or no feeling of buoyancy, of riding the air currents. It's almost as if an aircraft could suddenly plunge like a meteorite out of the cloudless cobalt sky.

This was the fate of the much-loved, much-respected Ewan McQueen, leaving the devastated Ruth alone with two children, Stewart and Enid, to rear. But Ruth is a great survivor. As soon as she could cope with her grief, she took over the reins, running the family's historic sheep station with all the energy and skill her husband had. A task nothing short of heroic, but Ruth employs something Ewan had never used: a ruthless hand forever poised in the air, ready to slam someone down. This has earned her many enemies. Something else Ewan McQueen never had.

So the McQueens are held in love and hate. They are the most powerful and influential family in the Northwest, their historic run, Wunnamurra, named after the fiercely predatory eagle hawks that patrol the desert skies. The founder of their dynasty, Dougray McQueen, a Scot who had traveled the world, noticed these birds of prey when he first made camp on the site of his future homestead. This was in the mid-1800s. A man of great strength, McQueen flourished in the harsh, remote environment, so different from anything he'd ever known or ever seen on his travels. It all but defied logic that he chose to build his life there.

His first bride, Fiona, a cousin and a young woman of

breathtaking beauty, was brought out from Scotland to
Dougray's immense pride and joy. Fiona lost her reason
within a year of arrival. The heat as good as killed her. The
isolation! The primitive, overwhelming landscape! The
strange indigenous people with their glistening black skin
and incomprehensible language. The terrible taste of creek
water. The food. The millions of strange birds with their
strange names—kookaburras?—their brilliant plumage,
their strident cackles and mournful calls. The deprivations
a gently reared young woman was forced to endure. It was
all too much to bear. Fiona, in a distressed state of mind
and in the absence of her husband, wandered off into the
bush and disappeared without a trace, despite a huge search
that employed the most skilled trackers on earth, the Aboriginals. A number of people over the years claimed to
have seen Fiona wandering the lignum swamps, her long,
curly red hair hanging unkempt and tangled down her back,
face pale and strained, glittery, staring eyes. She wears a
long flower-sprigged dress, the hemline dripping moss and
mud. The claimants were not fanciful people, either, but
iron-nerved family and tough stockmen already familiar
with the eerie nature of the Australian bush and its fore-
boding moods.

Dougray remarried a short time later. He wanted sons.
Another Scottish girl, Eleanor, not nearly so bonny, but full
of fight. This one had the advantage of an adventurous nature. From that point on, with Eleanor willing and able to
take over domestic affairs while producing six children
(two dying in infancy), Wunnamurra prospered. It rose to
a position of great wealth and prestige as Australia emerged
as the greatest producer and exporter of wool in the world.
Getting rich off the sheep's back, as the saying goes. Even
before wool sales went into a decline, the McQueens diversified, raising cattle as well, growing wheat on their

newly acquired properties in the rich highlands of the central Darling Downs, investing in oil and mineral exploration in a state with fabulous resources and tremendous potential for development.

So the McQueens remain big contributors to the state's economy. Their fortune, presided over by Ruth, is substantial. The family always figures in the *200 Wealthiest* list. Enid, the mayor, is democracy in an iron glove. Her CEO, her husband, Max, has been reduced to a peripheral figure after all these years with two dominant women. Max's own family were once wealthy landowners, but a series of financial downturns and the loss of two sons in the Second World War took their toll. Max and Enid have two offspring—the vivid, commanding Kyall, the heir, and his younger sister, Christine. Unable to thrive under her mother's domination and declared disappointments in her, Christine has fled to Sydney to find her own identity and make her own life.

There are other families in the town who make their presence felt. The Logans, the Hatfields and the Saunderses, all represented on the shire council and serving variously as town consulting engineer, finance manager, building inspector and the like. Then there's the town lawyer, dentist, pharmacist, mechanical engineer and the owner of the local pub, Mick Donovan, good-hearted, with a short-tempered wife who's never quiet. There are also the lone police constable (his city-born wife left him, screaming she couldn't stay another moment), town trucker, the plumber, the postie, the baker and the hairdresser. There's the artist Carol Lu, who could make a fortune with her beautiful landscapes if she so wished but clearly doesn't, and the mysterious and exotic Maya Kurby. Kurby isn't her real name. Her real surname is impossible to pronounce, let alone spell. Maya runs the truly excellent ballet school. Then there's the near-

blind violinist, Alex Matheson, who had a nervous break-
down when he was forced to abandon a brilliant career and
now conducts the town's orchestra guild. A man of mystery
is Evan Thompson, who arrived in town a year or so pre-
viously. Evan can fashion anything from wood, but it's obvious to everyone that at some stage of his life Evan
Thompson was "someone," not just a gifted woodworker.
Evan is a big man, with a dark, brooding presence. Of
course, the women of the town are attracted to his good
looks and smoldering dark eyes, but he acts as though he's
had enough of women to last him all his life. Charlotte
Harris (Lottie to everyone) is an extraordinary dressmaker
who could find a job behind the scenes at a Paris fashion
house.

Another important character in the town is the authori-
tative and highly respected Harriet Crompton, a spinster
and the town's lone teacher for the past forty years. Harriet
teaches the children and grandchildren of all the local families until they go away to boarding schools to complete
their secondary-school education. Harriet is no ordinary
woman but a woman of considerable culture (she founded
the town's theatrical society) and fine, upstanding values.
She has almost as much impact on the town as Ruth, of
whom she has been highly critical from time to time; such
is Harriet's standing in the town that Ruth has never been
able to have her removed.

The families of the outlying stations served by the town,
like the Claydons of Marjimba, have their role, too, although these stations, like Wunnamurra, are mostly self-
sufficient, dealing with their own problems and their own
affairs. Great technological advances have made station life
a lot easier, telecommunications and modern media opening
a door onto the world. All these families are admirable
people, but an underlying "cold war" with the McQueens

has been going on for decades. Ruth McQueen has earned a reputation for being absolutely ruthless in business, even when dealing with so-called friends. She is indeed a tyrant and her words are set in stone. Even her family, with the notable exception of Kyall, fear to cross her.

The McQueens are therefore loved and hated for a variety of reasons. Ruth is genuinely hated and perhaps should be. She has done things she had no right to do and all of Ruth's "crimes" are not known. Her grandson, Kyall, on the other hand, is universally admired. He is a splendid figure, striking of looks, clever, egalitarian, resourceful, innovative, with such charisma he appeals to everyone, men and women alike.

The McQueens are the pulse of the town, their money the town's lifeblood. It was Ruth McQueen who fought to get a hospital established in the town. McQueen money funded its construction and outfitting. The town has long boasted a resident doctor, a good one, Joe Randall. He's been there from the beginning, handpicked by Ruth (rumour spread early that he was her lover), but he's now approaching seventy and must retire. Depending on demand, Dr. Randall has up to six nurses to assist him. Nurses are easier to come by than ambitious young doctors, who can't be lured into rural and outback practices. Joe Randall can handle most everything in general surgery, but in the event of serious cases, he brings in the Royal Flying Doctor service. The Flying Doctor service, the "mantle of safety" over the outback, was founded in 1928 by Flynn of the Inland, a Presbyterian minister who saw the urgent need for medical treatment for the people of the region. Doctors from various bases fly almost two million miles a year ministering to the far-flung communities.

The Royal Flying Doctor service, like Joe Randall, has the gratitude of the town. Ruth McQueen shows her gratitude through big donations. Ruth isn't all bad. It's simply that she always has to have her way. Even if it involves playing God with people's lives.

For all her ability, Ruth has a strong vein of megalomania. Not so astonishing in a woman who's had so much power, can lay claim to a fortune, a fine historic sheep station and one of the grandest homesteads in the nation.

Love died for Ruth with her husband. She has never felt close to her children. She's been far too committed to running the station—or such is her excuse. But love sprang to life again when her grandson Kyall, crying lustily, was put into her arms moments after he was born. The great chunk of ice that entombed her heart for so long suddenly thawed. Love she had locked out for years flooded in.

What does it matter if Ruth brushes aside her only son, Stewart, who stands beside her at the foot of his sister's bed? Stewart who is destined, bruised and battered, to surrender his heritage rather than submit to a lifetime of endless clashes with his mother, in which he knows he can only come off second-best. As for daughter Enid? Enid will hang in for her son. At Ruth's insistence, the boy will be known as Kyall Reardon McQueen, an imposition Enid and Max are forced to accept. Kyall is the heir.

In Ruth's view, it is only fitting that he should carry the dynastic name. Indeed, before the boy is barely three, the "Reardon" is dropped as too much of a mouthful. Ruth has her way. Her grandson is Kyall McQueen—just as she has ordained. Kyall is more or less stuck with it, as this is the name the town, indeed the entire outback, becomes used to.

Ruth has never looked in the direction of Max, her son-in-law. As far as Ruth is concerned, she has "kept" him—although for years and years he's worked very hard. Max would never have been allowed into the family except for his impeccable background.

At the present time, Ruth is in her seventies. She still holds Wunnamurra in a tight grip, fearing that if she lets go she might die. And perhaps go to hell?

Ruth's heir, her beloved Kyall, has fulfilled her every hope and dream. She loves him so much he can even move her to tears when she hasn't shed a tear in all the years she's been widowed—including when she received news of the death of her son, Stewart, and his wife in a bus crash in Malaysia. They left a young daughter, Suzanne, safe in a Sydney boarding school. Ruth is her guardian.

But Kyall will succeed her. Ruth can die happy. Kyall will marry well. A young woman Ruth approves of from an "exceptional" family. A young woman who can take her place anywhere. Since his early teens, Kyall's had all the girls, one after the other, falling madly in love with him. Girls from the right side of the tracks.

Only once did Kyall cross into forbidden territory. Ruth never likes to think about that time although the terror of eventual discovery is coiled inside her like a hidden spring. This wasn't the first time Ruth tampered with other's lives, but it was the worst. Ruth would like to say she doesn't fear Judgment Day, but in her heart of hearts she does.

Not that Ruth wouldn't do it all again. Ruth McQueen is used to disposing of threats, even if they come in the form of a fifteen-year-old girl. Ruth won't have her beloved grandson's life ruined. Everything she did, she did for him. Even now she feels no remorse. There are certain laws laid down about who should be admitted into the McQueen family. The Dempseys would never find themselves on the list.

What does it matter that Kyall and Sarah Dempsey grew up together? That they formed a bond Ruth and Enid tried hard to destroy? Tried, but to no avail. For a grown woman to hate a mere child is demeaning. But it happened, and the hatred will continue unabated into the future.

In the end, Sarah Dempsey brought the whole unhappy business to a halt. She got pregnant. Ruth had to work fast to avert a scandal. Sarah's father presented no problem; Jock Dempsey is dead from a spinal injury sustained on Wunnamurra station, where he was an employee, one of the fastest shearers in the McQueen sheds. After that, Sarah's mother, Muriel, took on the running of the town's general store, with twelve-year-old Sarah handling the business side. Sarah is clever. But no match for Ruth. It was up to Ruth, the matriarch, to find a solution.

Sarah was removed from town, weeping bitterly. Her mother, a vulnerable woman, is made to keep quiet. Kyall McQueen is never told. Kyall at sixteen would have given up everything for Sarah. His future, his family. Ruth had to take care of it all. She'd hoped for a miscarriage. Sarah had refused point-blank to agree to an abortion, telling Ruth in a young, ringing voice that nothing and no one could make her get rid of her baby.

So the baby lived.

Ruth knows where she is, one of only three people who do. The fourth has since died of snakebite, although no one knows exactly how the snake, a desert taipan, got into Molly Fairweather's house.

Ruth to this day can't bring herself to admit that the child, already the age her mother had been when she'd stolen Kyall's heart, is her own great-granddaughter. That would take moral courage; Ruth only deals in the physical kind.

Life continues. Nothing goes terribly wrong. Ruth continues making plans, showing a rare smiling face to one

India Claydon, who springs from a good gene pool and will make Kyall an excellent wife.

Then one August afternoon around three o'clock, Muriel Dempsey, Sarah's mother, gives a great cry, calls her daughter's name and collapses behind the counter in her grocery shop, bringing down on top of her a pile of mail.

In the small space of time it takes for her assistant, the town stickybeak, Ruby Hall, to run for help, Muriel Dempsey dies at fifty-six without ever knowing she has a living, healthy grandchild. Muriel has been robbed of the great joy of knowing her only grandchild. Robbed by a cruel woman whose name is Ruth McQueen.

CHAPTER ONE

Waverly Medical Centre, Brisbane

THE SURGERY HAD BEEN chaotic that morning. Winter flu. The time of year no one looked forward to. The epidemic had hit the city in the wake of the August Royal National Show, a huge crowd-pleaser, with plenty of hot sunshine and flying red dust from the show ring to encourage the germs. The patients, coughing, sneezing, searching for tissues, others with their heads firmly buried in magazines, were either waiting for flu shots—injections of the vaccine, which was an attempt to second-guess what strain of influenza would strike or seeking medication to relieve the distressing symptoms. Antibiotics didn't work.

Sarah didn't prescribe them for the flu or a common cold, but she knew she'd always get an argument from some of her patients who thought that only drugs could kill off the virus. These were the days of Be-Your-Own-Doctor, with many a patient discussing his or her diagnosis and suggesting various drugs. Home remedies and bed rest simply wouldn't do. Small wonder the pharmaceutical companies were becoming enormously rich while bacteria became increasingly resistant to the most frequently prescribed drugs. It was a big problem and it worried her.

Around midday things got worse. Pandemonium broke

loose when a three-year-old boy with silky blond hair was brought in suffering severe febrile convulsions.

"Please, please. Where's Dr. Sarah?" The distraught mother registered her terror, appealing to the packed waiting room in general, tears pouring from her eyes.

"It's all right, Mrs. Fielding, you're here now. We'll take care of you." The clinic's head receptionist, Janet Bellamy, a kind, competent woman, closed in on the hysterical mother fast, while her junior, Kerri Gordon, ran for Dr. Dempsey, who had a wonderful rapport with her patients, children in particular. Dr. Sarah was the one everyone wanted to see. Especially the mothers of young children.

By the time Sarah, who'd been preparing to run an electrocardiogram on a male patient with chest pains, rushed into the reception room, the young mother was screaming her fear and desperation. Janet and one of Sarah's female patients, an ex-nurse, were trying ineffectually to calm the young woman and take the lolling, unconscious child from her arms. Another child, a little girl who'd been sitting quietly with her pregnant mother, was sobbing into her hands at this frightening new experience, while her mother placed a soothing, protective arm around her shaking shoulders.

Sarah remembered this wasn't the little boy's first brush with seizures. She had recommended further action at the child's first presentation, but his mother, Kim, had been fiercely against it, no doubt dreading a worse neurological disorder like epilepsy.

At Sarah's appearance, Kim Fielding seemed to gather strength. She stopped screaming when Sarah addressed her and immediately surrendered her only child to Sarah's arms. The frantic look left her eyes and in the examining room she watched calmly as Sarah swiftly administered an anticonvulsant medication. The seizure, however, proved of such severity and duration that Sarah called for an ambulance to take the child to hospital to be admitted for observation. Privately she thought the boy's high fever was only masking a more serious disorder. She grieved for the mother, and the anxious years ahead, squeezing her hand tightly as the young woman climbed into the ambulance to go with her son. These incidents involving children were deeply heart-wrenching for everyone, doctors and patients alike, but for the sake of her other patients Sarah had to refocus in order to deal with her caseload for the afternoon. It didn't help knowing she'd have to tell Megan Copeley the results of her mammogram.

Not good.

Megan's fat-rich, low-fiber diet alone had increased her risk of breast cancer by a factor of six. Despite every warning and every lecture Sarah gave her, she'd been unable to wean herself off it.

"But, Sarah, I can't go without all the foods I enjoy. Neither can my family. Mealtimes would be so dull. Jeff wouldn't stand for it. There's no history of breast cancer in my family, anyway."

There was now. Sadness crept up behind Sarah's fixed resolve to maintain a professional detachment. She could picture Megan sitting opposite her in a state of shock. Megan was only a handful of years older than her. Thirty-five, with two beautiful children. Some days Sarah could hardly bear the terrible burden and responsibility of being a doctor—telling patients their fears were confirmed or breaking totally unexpected bad news. There was no way out of telling the truth, of telling patients that life as they knew it was over. It was her job to help them deal with it. She knew she was a good doctor. She knew her patients liked and respected her, but sometimes she wanted to pull a curtain and hide behind it. To weep.

What Sarah didn't know as she agonized for Megan Copeley and tried to swallow the lump in her throat was that tragedy was about to strike *her*.

Not for the first time. Sarah was no stranger to loneliness, grief and despair. She had walked, talked and slept with it for years. Could she ever put the loss of her own child, her baby, behind her? Never. A mother doesn't suffer a blow like that and continue serenely on with life. Maybe she'd learned a deeper, fuller understanding her patients seemed to recognize, but the grief and the insupportable loss would go on forever.

Baby Dempsey, who had lived only a few hours. She'd already named her in her mind—Rosalind (Rose) after the grandmother she recalled with such love. From time to time, although it was fifteen years ago, she relived the long, empty months leading up to the birth. Hidden away with a middle-aged married couple Ruth McQueen had found. She relived the birth itself, which had taken place in a private clinic. My God, the pain! Her patients didn't have to tell her anything about that, not realizing because of her single status and lack of family that she'd given birth to a child. She remembered the morning after when she'd awakened, wanting to get up, to go to her baby. She'd wanted to tell Rose not to fear, she'd make something of herself. For both of them. *Don't be afraid, my little one. My little one.* There were moments when she could remember nothing but the feel of her baby against her breast. So fleeting a time!

Miss Crompton always told her she had what it took to be anything she wanted.

"You work hard, Sarah, and I see a future far beyond this little outback town. You're one pupil I know in my bones is going to make a name for herself. You have it here." At this point Miss Crompton always tapped her head.

She might've had the brains, but emotionally she'd been frail. At fifteen she'd been made pregnant by the great love of her life, the *only* love, and she was into her thirty-first year now, with all her friends either married or getting married. But she couldn't forget Kyall and the wonder of loving him. His spirit, like their baby's, was locked up inside her. Internalized. She carried Kyall within her, and his presence in her life sometimes seemed so real it was as if he was there, melting her spine with love of him. Other times she hated him with a shocking intensity, lowering herself to curse him to hell. How could he have abandoned her? Kyall McQueen, her soul mate. They'd each shadowed the other, despite the opposition of the all-powerful Ruth McQueen, his grandmother, and his mother, Enid. Even her own mother had found their unique bond a source of great worry.

"You can't be so daft, Sarah, as to think anything good can come of this. They're the McQueens! God almighty, they're royalty to the rest of us. We're nothing, nobodies. It takes all my time to put clothes on your back and shoes on your feet. With your father gone..." Here her mother used to choke on her tears.

In the end, her dear sweet mother had been right. A few secret hours spent together one starry night, one single glorious starry night cocooned in the bush, and she'd gotten pregnant when she was little more than a child. So much for Miss Crompton's pleasure and pride in her! Her whole future ruined. Kyall's splendid future already mapped out. Master of Wunnamurra, one of the country's most historic sheep stations. Kyall had been born not with a silver spoon in his mouth but the whole goddamn service.

Ruth McQueen had snatched her away from the town. Snatched her away from Kyall. Forced her devastated mother to keep her mouth shut about Sarah's baby. But the terrible hurt... How many times had Sarah gone to the phone during those long months of waiting, wanting to scream that she had to speak to Kyall. Of course they'd never have let her. Finally she believed what Ruth McQueen kept telling her. She would destroy Kyall's young life. She would ruin her own chances, having a baby so young.

"My dear, what you need is an abortion," Ruth had told her, voice very calm, very firm. "I can arrange it. Afterward I'll see to it that you have a good education. A private school in Brisbane. You would board. Harriet Crompton keeps telling me ad nauseam that you're a very clever girl, although you haven't been terribly clever about this, have you, my dear?"

She had been shocked at Ruth McQueen's utter callousness, especially when the baby in her womb was Ruth's great-grandchild. She had told the woman what she thought of her murderous suggestion, her own voice every bit as determined as that tyrant's. She believed that abortion was wrong, and she wasn't about to cower before Ruth McQueen. When she first knew she was pregnant, she was wild with panic like some trapped animal, but it didn't take all that long for her to settle down. She felt almost calm. Full of wonder. She would have the most beautiful child ever known to woman. *Her* child. Kyall's child. Her baby would have turquoise eyes like his, olive skin, blue-black curls. Her next baby would look like her. A brown-eyed blonde with a little dimple in her chin.

But she had lost her baby. She only remembered its little body lying on hers, its darling little head pressed into her shoulder while she crooned words of love. She'd felt that rush of maternal love, even exhausted and foggy from all the medication they'd given her. How her baby had hurt her coming out! The pain. Agony, really. She awoke sometimes at night crying out with that remembered pain. It was like being on the rack. The tortures of the Spanish Inquisition. And for what?

She learned the next morning from Ruth. Believing but never quite believing, somehow.

"No!" It was a scream that still resonated in her head. Not surprisingly, Ruth McQueen was much kinder to her than before. She attended to everything. It was McQueen money that sent Sarah to that exclusive boarding school, McQueen money that got her through medical school, though she'd worked hard at part-time jobs to pay as much of her own way as she possibly could. The McQueens were great benefactors. Sarah shivered as she took a breath. To lose her baby was in the order of things, wasn't it? She had never figured in Ruth McQueen's plans. She and her widowed mother were the ordinary people of the town. The baby, hers and Kyall's, had died without her ever telling a soul. Kyall never knew, and her mother had been advised to look on the whole tragic incident as if it had never happened. But her mother wasn't like that. Muriel carried the pain deep within her. Unspoken but never far from her mind.

Ruth McQueen had been grateful. She'd paid for their silence. Sarah never stopped long enough to think about how much she hated Ruth McQueen; she only knew she carried those suppressed feelings like a burden around her neck.

"Can you take a call, Dr. Dempsey?" Kerri was buzzing her, bringing her out of her unhappy reverie. "They say it's very important." From her tremulous tones, it was clear Kerri was still upset by the child's seizure.

"Not now, Kerri." Sarah had a patient with her. Mr. Zimmerman. She was in the middle of writing a referral to an ophthalmologist for him. Mr. Zimmerman had increased fluid pressure in his eyes, which needed looking at. He'd experienced no preceding symptoms, but Sarah knew glaucoma was all the more insidious because blindness presented with little warning. A pressure test really should've been done by the optometrist he'd recently visited. It was imperative at age forty and older.

"It's a Dr. Randall," Kerri persisted. "He's calling from the bush."

Sarah touched the tips of her fingers to her temple. Felt the pulse start up a drumming. "Put him through, Kerri," she said quietly, pushing the script across the table. "There you are, Mr. Zimmerman. You're going to like Dr. Middleton. He's a fine man and a fine ophthalmologist. The best around."

"I just hope I haven't left it too late," said Maurice Zimmerman as he rose to his feet. "You're the first to see a problem."

"Foresee, Mr. Zimmerman. Now the condition has been detected, it can be treated." She smiled encouragingly.

"Thank you. Thank you, Doctor." He sounded immensely grateful.

Joe Randall was still on the line. "Joe, how are you?" Sarah couldn't keep the anxiety out of her voice. This had to be about her mother.

"I have bad news for you, my dear." Joe spoke with infinite sadness. "I can't believe it myself."

Sarah closed her eyes, swinging around in her swivel chair so she wouldn't be facing the door and no one could see her face. "It's Mamma, isn't it."

"It is, dearest girl. With no history of heart disease, your mother has had a massive coronary. By the time I got to her—she collapsed in the shop—she was beyond help. I'm so sorry, Sarah. I grieve for you. Your mother seemed well and happy when she came back from her last visit. How she loved you. How proud she was of your being a doctor. Anything I can do for you—anything—I'll do it. I can make the arrangements if you want. I can do it all.''

''I'm coming, Joe,'' Sarah said, looking fixedly at a small photograph of herself and her mother that stood on her desk. ''I won't be able to get a flight out until tomorrow morning. I should be there by midafternoon. Where's Mamma now?''

''In the hospital mortuary, my dear.'' Joe's voice was low and shaken. ''You'll go to the shop?''

''Where else can I go, Joe?'' Sarah flushed deeply, then went paper-white. ''To the McQueens?''

''Sarah, Sarah,'' Joe answered, his gentle voice torn. ''You can come to me. You know that. I have plenty of room. I'm your friend. I brought you into the world. You could also go to Harriet. She's always been your great supporter. She'd do anything to help you.''

''I know that, Joe.'' Sarah's voice, like her body, was growing faint. She stiffened her back. ''I could never forget either of you and your kindnesses. No, I'll stay over the shop. Thank you for ringing, Joe.'' Sarah couldn't manage another word, so she hung up feeling as though she was dying herself. Swiftly she lowered her head to her knees. She would feel better in a moment. She *had* to feel better. She had things to do. She had to bury her mother. Her mother, her father and her child. She raised a pale, bitter face.

And, God—are you up there? She seriously doubted it. *I'm going to miss her so much!*

IT WAS LATER AFTERNOON when Kyall McQueen touched down at Wunnamurra's airstrip, taxiing the Beech Baron until it came to rest in the huge silver hangar with the station's name and logo emblazoned in royal blue on its roof. He'd been in Adelaide for almost a week, looking after McQueen business interests. Wunnamurra had always been among the nation's finest merino-wool producers, but the family had long since diversified. It was Kyall who had convinced his grandmother to buy Beauview Station, owned by the Youngberg family, winegrowers in the beautiful South Australian Clare Valley. Carl Youngberg, the grandfather and head of the family, had died, leaving the business in crisis. Seeing an opportunity and loving the whole business of wine, Kyall had moved in. The next step had been to secure the services of a great winemaker returning home from years in Europe. It hadn't been easy persuading the man to take over Beauview—he had a top name—but in the end they had stitched up a deal. It was, Kyall knew, a fantastic coup. Already the newly formed company had bounced back with the promise of wonderful wines from their new production manager/winemaker.

There were other developments, too. McQueen Enterprises, of which he was now CEO since his grandmother had vacated the position, had moved into specialty foods, growing olives and mushrooms on their properties on the Darling Downs. To prevent waste and enhance that region's culinary reputation, he had hired top people to open and run a factory making use of tree- and vine-ripened olives and tomatoes rather than see such splendid produce plowed back into the ground. Supermarkets only wanted produce that was picked green, which considerably affected the taste, especially of tomatoes. Now their factory made a whole range of sauces, relishes and preserves; these were proving a big hit in the specialty delicatessens.

So one way or another, he was doing his bit and making life a little easier for a lot of people.

Several members of the extended McQueen family had been brought into the company, boosting the capital. Every time he visited Adelaide, the family arranged a few parties, a mixture of business, pleasure and moneymaking. They were all delighted that he was so good at this. Hell, what else did he have to devote himself to but work?

Yesterday he'd talked over lunch with his great-uncle Raoul McQueen, a prominent merchant banker and Mc-Queen board member, and his uncle's lifelong friend, Senator Graham Preston. It was all very, very discreet, but he could see that they hoped he'd give running for Parliament a try in the not-too-distant future.

They were at his uncle's club, a haven of comfort and privacy, and a natural rendezvous spot for the country's power brokers when in town.

"May I remind you, Kyall, the McQueens have always been involved in politics," his uncle pointed out jovially. "It's time for you to do your share. After all, you've been promoting a whole raft of ideas."

"With which I agree absolutely," said the senator with a little nod of his snow-white handsome head. "If you decide to go in, I can tell you, we'll be right behind you. The party needs young men like you."

"And who exactly would run Wunnamurra?" Kyall had asked laconically, eyeing his uncle, who occasionally spent time relaxing at the family station.

"Didn't you tell me you'd found an excellent overseer? What's his name?"

"Dave Sinclair. Who will be excellent eventually. Right now he still needs a little help."

"But what about Ruth? Enid and Max, for that matter?" his uncle had persisted.

Kyall had answered patiently, "Gran doesn't play the dominant role she once did. You know that, Raoul. Maybe she's still a powerhouse, but she's seventy-five years old."

"You can work it out," his uncle had said then, plucking

at his mustache. "After all, Malcolm Fraser was a sheep farmer before he became prime minister."

"Fraser was a big guy."

"So are you," his uncle had returned, smiling. "You have a wonderful combination of assets. Financial and political expertise, brains, daring, imagination. A great sense of mission."

Kyall had had to laugh. "All of which could get me into trouble, if not destroy me. Those qualities aren't admired in some circles."

"They are in ours." The senator had met his eyes directly. "All we're asking is that you think about it, Kyall. There's no one I'd like to recruit more. It's no disadvantage to be a McQueen, either. The McQueens have had a sense of obligation to their country right from colonial days."

"People put their trust in you," his uncle had put in. "You can talk to anyone about anything—a whole cross-section of people—with equal charm and ease. It's a talent most politicians would give their eyeteeth for. You have a natural aura of authority, but you're not in the least arrogant. You have very real leadership skills. Lord, didn't they say that about you all through school and university? Not only that, you really care about people. God knows how many owe their livelihood to the McQueens. All we're asking you to do is think about it, Kyall. In my view and Graham's, you have the potential to rise to the highest office."

"Praise indeed!" Kyall had answered casually. "But wasn't I raised thinking my future was Wunnamurra? You know that, Raoul."

"There's a great deal more to it—to you—than that. As we've already seen. I've heard you debate political issues with a passion. Don't tell me you wouldn't like to be on the front lines solving the nation's problems. Think about it, Kyall. You've got the brains and the guts to make a difference. This nation is really on the move. You can be part of it.''

For a while their enthusiasm had swept him along. Of course, he'd always been interested in politics. He'd grown up talking politics. His family had always been vitally interested in a fair deal for the man on the land. A number of McQueens had played a role in public life, all of them members of the Country Party, then the National Party now in coalition with the Liberal Party currently in power.

Just as they were parting—the senator had gone off to another meeting—his uncle had asked him about his ''love life.''

''Is Ruth still pushing the Claydon girl at you?'' This with a long, steady look.

''Sometimes it's very hard to get through to Gran.''

''Ever hear from that little one, Sarah? Her father was a ringer, worked in our sheds. I've often wondered. The two of you were quite inseparable at one time. Lord knows how it went down with Ruth and your mother. An incredible pair of snobs. Sarah, ah, yes! As beautiful a creature as I've ever seen.''

At any mention of Sarah's name, anger and pain overtook him. ''Sarah and I lost touch long ago. For her own reasons she wants no part of me. She's been back in town a few times over the years to see her mother. Mostly her mother goes to see her. She's a doctor now. A good one. The Sarah I remember was always flooded with compassion for her fellow man.''

''Sounds like you're still in love with her, my boy. Maybe you should do something about it. Unless she's already married. A lovely creature like that surely would be.''

''No, she's not married, but like I told you, she no longer has the slightest interest in me.'' He didn't mention that the last time he'd seen Sarah at Tracey McNaught's wedding some eighteen months ago, she had turned her beautiful dark eyes on him briefly. For an instant those eyes had fired up as in the old days, then turned to ice, their message unmistakable. *Keep away from me.*

No, Sarah wanted nothing to do with him or the McQueens anymore. Something drastic had happened to her. He didn't know what. For a long time he'd tried to speak to her mother, only to have Muriel Dempsey shake her head and frown, her gaze fixed on some point over his shoulder. It was clear the woman didn't want their friendship to continue. She only saw trouble. But that hadn't stopped her from allowing Sarah to accept a McQueen scholarship to complete her education. From there, Sarah had gone on to med school.

Both his grandmother and his mother had been pleased—and enormously relieved—that Sarah had left.

"Darling, it's all for the best. She's a pretty little thing, but there's something a whole lot better in store for you." His mother had tried to soothe him. "You're a McQueen, after all."

A McQueen, that's me. Why was it some days it felt so bad? Not that he didn't know the reason. The reason was the unceremonious way Sarah had gone out of his life. The last time—the first time—they'd been together, with electricity leaping from her body to his, passion had blazed between them. Its excesses, the sheer glory and excitement of it, had left them both mute. He had always loved Sarah, but nothing like that. That was the one time they'd come together as lovers. Slipped the confines of adolescence and become adults. To this day, he was unable to forget. Unable for all his successes to pick up his life. Get married and be done with it. Have children. What the hell was he waiting for? A genuine miracle?

In all these years, there was no one who could oust Sarah from his mind, although he'd had his share of girlfriends. India Claydon was always around. His grandmother's choice. India seemed to think that fact alone would win the day. India was of his world. She knew all the things he knew. She liked all the things he liked. It was cruel to encourage her, but he'd never really done that. His grandmother was the one who kept pushing for an engagement because she truly believed India Claydon was the right wife for him. He could see it in a way. India was "suitable"; she could deal with being a McQueen wife. The big drawback was that although he was fond of her—he'd known India all her life—he didn't love her. It was going to take him a long, long time to forget what love was like. Love was Sarah. So beautiful, so bright, so real. So complex.

His grandmother said Sarah was ambitious. He knew that; Sarah had plans. Miss Crompton had encouraged her all the way. Sarah was going to make something of her life. She was also going to look after her mother, of whom she was very protective. He came to realize afterward that Sarah had never thought for a moment that she'd marry him.

"Darling boy, Sarah knew only a simple friendship was possible between you," his grandmother had pointed out, love and sympathy in her tones. "Your future is here, though it wouldn't come as a total surprise to me if someday you branched out into public life. You're a McQueen. You have the looks, the name, the money. You can always commute. Trust me on this. Sarah is from a humble background, and the press would always ferret it out. She was thrilled when I offered her the scholarship. So was her mother. For both of them it's a dream come true. Ask Harriet Crompton. Didn't she fill Sarah's head with lofty ideas? It was inevitable that Sarah Dempsey would leave like this.

Surely you know that in your heart. You had a childhood bond, but that's all over. Outgrown, because it's unworkable. I understand these days Sarah's set her mind on becoming a doctor. I'll see to it that she gets help. This is the way life is, my darling, and this is the way it will remain. A door may have closed, but you'll see another one will open.''

Lots of doors had opened over the years, but in all that time Sarah Dempsey had never walked through one. She'd only had a dozen words to say to him on the few occasions he'd seen her. Once it had seemed to him she'd been almost afraid. That didn't fit with the Sarah he knew. Another time she'd told him flatly to stay away. ''Stick with your own crowd!''

Though he had taunted her cruelly in a desperate bid to get at the truth, she'd turned into a cold stranger right before his eyes. Probably he was the only one who had loved, inventing a Sarah who'd never really existed outside his own mind. When she was offered the chance to be someone, Sarah had jumped at it. That was real ambition, just as his grandmother had said. High time he just gave up.

When he arrived at the house he found his grandmother and his mother in the plant-filled solarium. High walls of glass allowed for a superb view of the garden with its huge ornamental fountain and beyond that, rolling plains to the horizon. On a small circular table in front of them sat a sterling-silver tea service with beautiful china. Unless the family was entertaining, the very grand drawing room, too elaborate in his view, and the equally grand dining room were never used. He wondered if either woman knew or cared just how much it cost to maintain a mansion of this size. And that didn't include the home grounds. But then, they were so used to being rich, they didn't care about anything. Or anybody. His father had lived his married life largely unnoticed, left out of family councils, never making inroads into his mother-in-law's affections. Why the hell had he stayed? There didn't seem to be any real feeling between his mother and father, yet the relationship was civil enough, built on the premise that no one could alter the status quo. Marriage was a serious and solemn business entered into for life. Solidarity was important for the family. No scandals. Still, his uncle Stewart had left Wunnamurra behind. So had his sister, Christine, both of them determined to find their own happiness.

Stewart had died in Malaysia. Chris, who looked very much like him, traveled the world as a fashion model. The last time he spoke with her, she was doing some fashion shoot in New York. They always kept in touch.

"I'm never coming back to that bloody place, Ky. You and Dad are the only ones I love."

He knew his sister had sought their mother's love, but his mother had treated Christine less than kindly, forever finding fault. God knows how many times he'd told her as much. Chris, the "perennial disappointment" and, strangely, the "ugly duckling" when she was growing up. By the age of seventeen, just as he'd predicted, Chris had turned into a swan, still hording the endless criticisms her mother had directed at her, often in front of people. Their dysfunctional relationship had made Chris a very angry young woman. But she was fine now. The talk of the town. No one minded a bit that she was six feet tall—it was actually an asset—although their mother had deplored her height for years. He must have recognized very early, probably in the cradle, that he had to be his own person. Neither his grandmother nor his mother had ever come anywhere near pushing him too far, as they had with the others. The fact was, he wouldn't stand for it.

Like Chris, he loved his father, but he wasn't *like* his

father, though they both owed their height to him—he and his father were six-three—their flashing smile and the turquoise eyes. The rest of them, the dark hair, the olive skin and the bone structure, was pure McQueen. He'd had enormous advantages. He knew that. But he was no playboy. He worked extremely hard. One reason was that he liked work. Another? He wasn't happy. So he kept himself occupied.

When he walked into the solarium, the women looked up.

"Hello, darling." Both spoke together. What had he done to deserve this damn-near hero worship? Was it because he was the heir? Didn't they know that didn't matter to him?

He stared at them, silent for a moment. "Hi! What's up?" He was nothing if not observant.

"A bit of news, darling," his mother replied, putting her hand to her thick dark hair, which she wore very short. "Muriel Dempsey died. Apparently she dropped dead in the shop. Just like that."

"Good God!" He felt something like an electric shock. "How awful. She couldn't have been more than fifty-five or -six. What was it, heart attack?" He lowered himself into a chair, his mind immediately and inevitably springing to Sarah.

"So Joe said." Now his grandmother spoke, her voice not quite as strong and self-assured as usual. She'd lost weight recently and suddenly she looked her age, instead of nowhere near it. Only the eyes remained brilliant, sharp and searching. "The extraordinary thing is, I've been thinking about Sarah all day."

"So it was today?"

"Only hours ago."

"How dreadful." He knew genuine grief. For Muriel

Dempsey and for Sarah. Muriel hadn't had much of a life, although he'd heard through the grapevine that she'd resisted Sarah's pleas to come to Brisbane to live with her. Muriel Dempsey had always struck him as completely unselfish. She'd probably thought she might be a burden to Sarah in some way.

"Then Sarah will be coming home. Home, sweet home," he finished ironically.

"That's what we're afraid of," said his mother, then flushed when Ruth sent her a frown.

"So what's the problem there?" he asked, his own voice sharpening.

"We'll be expected to put in an appearance at the funeral or send a representative. The town expects so much of us."

An angry feeling rose from his heart to his throat. "Perhaps because we have more than enough. I can't understand what gets into you, Mum. Aren't you the bloody mayor? Haven't we known the Dempseys forever? Wasn't Sarah's father one of our best ringers? I can't compel you to go, but *I* certainly will."

"We'll all go," Ruth said, signaling her daughter with her eyes. "Joe had already contacted Sarah before he rang me. She'll be in town by tomorrow afternoon. She'll be staying over the shop." One of Ruth's arthritic hands closed tightly over the other. "The funeral is scheduled for Friday. Muriel wished to be cremated and her ashes scattered over the desert like her husband's."

"It's just so very tragic," Kyall said. "Sarah's had so much suffering in her life."

"What do you mean?" Ruth asked very suddenly, her voice like a blade. She leaned forward in her upholstered rattan armchair as though hanging on his answer.

"Why so surprised?" His expression conveyed his reaction. "She lost her father, and now she's lost her mother, Gran." Emotion tightened his striking features.

He's never forgotten her, Ruth thought. The knowledge made her feel more vulnerable and frightened than she'd ever felt in her life. What if he found out? What if Sarah suddenly decided to tell him? Well, if Sarah tried it, she wouldn't know what she was letting herself in for.

"I did my level best to help her, Kyall. I didn't *have* to pay for her education, then send her on to medical school. Sometimes I think I was a damned fool. She's never appreciated it. One doesn't like to speak ill of the dead, but Muriel was the same, even though I put plenty in her pocket. She didn't have to continue to work at that shop. She wanted to."

"Why exactly did you do it, Gran?"

Shocked, she detected an undertone of bitterness and skepticism in the way he said it. "I carried on from your grandfather and his father before him. The McQueens are philanthropists. Isn't that the truth?"

"When it's worth it to you."

"Kyall!" his mother gasped, her strong-featured, aristocratic face turning pale.

"Mum, must you always be such a hypocrite?" he asked coldly. "Let it go. This news has upset me if it hasn't upset you."

Ruth's glittering black gaze flickered. "I can scarcely believe that my grandson, my splendid grandson, never in awe of me or our fortune, can't escape that girl. Did she steal your heart, my boy?" For once Ruth allowed herself to show her contempt for Sarah.

Kyall stood up, the last rays of the sinking sun striking blue out of his raven hair and turning his skin gold. "Don't overplay your hand, Gran. You have a tendency to do that, but I'm not one who's going to listen."

"Kyall, darling, don't!" his mother pleaded, stretching out a hand that shook slightly with nervous tension.

"I certainly never meant to hurt you, Kyall," Ruth said, aware that someplace inside her was trembling, as well.

"But that's your problem, Gran," Kyall said, standing up and turning away, not waiting for her answer. "You do hurt people."

Normally charming, courteous, above all a gentleman, he spoke like a man who could say anything he wanted to.

These next few days were going to be terrible, Ruth thought. She could hardly have foreseen that Muriel Dempsey would die so soon.

CHAPTER TWO

A FUNERAL WAS an opportunity for the whole town to come together, to reaffirm the bush tradition of "mateship," of offering real comfort and support in times of trouble and grief.

Father Bartholomew of the Aerial Ministry conducted the service, talking about Muriel Dempsey and her late husband, Jock, in a way that Sarah really appreciated. She'd known Father Bartholomew all her life. He had never failed to give Sarah and her mother comfort and hope. Father Bartholomew was a man you could really talk to, laugh with, whose shoulder you could cry on.

There were no tears today. Sarah sat in the front pew of the small all-denominational church, her features composed. In her short years as an intern and then in private practice, she had seen many tragic things. Everybody lost a loved one at some time or other, many of them far too early—children with terminal leukemia, young women with breast cancer, adolescents overdosing on drugs, young drivers involved in horrific road accidents. She had seen and attended them all. That was part of her profession, what she believed with all her heart was a noble calling.

But this was different. This was saying her final goodbye to her cherished mother. The one who'd loved her absolutely, unconditionally.

Her mother. So lovely. Her mother had always called her "my angel." Her long mane of curly blond hair, Sarah supposed, plus she'd never been a moody, rebellious child. She and her mother had been too crucially interdependent to allow disharmony into their lives. They'd been mutually supportive and caring. Her mother had continued to call her "my angel" even when she'd had to confess in floods of tears that she was pregnant.

My Rose. I, too, would've had a girl. I would've had a wonderful, meaningful relationship. Little more than a child she'd been, but she had really wanted her baby. The child in Kyall's image. Rose Red. Just like in the old fairy tales. She had since learned that everyone had to cope with dreadful losses over a lifetime, but it was something that shouldn't have happened to her at fifteen.

Joe had tried to talk her out of attending her mother's cremation. He and Sister Bradley would act as witnesses. But she intended to be with her mother to the very end. Afterward she would borrow Joe's vehicle to drive out into the desert to scatter her mother's ashes. She knew where. Around a particularly beautiful ghost gum that had held some special message for her mother. Sarah never knew what.

She would've given anything to be talked out of the wake, but she knew she had to go. Her mother had many, many good friends in the town. Attending the wake was expected. Harriet, that eternal tower of strength, had arranged it at her place. "Harriet's Villa," the town had always called it. A building considerably grander than those usually allotted to an outback town's schoolteacher. Convincing evidence of Harriet Crompton's regal, no-nonsense presence. The villa was really a classic old Queenslander with the usual enveloping verandas, lacework balustrades and valances. As a child Sarah had loved it. What made the villa truly extraordinary was Miss Crompton's remarkable collection of native artifacts. She'd gathered them from all over—the Australian outback, New Guinea, where she'd been reared by her English parents on a coffee plantation, New Zealand and the Pacific Islands, which she'd visited in her youth. There was hardly a field of learning Harriet didn't know about or couldn't talk intelligently about. She was an inveterate reader with an insatiable appetite for knowledge. Miss Crompton—she hadn't become Harriet until a few years ago—had sensed the day after Sarah and Kyall had made love that something new had taken over her favorite student's life. Sarah had sometimes thought Miss Crompton had sensed the very day she knew she was pregnant. Certainly Miss Crompton had said Sarah could come to her at any time if she needed help.

"My door is always open to you, Sarah. Whatever problems we experience in life, we can get through them with friends."

She was two and a half months pregnant, her body as slim and supple as ever, showing no outward changes, when Ruth McQueen put a name to her condition and in so doing put a name to her.

"You little slut! What were you thinking of? What were you and your *mother* thinking of? That you'd trap my grandson? As though I'd allow it for one minute! It's unthinkable. You'll go away and you'll stay away. You have no future here."

What did it concern her that the baby was someone she and Ruth McQueen's adored grandson had created together?

"I'll protect my grandson in any way I have to. Understand me. I'm a powerful woman. Do you think I'll listen to your stupid prattle about loving Kyall? This will ruin him, bring him and my family down. It will never happen. You'll go away if I have to drag you off myself. If you truly love my grandson, you'll recognize that this pregnancy has the potential to destroy his life. God almighty, girl, he's only sixteen! Do you think I'm going to allow him to waste his life on someone like *you?* You're fortunate you haven't told him your little secret, or God knows what I'd do.''

Sarah hadn't doubted then, nor did she now, that Ruth McQueen would have taken drastic steps to shut her up. But basically it had come down to one thing. She did love Kyall. His happiness was very important to her. She'd never seen them in terms of a committed relationship; their backgrounds were too far removed. She'd accepted what Ruth McQueen and to a certain extent her own mother had told her. Exquisitely painful as it was, it would be better for her, for her baby and for Kyall if the child was adopted out to a suitable young couple who would give it a good, loving home.

She remembered how frightened her mother had been of Ruth McQueen. ''Everyone is, my angel. She's done some terrible things to people in business. Her own son was forced to leave. She simply doesn't have it in her to love anyone. Except Kyall. This is a real crisis, my angel. I have no money. Nowhere else to go. No husband anymore. I know it's dreadful to accept what she's offering, but she proposes to look after us if we do what she says.''

So the answer, although it was terrible and not what she wanted, was very clear. She was to go away and put her baby up for adoption. Afterward, as though nothing monumental had happened, she could resume her education, one important difference being that she'd never go back to the town but be enrolled in an excellent girls' boarding school.

NOTHING HAD PREPARED HER or would ever prepare her for the sight of Kyall. She thought she gave a stricken gasp, but in fact she hadn't made a sound. She stood outside the

church, flanked and supported by Harriet and Joe, surrounded by people of the town, the mourners, as her
mother's casket slid into the hearse and then began its final
journey to the funeral home on the outskirts of town. It had
been decided that she would attend her mother's wake first
before the cremation. Harriet and her mother's best friend,
Cheryl Morgan, would accompany her.

There was something eerie about seeing Ruth McQueen
again. She had aged. Lost height and weight. Never a tall
woman, she'd always had such an imperious manner she'd
managed to overcome her lack of inches. From this distance—and Sarah hoped she'd keep it—Ruth McQueen
looked almost frail. Wonder of wonders! Hard to believe
that, but she still had the incredible aura of glamour her
daughter Enid, though a handsome woman, totally lacked.
Both women were dressed in black from top to toe—a lot
of people weren't—but the McQueens always did things by
the book. Kyall's father, Max, a tall, handsome man with
lovely manners, glanced in her direction. He lifted his hand
and smiled, somehow indicating that he'd see her at the
house.

The McQueen women had already turned away as Kyall
cleared a path for them to the old, meticulously maintained
Rolls Ruth McQueen kept for her dignified entries into
town. What was more of a surprise—but then again, perhaps not—was the presence of India Claydon of Marjimba
Station, who now stood beside Kyall, suggesting she was
a young woman of some significance in his and his family's
life. India did not look in Sarah's direction. Her concern
was solely with supporting the McQueen family, as though
they were the chief mourners.

India, a tall, athletic young woman with a long fall of
glossy brown hair and bright blue eyes, appeared cool and
elegant even in the heat of the day, which had most women

waving decorative straw fans. India Claydon was a few years younger and had never been a friend. India, as heiress to Marjimba Station, liked the locals to keep their distance. Certainly she had looked down on Sarah and made the fact very plain. India had been educated at home until age twelve, when she was sent away to boarding school. As fate would have it, she'd attended the same prestigious school Ruth McQueen had picked out for Sarah. An excellent school was something Muriel Dempsey had found the strength and the courage to insist on for her clever daughter. Right from the beginning, India had made it her business to let the other girls at school know Sarah was there through the charity of that philanthropic family, the McQueens, her own family's close friends. If it was meant as an embarrassment, the ploy backfired. No one cared. Sarah Dempsey was a bright girl, a real worker and she excelled at sports. Everyone liked her. She was kind and courteous, respectful to her teachers, who couldn't praise her enough. Eventually she was "dux" of the school, the top student, as well as school captain. Impossible to believe Sarah Dempsey had ever put a foot wrong in her life. Impossible to believe that behind the sweet seriousness of her expression lay a grief and a guilt that had never been resolved.

What did I do wrong that my baby was born without a chance at life? Sarah agonized endlessly as she faced the future without her child. What had happened? During all that long, lonely waiting time, she'd tried her very best to take care of herself. She had felt physically strong, never questioning that she would deliver a healthy child.

But I slept while my baby died.

LEAVING THE CHURCH, Kyall kept moving forward, unaware that his face was still and somber. People greeted him on all sides, saying the usual things one said at funerals. Untimely…sad occasion…no nicer woman than Muriel… He could see they were pleased he and his family had come to pay their respects. Some were a little awkward about mentioning Sarah. These good-hearted people knew all about the adolescent bond between him and Sarah Dempsey. They had been inseparable. He knew there'd been lots of whispers when Sarah had gone away so suddenly to boarding school, everyone certain his grandmother had put an end to an "unsuitable" relationship. No doubt in the town's view it had been for their own good. Kyall had to admit their bond had amounted to near obsession. They were both too young for it. Probably the townspeople felt that the breakup had been inevitable from the start. Such a friendship would never culminate in anything, given the fact that his family reigned supreme and the Dempseys, though respectable people, were nevertheless working class. That would be the reasoning.

Still, Kyall knew the town had a soft spot for the remarkably bright Sarah, Miss Crompton's protégée, fatherless child and a great comfort and help to her widowed mother.

There were just too many obstacles, too much formidable opposition from his family. His grandmother Ruth, who showed little or no affection for anybody, doted on him. Who knew why? But the upshot had been the severance of the greatest bond of his young life. With some bleakness, Kyall pondered that. *I could never forget her, but Sarah quickly enough blotted out all memories of me.*

Now his family was attending Muriel Dempsey's funeral, an odd gesture, perhaps, but one that was obviously much appreciated. It was, everyone seemed to agree, in the true spirit of the bush, yet the pain in his heart was so bad Kyall thought he might groan aloud with it. Across the room he could see the women of the town, one by one, go to Sarah and wrap their arms around her, hugging her, their faces full of sympathy and compassion. The men gripped her hand. Some of the older men, the grandfathers, hugged her close. He saw India's brother, Mitchell, a friend and in his view the pick of the Claydons, kiss her on both cheeks; he wasn't surprised when she lifted her beautiful grave face and gave him a heartbreaking smile. Sarah had always liked Mitch. It was Mitch who'd christened her at age ten the "little Queen of Koomera Crossing" a reference to some quality in Sarah that put her above the rest.

She was more beautiful every time he saw her. Even now, when he knew she was filled with desolation, she managed to keep the tears at bay. She was…gallant. He knew she wouldn't break down until she was entirely on her own.

She wore a simple black dress that made her skin glow and her hair glitter. That extravagant blond mane was pulled back from her face and arranged in a thick upturned roll, though wisps like little golden flames found their way onto her temples and cheeks and clustered on the creamy nape of her neck. Taller than most of the women around her, she was slim to the point of thinness.

Even as a child she'd had presence. Now, her natural beauty allied with her focused demeanor and high intelligence gave her real power. Not the power his grandmother possessed and had basked in for most of her life but the power of the spirit. Sarah was the sun, on the side of the angels. His grandmother? Well, his grandmother was his grandmother. He'd always thought of her as a woman full of darkness, full of secrets. Her eyes, for instance, were so dark one could look into them and never see the bottom.

His grandmother and mother weren't among the women who reached out to Sarah with consoling arms. They stood together as people expected them to, overdressed in this company, faces pale, clearly saying the necessary words, words that covered up what both women wanted most. For Sarah to go away. Miles and miles and miles away. Back to the city and her medical practice.

They were out of their minds if they thought he'd forgotten Sarah. It was just something he couldn't give up. Like a powerful addictive drug. Soon it would be his turn to speak to her, although he knew she wouldn't want it. The last time they'd confronted each other, she'd told him she never wanted to see him again. You'd have thought he and the McQueens had personally run her out of town, instead of financing her education. It was all so inconsistent with the Sarah he thought he'd known and with whom he'd shared such a remarkable friendship.

That friendship had ended literally overnight. Maybe his daring to make love to her, to take her virginity, had shaken her to the very core. He remembered—how he remembered—that she'd cried. He'd thought it was with rapture. Hadn't tears filled his own eyes? It hadn't been rapture, though. It'd been something else. Things hidden in a young girl's soul. All he knew was that she'd stepped away from him as if it was the only possible way she could protect herself. As if this perilous new dimension in their lives could only damage her. Of course, she would've feared having a child; any young girl would have. But *their child*. Wouldn't that have been the most wonderful thing? That was his spontaneous reaction, years later of course, although he realized it would have changed their lives.

Ultimately he'd discovered that Sarah had wanted more for herself. And why not? She'd gone away. Withdrawn her body, her mind and her heart. In effect, his own family's money had sealed her off.

A few moments more and he saw his mother and grandmother turn away, both formidable figures, as Miss Crompton returned to Sarah's side. She was a spare, birdlike woman, but elegant, erect, albeit dressed like a woman from another era—Edwardian?—with hairdo to match. There was a troubled look on Harriet's face, her English skin weathered to crazed china by an alien sun. It was a face that would've been outright plain except for a fine, glinting pair of gray eyes that were normally filled with sardonic humor. He liked and respected Miss Crompton. Many times he'd sought her out in the late afternoons when he was in town and knew she'd still be in the schoolhouse, her second home. He felt with certainty that she enjoyed his company as much as he enjoyed hers. She was a very interesting woman with a keen mind. As a boy she had taught him, reined in his high spirits. During those years he thought she took as much notice of him as Sarah, showing her pleasure in their learning skills, knowing he would soon go away to his prestigious private school to complete his education. What had she called him?

"The princeling." That was it, although she never said it to hurt him. It was more like taking a shot at his grandmother for whom, he came to realize, she had a deep, unspoken distrust. It had been strange growing up knowing most people regarded his iron-fisted grandmother as a terrible woman. No, not a woman at all. A vengeful deity. Get on the wrong side of her and all manner of afflictions would be called down on you. He had never wanted to believe it—since he was completely unafraid of her—but he came to see over the years that it was true. Yet it was due to his grandmother that little Sarah Dempsey, who lived with her mother over the shop, was now the well-respected Dr. Sarah Dempsey. Her aura of calm poise and balance, of caring, would inspire confidence in her patients.

Yet the sparkle, the vivaciousness, the youthful high spirits he remembered in his Sarah now lay below the surface.

Hell, would the pain ever stop?

He made his way across the packed room, the press of bodies raising the temperature to an uncomfortable degree. Sarah looked cool, though. Was that because she was so blond? Or maybe the hot blood no longer raced through her veins....

"Sarah. Miss Crompton." He stood in front of them. Sarah didn't raise her eyes. Hadn't she told him she didn't want to see him again? But pride, and he had plenty of it, didn't seem worth bothering about where Sarah was concerned.

"Good to see you, Kyall." Harriet Crompton smiled up at him—encouragingly, he thought. "I'll leave you and Sarah alone, although I'd like to speak to you later, Kyall, if you can spare me a few minutes."

"Of course," he said, his faint smile sardonic. Acknowledging what they both knew: it didn't do to keep Ruth McQueen waiting.

"I want you to know how sorry I am about your mother, Sarah," he said, trusting that his voice carried his utter sincerity.

"Thank you, Kyall." She flushed, then paled. "My mother always thought the world of you."

"Did she?" he asked quietly, his skepticism plain. "Estranged wouldn't be an overstatement. Our relationship became extremely complex after you left. When I was a boy, I knew your mother liked me. She said so. I made her laugh. But once you were gone, she presented a different face. She couldn't have been more distant. No, not distant," he mused, looking over Sarah's golden head. "What? As though the whole situation overwhelmed her."

"Perhaps she was afraid your grandmother would turn

really nasty if your friendship with her persisted," Sarah answered, as the dark whirlpool of the past swept her on.

"What else could have accounted for her nervousness?" he said, shrugging. "Anyway, I never lost my affection for her. And she did love you, Sarah. I've never felt that kind of love."

"No. You just have to get along on idolatry." She spoke without thinking, her words dredged up from that deep well of bitterness.

He stood looking down at her, knowing this yearning to do so would never stop. "If that was said to hurt me, it missed the mark. Idolatry, as you put it, isn't something I crave. It's not easy living up to a million expectations, either."

"But you do. I'm sorry, Kyall. I know you wanted none of it. But your grandmother's and your mother's fixation on you left your father and Chris out in the cold. How *is* Chris?" Sarah had a lot of affection for Christine, who was three years younger, feelings that were reciprocated. But she'd never been tempted to confide in Chris. That really would have started something.

Kyall turned toward the cool breeze blowing in the window and fluttering the filmy lace curtains. All in keeping with the house, except that the windows were flanked by two pretty-scary wooden witch doctors from New Guinea. "Chris is in the States at the moment. She gets plenty of work."

"She's stunning," Sarah said, carefully pushing a few tendrils of hair away from her face. "I always said she would be. She's got a ton of grit. She paid me a visit the last time she was in town—it has to be a year ago now."

"She told me."

Sarah nodded, knowing how much Christine loved and confided in her brother. "It says a lot for Chris that she never resented you because of your mother's attitude—endlessly, openly criticizing Chris while lauding you. Chris would've given anything for some love and encouragement.''

Fire sparked in his brilliant blue eyes. "She got it from me. And Dad. It wasn't all terrible.''

Sarah started to apologize. Stopped. It was much too late to forgive the McQueens. "No, I suppose not.'' Sarah sighed deeply, knowing she was only doing damage to herself by standing there talking to Kyall. Their problems would never be resolved. "I've spoken to your father. I always liked him. But I find it difficult to speak to your grandmother and your mother. You know that.''

"So nothing's changed?'' What was that expression flickering in her eyes? She wasn't as indifferent to him as she pretended.

"Nothing can change, Kyall.''

"Why is that?'' he challenged, desperate to get somewhere near the truth. "You've never had the guts to tell me.''

She lifted a hand, let it fall. Wordlessly.

Somehow that broke his heart. "Forgive me.'' Swiftly he reined himself in. "This is hardly the time.''

Someone else, a male mourner, was approaching. "Sarah, are you willing to spend a few hours with me?'' he asked urgently. "There are so many questions you've never answered. I know I made one terrible mistake, God forgive me. But, Sarah, I loved you. I shouldn't have touched you until you were a woman. I've had to live with that. Excuses are no good. I know that. When are you leaving?'' He held up a hand to stay the other man—he didn't know him—who appeared determined to speak to Sarah.

"Two or three days. I have things to attend to.''

"Tomorrow. Can I see you tomorrow?''

"Kyall, there's nothing more to say. You're wasting your time." Was she a total emotional coward? Simply that? Loving Kyall McQueen was like a terminal illness.

"Look at me." He knew his demeanor was pressing, but he couldn't help it. "You're not looking at me. Why? Does my face upset you? Do you hate me so much?"

"I don't hate you at all." Her voice was low and stricken.

"But apparently you've got so much against me."

"Kyall, please don't." Being with him, within touching distance, was so disturbing she was afraid of it. Even on this day of sorrow, her flesh was responding the way it once had.

"How can I when there's something in your eyes that…" He lowered his dark head. He wanted to lift up her chin with its ravishing dimple, *force* her to look at him. "I'm not a fool. Don't treat me like one. Tomorrow?"

"So I can be cross-examined?"

"It's a sad thing, Sarah, to be left completely in the dark," he said, the severity of his hurt never forgotten. "It's like being blind. If you despise me for what I did, you must tell me." He broke off, glancing over his shoulder. "Wouldn't you think that guy would go away?" he said in frustration.

"People want to speak to me, Kyall," Shockingly Sarah felt like laughing.

"Okay, but you can't shelter behind your wall of silence forever. I'll be back in town tomorrow afternoon. Say, around three," he said, looking every inch the arrogant, always-gets-what-he-wants McQueen. "I'll come and fetch you at the shop."

"Kyall. I thought I made it clear—"

"That's just it." He mocked her with the merest flash

of his marvelous smile. "You never have. To this day. I almost have to wonder if you were part of some conspiracy." He strode away.

MURIEL DEMPSEY'S FUNERAL was, in every way, an event no one was destined to forget. It brought Sarah back to town, the one place she'd planned never to go again. It brought her back into Kyall McQueen's orbit with its powerful emotional pull. It struck fear into Ruth McQueen, watching their intense conversation from across the room. Sarah had never spoken out in all these years. Neither had Muriel. Now with Muriel gone, what would happen? Sarah might think she could tell her story with impunity. As always, Ruth would be ready to step in. Nevertheless, fear pounded forcefully through her veins, raising her already elevated blood pressure.

There were anxious stirrings inside Harriet Crompton's breast, as well. Harriet had once believed young Sarah was pregnant when she left town. She would've done everything in her power to help, but Sarah had gone off with Ruth McQueen in the unlikely guise of benefactor and protector. Harriet couldn't dispute the fact that McQueen money helped many. The child had gone willingly, seduced by education. Lord only knows, *she'd* been the one to encourage Sarah. Sarah had written to her frequently over the years, sounding fulfilled and happy. Why, then, did she continue to think there was some mystery? Obviously it hadn't been a pregnancy, after all. Harriet was certain Sarah would never have given up her baby. Muriel, too, would never have given up a grandchild. And Sarah wouldn't have kept such momentous news to herself. She would've told Kyall. For surely Kyall McQueen was Sarah's first and only lover. Both of them so young, so beautiful, so radiant and careless, suddenly thrust into adult love.

It was a puzzle Harriet often brooded about. Both of them had locked up their hearts. And Muriel…

Harriet didn't want to consider whether poor Muriel had died of a broken heart.

CHAPTER THREE

LATE THAT AFTERNOON Sarah drove into the desert to scatter her mother's ashes. Harriet sat beside her in the passenger seat, her mother's friend Cheryl in the back.

Red sand streamed off in the wind, the four-wheel-drive bouncing over the golden spinifex clumps that partially stabilized the dunes. It was an unending vista, awe-inspiring in its vastness. Low sand plains and ridges extended to the horizon, dotted here and there with a tremendous variety of flowering shrubs and stunted mallee, the branches of which were bent into weird scarecrow shapes.

Desert birds flew with them—the lovely swirls of budgerigar in flocks of thousands, trailing bolts of emerald silk across the sky, the countless little finches and honeyeaters, the pink and gray galahs, the brilliant mulga parrots and the snow-white sulfur-crested corellas that congregated in great numbers in the vicinity of permanent water holes. Apart from early morning, welcoming the sunrise, this was the time of day the birds were most active. In the noontime heat they preferred to preen or doze in the trees to escape the blinding intensity of the sun.

Sarah crossed Koomera Creek at a point where the iridescent green waters had subsided to a shallow, tranquil pool that, up until their approach, reflected the fresh, light green foliage of the river red gums. The brassy glare of the sun was now giving way to a sunset that spread its glory across the sky, innumerable shades of pink, rose and scarlet

streaked with yellow and mauve, the whole brushed with
deepest gold.

Sarah knew where she was headed. A solitary white-
trunked ghost gum that grew out of a rocky outcrop some
quarter of a mile on. It was a marker for anyone who got
temporarily lost or disoriented in the dizzying wilderness,
with its head-spinning, extravagant colors. Burned umber,
fiery reds, glowing rust and yellow ochres, pitch-black and
a white that glared in the sun.

"We're here." Sarah spoke quietly, looking up at the
stark white bole and delicate gray-green canopy of the
ghost gum, which stood like a sculpture against the incan-
descent sky.

All three were silent as they approached the curious
stony outcrop, its surface so polished by the windblown
sands that it reflected all the colors of the setting sun.

When it was time to release her mother's ashes, Sarah
walked alone to the base of the ghost gum, while Harriet
and Cheryl stood side by side, quietly saying a prayer for
their friend.

"No more heartache, Mamma," Sarah told her mother
silently. "What I did cost you dearly. Forgive me. The Lord
will protect and look after you now. You'll never be alone.
Dad will come for you now. Life wouldn't have been so
hard for you had Dad lived. But that's all past for you,
Mamma. Go with God."

WHEN THEY ARRIVED back in town, Sarah dropped Cheryl
off first, both women hugging silently and swiftly. But Harriet's thick dark brows knit when Sarah drew up at her old
colonial, the front door guarded by an eight-foot-high
Maori totem pole.

"How do you feel, my dear?" Harriet asked.

Sarah let her head fall back. "Empty. I think that's the

word, Harriet. My mother didn't have a happy life or an easy life. I wanted her to come to me, but she wouldn't.''

Harriet thrust out her strong chin. ''Listen, my dear, don't blame yourself for anything there. You were a fine daughter to your mother. I remember very clearly how Muriel's face lit up every time we talked about you. You realized your ambitions. She was proud of that.''

''They came at a cost.'' The words left Sarah's lips before she could draw them back.

Harriet, too, sat back, still frowning. ''I've always thought that, Sarah, although you've maintained a poised and dignified facade.''

''I learned that from you.'' Sarah turned her head to smile.

Harriet's thin cheeks crinkled into an answering smile. ''Ah, my dear, with a face like mine, dignity's all you've got,'' she announced mock mournfully. ''You were the best pupil I ever had and I've had a few that have gone on to make names for themselves, like Charlie Garbutt.''

''I was never as brilliant as Charlie,'' Sarah gently scoffed.

''Charlie was and is entirely focused on other planets. He's brilliant and respected worldwide as an astronomer, but you were more of an all-rounder. Interested in earthlings, mostly. I don't think I could've wished for three better pupils than you, Charlie and Kyall, who found passing exams with flying colors a piece of cake. Even when you didn't study. Incredible, the bond between you and Kyall,'' Harriet mused, touching the lace on her rather grand, faded gray dress. ''Then it was all over.''

''It had to be, Harriet. You know that.'' Sarah sighed uncomfortably.

''I know no such thing!'' Harriet ripped off her glasses

and rubbed furiously at her aristocratic high-bridged nose. "There's so much I didn't understand, Sarah."

"Yes," was all Sarah could muster.

"Are you coming in with me, my dear?" Harriet heard the exhaustion in Sarah's voice. "I've got a bed made up for you. I don't like the idea of your going back to the shop."

Sarah shook her head. "You don't have to worry about me, Harriet, but thanks all the same. There are things I have to do. Pack Mum's clothes—" She broke off.

"Cheryl and I can help you do that," Harriet answered crisply. "You look done in."

"I'm not a girl any longer, Harriet. I'm not even particularly young. I'll be thirty-one this year."

"That's hardly old! You've never looked more beautiful. You have the sort of bone structure that will last. You know, Sarah, if something's wrong I'd want you to tell me what it is."

"Plenty is wrong, Harriet," Sarah found herself saying, staring fixedly at the street lamp and beyond that, the evening star. Was there a place called heaven? Was her mother there? She made a distraught movement of her hand. A hand that Harriet, thin face pinched, caught and held.

"Can't you trust me, Sarah? You know that anything you tell me in confidence I would never tell anyone else."

Sarah swallowed the lump in her throat. "I know that, Harriet. I'd trust you with my life. But there are some things we can't unload on others. I'm fine, really."

"That's what your mother used to say when she was in the doldrums. 'I'm fine, Harriet. Don't you worry about me, Harriet.' Of course I did." Harriet paused briefly. "I couldn't help noticing you and Kyall this afternoon. Neither of you is happy. You're not married. Kyall's not married."

"Surely Ruth will get her way," Sarah burst out scornfully. "God knows, she always does. I spoke to India briefly. She came up to me to say a few words. For appearance's sake, only."

"That's right!" Harriet agreed. "She's so different from Mitchell. But Ruth doesn't run Kyall's life, my dear. Pay attention, Sarah, because I'm right. Kyall is his own man. He has a different strength from Ruth's. A better, brighter strength. So much time has passed, but I don't think either of you has forgotten the other."

"Isn't that strange!" Sarah gave an odd little laugh. "Whenever I read an article about obsession I think of Kyall and me. And I think of a long-ago day when I made the decision to seek a new life. You have no idea how powerless I felt then."

"I think I do. In fact, I swear I do." Harriet sighed. "Am I right in thinking you still love Kyall?"

"Harriet, Kyall is a sickness. Nothing more."

"That splendid young man a sickness?" Harriet snorted disgustedly. "I ain't stupid, as the bad guy invariably says in the movies. I think for your own sake you have to get a few things out into the open."

"I don't have a child tucked away somewhere, Harriet, if that's what you're thinking."

Harriet didn't answer immediately. "It's not what I was thinking, not at all, because I never dreamed either you or Muriel would hide your own. All I know is, *something* is wrong. I'm speaking out because I feel you can't go on this way. You deserve a full life, Sarah." Harriet frowned. "A full life includes the man you love. Marriage. Motherhood. I had my chance at marriage when I was young, but I missed it. I was never pretty—not even a tiny bit— but I had a good figure, good hair and good eyes. But I played it too cool for too long. The chance never came again. I don't want that to happen to you."

SARAH SPENT THE EVENING sorting through her mother's things. It was a heart-wrenching job, but she was desperate for something to take her mind off her despair. A comment of Harriet's had upset her. The remark about her and her mother never hiding what was theirs. The terrible reality was that her mother had given in to Ruth McQueen's demands for adoption, persuaded it was for the best. An absolutely harrowing decision, and it had returned to plague her. Her mother had gone into a kind of inconsolable bereavement. As she had herself. Except that she'd never signed the adoption papers, fighting it to the end.

Once that awful woman, the midwife, put the baby on her breast, there was no way she was ever going to part with her. A profound spiritual and psychological connection had taken place. Woozy, not exactly sure of her surroundings, she'd still protested, telling Ruth McQueen in the absence of her mother that she was going to keep her child.

"I'm keeping her, no matter what!" she'd cried, finally finding the decision so easy. "I haven't signed your damned forms. I know I said I would, but now I'm not able to. This is my child. Mum and I will move away. We won't bother you, but you'll never take her from me."

Words that must have brought down the wrath of God, for her child *had* been taken from her. She'd never seen her again, though she'd demanded in hysterics that she be allowed to kiss the lifeless little body.

She'd been given a sedative. And afterward she'd fallen into a deep depression, thinking she could still hear and see her tiny Rose.

God knows what had brought her back from the brink. Some inner strength she didn't know she had. Or just the resilience of sheer youth.

"What you have to do now, my girl, is put your mistake

in the past,'' Ruth McQueen had told her, black eyes mesmeric. ''You're not the first and you won't be the last. Get on with your life. It may seem hard now, but you'll survive. My grandson will, too. You'll realize in time that you've done the right thing by not telling him. Especially now that the child has died. Make no bones about it, he would blame you. For keeping him in the dark about your situation and for losing the baby. I know my grandson. Do what you're told and you'll have me as a friend.'' There was a short pause. ''Do you really want me as an enemy?''

Ruth McQueen. How did you protect yourself from a woman like that? How did you protect your mother? So the woman she hated gave both of them a helping hand. With McQueen money, along with her job working nights, Sarah had become Dr. Sarah Dempsey. Battling her aversion to taking McQueen money, she came to reason that they owed her. After all, Kyall had been involved in making their baby.

The going had been tough, but she'd made it.

Until now. Her mother's death was a powerful turning point.

It was midnight before she went to bed, sleeping with her mother's pink cotton robe wrapped around her. A robe whose front was soon soaked in tears. Having used up all her strength, Sarah fell into an exhausted sleep.

SHE RETURNED Joe's four-wheel-drive first thing in the morning, parking it on the hospital grounds, then walking into the building to speak to the man himself. Looking around, she had to applaud what she saw. McQueen money had provided this hospital for the town. No expense had been spared in its construction, its neat gardens, its medical equipment, its cheerful interior.

She found Sister Bradley at the nurses' station and exchanged a few words before moving down the corridor to Joe's office. Joe had said he particularly wanted to speak to her. What about? Word in the town for more years than she could remember was that Joe had been Ruth McQueen's lover. A rumor Sarah had found so overwhelming she'd tried to discount it. She liked and respected Joe. Everyone did. He was a fine, caring doctor, devoted to his patients and the well-being of the town. Joe had brought her into the world. It was impossible to dislike or distrust him.

But his relationship with Ruth McQueen…it couldn't be true. Wouldn't Ruth have a problem mating with a mere mortal? Sarah wondered if this was some wild story people chose to believe simply because it was so bizarre. Not that Ruth McQueen was without a lethal sort of attraction. Even now that she was a woman in her seventies, you could see that she'd possessed sexual magnetism.

Imagine trying to make love to her, Sarah thought. Joe would've had to manage the whole business on his knees. When she tapped on the glass door, Joe raised his head, his gentle, worn face lighting up.

"Come in, Sarah. Please sit down."

"I've left your car out front."

"Thank you, my dear. Did you manage to get a little sleep?"

"Not right away, Joe. I don't have to tell you what it's like. Now, what's this you want to talk over with me? You look awfully tired. Are you all right?"

"Sort of." Joe responded.

"That's not much of an answer."

"All right then, my dear. I have cancer. I'm not telling anyone else."

"Joe!" Sarah was saddened and shocked. "If you can bear to, please tell me more."

Joe did, going into clinical detail. It was clear he had only six to twelve months to live. "As I say, Sarah, and you will know, it's the end of the line."

"You're so calm, Joe." Sarah said, finding it difficult to swallow.

"I'm seventy. I've had a good innings."

Sarah couldn't contain her distress. "Oh, Joe, how I wish we doctors could change things that desperately need changing."

"I have my faith to sustain me, Sarah. I believe in God. I believe in an afterlife. I don't know how I'll do getting through those pearly gates, though." He briefly closed his eyes. "I lost myself for a few years there along the way."

"You mean Ruth McQueen?" Sarah asked as gently as she could.

Joe laughed wryly. "Ruth had—still has—a certain technique for mesmerizing people. She mesmerized me from the start. I know it sounds weak, but for years she had an uncanny power over me. I knew she was only using me— Ruth had a very strong sex drive. In fact, to my shame, she threw me over." He shook his head. "This is old stuff, Sarah. I know you chose not to believe it, but... The point is, I never neglected my patients."

"I know that, Joe. You've made a real difference. The town owes you a great debt."

Joe shrugged that away. "Caring for people, trying to cure them, is our role, Sarah. What I'm trying to get to is— Forgive my shaky hands. It's the drugs I'm on. Would you consider for one moment replacing me? I hear all about you from colleagues. You're a fine doctor and there's plenty of doctoring to do in this town."

"I couldn't, Joe."

"What's your biggest obstacle? Unfinished business with Kyall?"

Sarah dropped her eyes. "I was over Kyall McQueen half a lifetime ago."

"I don't think so." Joe reached a hand across the table, his voice so strange Sarah lifted her head to stare at him. "You've never told me, but did Ruth threaten you?"

Sarah almost broke down. "Ruth McQueen has been a very threatening presence in a lot of people's lives."

"I know she was desperate to break you and Kyall up. I wasn't happy about that and told her so. She used to talk to me. She doesn't any longer."

"Does she really talk to anybody, including Kyall? I hate that woman."

"Why?"

"Because she ripped me from Kyall's side. I know it sounds extravagant, but Kyall meant the world to me. He was the sun, the moon, the stars. He was my brother, my soul mate, my very best friend."

"Forgive me, Sarah. There's so much I don't know. Was he your lover?"

"It doesn't matter now," she said.

"I'm dying, Sarah, so your secret is safe with me. I'll file it away and take it to the grave. Somewhere inside me, I feel a terrible guilt, as if I failed you and your mother."

"No, my dear friend." Tears sprang to Sarah's eyes. "Don't punish yourself, because there's nothing for you to punish yourself about. Ruth McQueen persuaded me that I had to be brave and give Kyall up."

"So she made you leave Koomera Crossing. I know you wouldn't have gone easily."

"She was afraid we would become lovers."

"Are you telling me the truth? I won't let Ruth hurt you."

Sarah looked at him levelly. "What would you do, Joe? Kill her?"

Joe answered in a shaking voice. "Ruth doesn't entirely have the whip hand. I've long suspected she was somehow involved in Molly Fairweather's death. I've never told anyone. There was nothing substantial to go on. Just a feeling."

"Good God!" Sarah revealed her shock. "Who's Molly Fairweather, anyway?"

"Oh, I remember. You wouldn't have met her. She came to town a year or so after you left. Big woman. Very gruff. People used to think she was crazy. Sure acted like it from time to time. 'Mad Molly' the kids called her."

"Mum never, ever mentioned her."

"No reason to, I suppose. She kept to herself. Had everything delivered to her door. She bought the Sinclair family home from Ruth, I believe, so I suppose she had private money. She was a trained nurse, but apparently she'd injured her back."

"What has this got to do with Ruth McQueen?"

"I might go straight to hell for suggesting such a thing, but Mad Molly died of snakebite. Somehow a desert taipan got into her house."

"How did it get there? They don't usually choose someone's doorstep.

Joe shrugged. "It was a bad year for snakes, but no one else in town spotted one in their garden. By the time I got out there—the postie raised the alarm—Molly Fairweather was dead, lying facedown in the hallway with the front door open. Later when I spoke to Ruth about it, I knew in the blink of an eye—or thought I knew—that she'd had something to do with it. Molly Fairweather's will handed the house back to Ruth, which I thought decidedly odd."

There was something else, Sarah felt, about that terrible story. In a sudden flashback, she remembered the midwife who'd brought her little Rose into the world. A big woman

with an aura of competence, but taciturn with rigid dark
eyebrows. A woman who had appeared consumed with the
desire to serve Ruth McQueen any way she could. *Why am
I thinking of her?* she wondered in dull surprise. All these
years, she'd never been able to rid herself of the sight of
Ruth McQueen's face, yet she'd all but forgotten the midwife. Mad Molly couldn't be the same woman, could she?
Still, Joe's story was disturbing. She stared at him.

"How could you use a mere feeling against someone like
Ruth McQueen? There must've been some inquiry."

"There was an autopsy. I performed it myself. The ver-
dict was bloody bad luck. But the whole business got to
Ruth in some way. Don't forget, I knew her very, very well.
Or as well as anyone could know her. For all her fine family
name, her power and influence, Ruth McQueen wouldn't
hesitate to walk on the wild side."

"Kyall and Christine are nothing like her. And they only
resemble Enid a little."

"Enid's just a shadow of her mother."

"She certainly knows how to be cruel," Sarah offered,
feeling as though she had a splinter in her throat.

Joe nodded and put a trembling hand to his chest.

"Are you all right, Joe?" Sarah stood up abruptly.

"It comes and goes. Sit down, Sarah." He spoke like a
father. "I'm not quite sure why I feel this way, but I believe
you were destined to return to this town. I've never given
much evidence to dreams, but I've been having some odd
ones lately. I know—" he held up a hand "—the medication. But the voice in my dreams tells me to beg you to
take my place. There are unanswered questions surrounding
you, Sarah. I believe the only way you're going to find the
answers is to return to Koomera Crossing. The way has
been paved for you. Muriel is at peace. And here I am,
dying, ready to hand over the running of the hospital to

you. I don't suppose it was ever what you had in mind. But for a few years? Would you mind so much leaving the city and the medical center you work for?''

"Joe, it's not possible," Sarah said. "Ruth McQueen drove me out of town. She'd do it again. Lest we forget, they own the town. They built the hospital. The dedication stone bears Ewan McQueen's name."

"Aren't you forgetting Kyall is a man now? Not a boy. A lot of the power has passed to him. He's enormously popular, not only in the town but the entire southwest. If you spoke to Kyall about taking over, what are the chances he'd say no? He'd back you to the hilt. I know Ruth's been trying and trying to marry him off to India Claydon, but with no luck. The girls have always been after Kyall, but for him, it appears, there is only you. Unless there's someone in your life?''

"No." Sarah shook her head. "I've had a few relationships that didn't work out. One almost came to something but in the end, I couldn't commit myself. We're still friends, though. He's a fellow doctor."

"Would you think it over for me, Sarah?" Joe looked at her out of strangely light-filled eyes. "You'd have plenty to do. Probably much more than at your city surgery. Challenges, too. You're the kind of doctor who could run this place. You could manage the nurses. People warm to you, Sarah. They always did."

"I'm afraid of coming back, Joe," Sarah confessed. "There's so much grief inside me. So much anger."

"There always will be until you exorcise the pain." Joe's almost messianic gaze locked on to Sarah's. "Don't say no, Sarah. Talk to Kyall about it. You're going to see him, aren't you?''

"How do you know that?" Sarah stared at Joe, taken aback.

"I saw the two of you together, Sarah. God, I've known you both from babyhood. Ruth may not have considered you grand enough for her grandson but in my opinion she'll never break you up."

Sarah's tone came out more harshly than she intended. "Wouldn't your plan to bring me back to town put me in danger, Joe? You've as good as accused Ruth of conspiracy to murder."

"I've never spoken a word of that to anyone other than you, though I nearly did to Harriet. Maybe I've found my calling as a psychic," he said with a quiet laugh. "Either that or when you're dying, you give your whole life a good going-over."

"I see it like that, too, Joe," Sarah said much more gently. "But although McQueen money assisted me, nothing's changed behind the scenes. I only spent two minutes in their company, yet I felt their clear message. *Go away. Go far away.*"

Joe slapped his hand on the side of his swivel chair. "Listen, you've got the right stuff, Sarah. You've got plenty of guts and, I'm betting, a lot of resilience. You're not afraid of Ruth, are you?"

Sarah knew in her soul she wasn't. "I'm more afraid of Kyall," she said after a long moment. Of his condemnation if he ever found out the true story. "I've gained some peace of mind, Joe. I don't know that I can handle opening old wounds," she added bleakly.

"Think about it, Sarah," Joe urged, coughing a little. Sarah heard the rattle in his lungs. "That's all I ask. I think I can hang on here for another few months. After that, I'm not sure. You know how difficult it is to get doctors for rural areas, let alone a place as remote as Koomera Crossing. Could you manage it for just a few years? You'd not only be doing the community a great service, you'd be doing something I feel is absolutely crucial for yourself."

CHAPTER FOUR

NOT UNTIL THE LAST MOMENT, when he saw her exit the shop, put on her sunglasses, then look toward where he was parked across the street, was Kyall sure she was going to come at all. He saw the town nosey parker, a woman he disliked, Ruby Hall—Muriel's helper in the store—peer through the blind. She obviously figured he couldn't see, so he gave her a little salute.

It would be all around town within minutes that he and Sarah had driven off together. Ruby couldn't keep a secret to save her life. At least she wouldn't know where they'd gone, but he wouldn't put it past her to jump into her little shoe-box car and follow them, ducking and weaving down the main street. She should've been a private eye. She would have loved it. The trouble was, there was no excitement in Ruby's life. She was in her forties, uneducated and unmarried; her sharp tongue had put off the odd admirer. Ruby's idea of excitement was loitering for the purpose of spying on other people. She wasn't exactly harmless, either. It was Ruby who'd told Vera Saunders that her husband was having afternoon trysts with a certain young woman who used to work at the pub.

Sarah was moving gracefully in his direction, so Kyall abandoned himself to simply staring at her. Her hair was pulled back in a thick braid, those glittering little ringlets springing in an airy halo around her face. She looked little more than a schoolgirl, her body slender and supple. For a moment he was swept by nostalgia.

Sarah! Why did you do this to me? Why didn't you write? How many years was it before he finally gave up? Surely what they'd felt for each other hadn't completely died? He never ceased to marvel at what a poor, deluded fool he was. Whoever said women were the romantics had got it all wrong.

She wore yellow jeans that showed off her slim hips and long legs. Instead of the usual T-shirt India favored, albeit with designer label, Sarah was wearing some gauzy cream top that had bands of cream lace on either side of the low V front. Very feminine and sexy enough to make him catch his breath. There were boots on her feet, a yellow leather bag slung over her shoulder. Sarah had always had style. Not something she'd learned but something that must have been with her from birth.

"Hi!"

She nodded briskly. No smile. "Could we please go, Kyall? Ruby—I had to let her open the shop—has her nose poked through the blinds like she's on to something important."

"That's okay. I've already spotted her." He lifted a non-chalant hand, waved again. "I have complete confidence in Ruby to inform the town that Sarah Dempsey and Kyall McQueen have picked up where they left off."

"Then she'll be pointing them all in the wrong direction." Sarah stepped into the Range Rover. "So where are we going?" she asked tautly when he was behind the wheel, so dynamic in that confined space she didn't know whether to jump out, cry with frustration or both.

He placed both hands against the wheel. Beautifully shaped hands, strong, darkly tanned, long-fingered. She considered them for a moment, remembering their unique touch, then looked away.

"Listen, I'm not trying to kidnap you, Sarah," he said mildly. "I just want to grab a few minutes of your valuable time. What do you say to getting out of town?" He searched her face for understanding. "How about our old pocket of the creek, or does that have too many traumatic memories?"

"I don't care." Her face twisted a little as she said it. In her body, perhaps, she'd always be fifteen.

"Oh, yeah, I'm sure you scarcely remember." He was silent until he pulled out of the parking bay and drove to the end of the main street, which was, in fact, the only street of any significance. People conducted their business there. It was called O'Connor Street after an intrepid young adventurer who really didn't know a lot about adventuring. Or not in the Australian outback, at any rate.

Dominating one side of O'Connor was the shire council building, pristine white, surrounded by palms and beds of decorative grasses. It had been built with McQueen money and designed by a talented architect. It looked impressive enough. Air-conditioned for the comfort of the mayor, his mother (Kyall hadn't been a bit surprised when she was elected) and the councillors, ten at last count. The pub on the other side. The Sweeney. Version three. Two had burned down, but photographs of the original quaint old building with its corrugated iron roof lined the current pub's walls. The hospital had half a block to itself. The theater stood on the corner—the Endeavour. That was Harriet's baby. It served as a cinema, as well. Again, mostly McQueen money. In some respects his grandmother was generous. In others? Well, she was miserly as hell.

"How are you, anyway?" he asked Sarah, at the same time lifting a hand to hail another driver, someone Sarah didn't know. A big man with a large, handsome head, and probably a body to match. Normally she would've asked who it was, but didn't. Not the way she felt.

"How would you expect me to be?" she asked. "My world will be a different place without Mum. We mightn't have seen each other all that often, but we always kept in touch. I knew she was there."

"I'm sorry, Sarah." He glanced at her lovely wounded face. "It was obvious to everyone how proud your mother was of you. How proud the town was. Harriet in particular. So my grandmother did *some* good things. You'd never have become a doctor without her. Takes a lot of money."

"And we had none."

He sighed. "I meant gifted people sometimes need a helping hand with the practical realities—like medical-school fees. You always were good at healing. Remember how you used to find berries and fungi in the bush? Water roots? You used to rub them on my cuts and scratches."

"Loaded with antiseptic properties. I found them because I used my eyes. And I listened. There's so much to be learned from the Aboriginals. They're the ones with the special relationship to this land."

"They never plant gardens," he mused, thinking how denuded the homestead would look without its gardens. "They're not interested in cultivating gardens at all. Even vegetables to fill out their diet. I know they look on the whole natural environment as their garden, but to me and the rest of us who spend a lot of money and time surrounding our houses and public buildings with beautiful gardens, it seems they're somehow deprived."

"They don't see it like we do," she said simply. "Nature *is* their garden. Ancestral beings left them enough to eat. They have intimate knowledge of all the plants and trees. What they can eat, what they can use to heal. They use everything to the full. They can find water where we see a barren desert. Remember old Jalgura showing us how to extract water from the roots of the mallee? We were just kids and he must've been nearing a hundred.''

Kyall nodded. ''I also remember that you became interested very early in the healing side of it. I was more interested in bush tucker for survival.''

''We had a wonderful childhood.'' Her gaze blurred with tears and she tilted her head away slightly, pretending to look out at the town's buildings.

''You were my shining light.'' His voice deepened. ''You always wore your gold hair the way you're wearing it now. Exactly the same. Except for special occasions, when you let that glorious mane loose. You always knew how to look wonderful. Remember that last time when everyone for hundreds of miles around was invited to Bonny Hatfield's wedding?''

''I'll remember it all my life.'' After that, everything had changed.

''So will I. Lottie Harris made you that beautiful dress. What was it made of, moonbeams?''

She couldn't speak for a moment. ''Tulle over a silk slip with little rose appliqués,'' she managed eventually. ''So pale a blue it was almost silver. How wonderfully generous Lottie was. Mum paid for the material, but Lottie made the dress for nothing. And she made the rose trim for my hair. I felt like a princess the night you stole my heart away.''

''And your honor,'' he responded harshly. ''Do women still think of their virginity as their honor?''

''It matters,'' she answered carefully. ''Perhaps to some more than others. It's the moment of changing from a protected child to a vulnerable woman. Self-esteem is affected by the experience.''

''Did the loss of your virginity give you so much grief?''

He threw a brilliant blue glance at her. "God, Sarah, I didn't rape you. I hope—I can't remember exactly, because I was so crazy about you—but I would've stopped if you'd uttered one word of protest. Whatever happened to account for your subsequent behavior? You not only went beyond my reach, you treated me like a…like a criminal."

That was the truth, and in its way dreadfully cruel. "Please, let's not talk about it, Kyall. It's so long ago. What can be gained from going over the whole thing again?"

"Because it matters, Sarah," he muttered, echoing her earlier words. "To me, anyway. You're an intelligent woman. You're also a doctor, used to dealing with trauma. What was it about your first experience of romantic passion that made you want to cut me so violently out of your life?"

To tell him would be playing with fire. "It was all too much for me to handle."

"So you hated me for it—even though no grown woman could have responded more passionately," he said. "Then, almost overnight, you had no greater wish than to be separated from me. You might as well have left me stranded in the middle of the Simpson Desert."

"I'm sorry." She looked down at her shaking hands.

"Why did you come with me today?"

"I thought I owed it to you."

"Now, doesn't that beat everything!" he heard himself saying in a hard, derisive voice. Then he blew out a calming breath. "It's not really the time, is it, to get anything out of you. Losing your mother has hit you hard. I'm sorry, Sarah. I don't want to hurt you, but I'd be lying if I said you haven't hurt me."

Neither of them spoke on the journey out to their old haunt, a hidden and beautiful pocket of the creek that was always filled with volumes of opalescent green water. The water swirled whitely around and between a handful of large, oddly shaped rocks that stood up from the creek bed like primitive sculptures. When they were children, this had been a fairyland to them, full of beauty and mystery. The bauhinias always seemed to be in bloom, pink, white and cerise, along with the flowering kurrajongs and the tall pink masses of mulla mullas. Their secret place had been a haven for large butterflies, too. Beautiful species that fed on the blossoming shrubs.

He helped her from the vehicle, acknowledging her thank-you with a curt inclination of his head. The native boronia was in flower. The heavenly scent, so filled with old memories, wrapped around them. In the old days they'd maintained a twisting track down the slope to the glittery sand. Now the track had long since overgrown with grasses and trailing vines covered with tiny mauve flowers.

It was a mistake to come, Sarah thought, torn between melancholy and a knife-edged excitement.

"Let me go first to clear the way," Kyall said in a businesslike voice. "It amazes me that other kids haven't found this water hole."

"How do you know they haven't?"

He gave her a half amused, half scornful smile. "Sarah, look around. No one's been here for years. The whole area is totally undisturbed. Watch those vines. They're inches deep. They might trip you up."

"I'll follow you." Hadn't she always?

Nearing the bottom of the slope, she gained an unexpected momentum, slamming into his broad back. It was too late for regrets now. She was here alone with Kyall.

"Steady." He caught her around the waist.

Don't let me go. Don't ever let me go. She wanted to say the words aloud, but they were stuck in her chest.

"It's uncanny," he said. "It's like we were here yester-day."

She didn't answer, moving to the water's edge. There was a subterranean spring in the center that kept the water deep. One section of the oval pool was aglow with a flotilla of blue lotus, the water so clear she could see the sandy bottom in the shallows. She couldn't begin to count the number of times they'd swum here, racing one another from end to end.

Try to catch me!

The memories kept breaking out all around her.

Careless of her boots and the hems of her jeans, Sarah waded in a little way, dipping her hands in the cold, flowing water. Cold even in the shimmering heat. Gratefully she splashed her face several times, throwing back her head to send a silvery spray of water into the air. She would've liked to wade out to the rocks. She and Kyall used to sit there, with her perched on one rock, him on another, having one of their endless conversations, sometimes arguments. Her mother had jokingly called them "the twins."

Impossible to shake off her nostalgia, but this beautiful place, so important in her life, was diminishing her grief. It had changed so little that time might've stood still. She dared to chance a look back over her shoulder, feeling the sensual intensity gathering inside her. Desire was such a powerful force. She could feel her nipples harden and the muscles of her stomach tighten. Kyall was watching her from the shade, his tall, powerful body elegant even in a relaxed slouch. She didn't want to know what he was think-ing. No—not true. Of course she did! There was always that thread of apprehension mixed up with the longing.

Across the stream, the wilderness blossomed and beck-oned. One starry night, she and Kyall had sought shelter there in the wild bush. A place for young lovers to meet, curtained off from the world. There their child had been conceived.

Suddenly she was crying—afraid of revealing herself, afraid of pity, anger, condemnation. But she couldn't help it. She hid her face in her hands, allowing her hair to fall forward like a shield.

"Sarah!" It took mere moments for him to reach her.

"Can't you see…can't you see…" She was breathless. Her voice trembled.

"What? Please tell me."

Her weakness lasted perhaps ten seconds. She shook her head fiercely. "I've got to stop," she said fiercely. She could melt away just from looking at him. She refused to. That would be inviting fire down on her head.

He heard her desperation, the conflict behind it. "Why not give in to it?" His voice was low-pitched, unconsciously thrilling.

It filled every space in her. The walls she'd taken refuge behind abruptly collapsed. Kyall's arms were around her, hers locked across his wide back. *This is what arms are for,* she thought helplessly. *Holding one another. In love.*

He pulled her closer. Murmured something in her ear.

Old endearments? She couldn't tell.

"Sarah!" His caressing hands were simmering with electricity, touching every chord beneath her sensitive flesh.

Just for a moment, a little while, she let her head rest against his chest. To lay down her burden. His hands were moving along her back, so carefully he might have been an anatomy student studying her bone structure. Even through her grief, she couldn't fail to respond, her little sobbing gasps growing shorter as he began to nuzzle her neck. Her body was moving into another dimension now. She'd dreamed of feeling like this…

Dark eyes stormy, she looked up at him, felt the wavelets

of panic, swirling resentments, then a flowering, flashes of color. The world wasn't wide enough to separate her from Kyall. She could want no one else.

"This is me, Sarah," he muttered, contending with his own confusions and frustrations. "How I've missed you! God almighty, every day!" He drew her into a kiss that sent her heart spinning, a kiss full of heartbreak and undying passion. Then for long moments he felt the bliss of utter forgetfulness.

The last time he'd kissed her, he had been on the threshold of manhood; now he was a man, with volcanic desires locked up inside him. He could feel her melting, melting, the heat of her skin proof of her blood surging hot.

Her breath was as clean and fresh as creek water. It had a citrus quality, too, that he had never forgotten. She couldn't and didn't deny him, her mouth wide-open to his exploration. What were words, when he could put his heart into his tumultuous feelings? He had lived with betrayal and a hurt so deep it had cut to the bone. He should push her away, seek retribution. But in his arms, she was the old Sarah. His Sarah. Her flesh was burning at his touch.

It was a kiss that he held on to forever, thinking that when he let her go, she would return to her hiding place. His hand sought the swell of her breast, not wonderingly as it once had, but confidently, possessively, his thumb working the nipple through the fine fabric. He had seduced her—but didn't she know he would love her forever? She'd never given him a chance.

My Sarah. My first love. My only love.

"Kyall, we can't do this." She wrenched her head away, running her tongue over her lips. "We can't start again."

He swore softly, fervently. "Why the hell not? Why are you so different from other people? Always running away from the things that hurt you. Obviously I'm one of them.

But we're not kids anymore. Our lives are in our own hands. You couldn't kiss me like that if you didn't mean it. Look at you! You're like me. Aching for physical release. For God's sake, you can't remain a girl forever. Let's just get married and end this nightmare. There's no life for either of us otherwise.''

Now. Now. Make a move. Tell him. Sarah felt the challenge to her integrity and her courage. At the last minute she backed off. ''And what then?'' she demanded, her taut nerves evident. ''Everything's going to be great? No damned way! I'd be no more welcome in your family now than I was years ago. You and I aren't going to happen, Kyall. That's just how it is.''

He held her fast, although she pushed back against his arms. ''So you've chosen to be forever on the run?'' He stared accusingly into her face. ''What I should've done was make you pregnant years ago. Then you'd never have been able to leave me. We would've been together— would've stayed together.''

She turned her head away.

''I could make you pregnant now.'' He fought to block a powerful, near-violent flood of emotion. ''God knows that's what I want. You made a mess of my life, Sarah, not just yours. If I meant so little to you, why aren't you married? Has what happened between us made you frigid? We were in love—it wasn't a sin.''

''Then why do you feel so guilty?'' she asked tempestuously. What did he know of her pain? He'd been spared.

He caught the back of her head. ''Sarah, you're a highly intelligent woman, a trained doctor, not a neurotic with sexual problems.'' His tone was deliberately controlled, bone-dry. ''You've always denied it, but I can only conclude my grandmother threw a scare into you and your mother.''

''What would you have done had you known?'' she

asked, trying to speak more quietly. "How could you have helped? You were sixteen!"

He studied her tormented, unsmiling face. "My grandmother has never ruled my life the way she has others. I'd almost become a man. *Was* a man after that night. I would've defended you, Sarah. You and your mother. You only had to tell me. My grandmother holds no terrors for me. Or mine. I could never in my heart believe what she told me—that you were ambitious. That you wanted an education above anything else. That you wanted to be a doctor and didn't want the distraction of adolescent love."

"I had to start looking after myself, my future," she responded bluntly, thinking she couldn't bear his anger and bitter disillusionment.

"This is a good time to ask. You weren't pregnant, were you? I've tortured myself with that."

"Oh, Kyall…" It sounded like a lament. For lament it was.

"All right, all right, I'm sorry." His apology was swift. "I know you would've told me. But it seemed a real possibility, so I had to consider it."

"We only made love once."

He threw her a derisive glance. "Once is all it takes. You know that better than I do. Have you had other partners, Sarah? Other lovers?"

"Fabulous ones!" She gave a short laugh and looked skyward. "No, I haven't been able to form any long-term relationships, Kyall. Anyway, I've been too busy."

"Yet you're a passionate woman. You wouldn't have given up sex."

She shrugged. "Sex is great, but I couldn't get serious about anyone. Consider that. I'm the victim of a forbidden love." She laughed ironically. "In the grip of an obsession. I don't know if I love you or hate you, Kyall McQueen, but I have to tell you this. I utterly and completely refuse to marry you.''

He suppressed the urge to shake her. ''Could it be that you're emotionally stunted?'' he demanded angrily. ''If it were anyone else, I'd take it as a sign of immaturity. Poor Sarah,'' he mocked. ''Do you really think you can admit to loving me or hating me—what's the difference?—and then run off again? What sort of crazy strategy is that? You'll never be free of me. You'd better understand that.''

''What about India Claydon?'' she flung at him. ''She's madly in love with you.''

''India is no match for you, Sarah.''

''But you keep her around.''

''My grandmother keeps her around,'' he corrected. ''India is one of the few people she approves of. God knows why.''

''Because India will carry on the grand tradition and she'll never be fool enough to cross your grandmother.''

''Exactly. But I'm not going to marry India. I want you. That's not about to change.''

A cooling breeze came off the water and she turned her heated face toward it. ''I dreaded coming back to town.''

''It's not the town you dread.'' He spoke with a hard edge of disgust. ''It's me. Why? You or your mother didn't sign some agreement with my grandmother, did you? Some legal document? If you did, tell me. I'll fix it. This whole business is bizarre. Something wrong at the heart of it. Can't you meet my eyes?'' He took hold of her, communicating his urgency.

She shook her head. ''No need to get angry. I signed no agreement, Kyall.'' In fact, unbeknownst to her, her mother had. She had found it among her mother's papers. Agonized over it.

''Well, that's a relief,'' he muttered with acid humor.

Above their heads the branches of the bauhinias were whispering to one another. The Aboriginals considered them fairy trees. The fairies that lived in them were urging Sarah to confide in him. Only she wasn't brave enough. She broke away blindly, making for the track, although the strength had gone out of her arms and legs.

There was comfort in silence.

ON THE RETURN JOURNEY Sarah confounded Kyall by telling him about Joe Randall's proposal that she take over from him at the hospital.

He'd been driving across the open plain, dodging the clumps of spinifex. Now he hit the brakes and drew the vehicle to a halt. "Sarah!" he exploded. "Why didn't you tell me this before?"

"I don't know," she said. "This is a very traumatic time for me, Kyall. I've settled into a kind of life. I have spells of being happy. My patients think I'm a good doctor and I do get results, so I must be doing something right. I deal with very sad things, but I try not to let my emotions get the better of me. Most doctors have to do that. But whenever I come back here, it all starts up again. The desperate memories…"

"Memories I share, Sarah," he told her. "You don't want to love me. But don't you think I've been through that? I've tried to stop loving you. I wanted to get on with my life, but so far it hasn't worked. For either of us, obviously. But we can't go on and on and never find a resolution. What did you think of Joe's suggestion? He's ill, isn't he. He keeps putting me off when I ask him."

"He has a condition that's very worrisome," Sarah said evasively, Joe having sworn her to a secrecy of sorts.

"Go on," Kyall urged. "I should tell you I'd never expect you to give up your profession. Everything you've worked for."

"You mean you'd come to the city?" Her voice held disbelief. "A McQueen of Wunnamurra Station. Scion of the McQueen dynasty."

"Why not?"

Sarah turned fully to stare into his eyes. "You, give up your heritage? Devastate your grandmother?" she asked incredulously.

He laid a hand on her shoulder, his lean fingers automatically caressing. "Who said anything about giving up my heritage? My heritage is intact. Gran is only the custodian. She can't disinherit me. She won't even try. Legally she wouldn't have a leg to stand on. I can administer our affairs from anywhere. We have a station overseer and there's Mum and Dad. Gran's never given Dad credit for all the hard work he's done. He's too much a gentleman of the old school—he should've put her straight long ago. My mother's been too busy staying on Gran's good side to support her own husband. It's all too sad." He flashed a sardonic smile. "We all live under one roof, but we're not a proper family."

"Whose fault is that?" Sarah retorted. "It's a tragedy that your grandfather, Ewan, died so early. He'd have kept your grandmother in line. She would never have been able to adopt the role of dictator. She seems to enjoy making everyone around her feel insecure."

Kyall acknowledged Sarah's words with a grimace. "Still, she's shown me nothing but affection."

"A bond that can't be broken." Sarah leaned her head back, her expression plainly unhappy.

"If she's ever hurt you, Sarah, she'd learn very quickly that her love—her kind of love—is not enough."

A curious expression rippled across her face. "You say

all this, Kyall, but you don't really want to cut your ties with the land. Your love for it has a spiritual dimension. I feel it myself, although I'm not from an outback dynasty. My father just happened to be your top ringer.''

He gazed at her, so beautiful, so desirable, so maddening, she made his head spin. ''Your father knew everything there was to know about shearing. He had the reputation of being a great bloke. You have no reason to look down on your father.''

''Who said I did?'' Sarah burst out. ''It's your family and the likes of India Claydon who make judgments like that.''

''She's jealous, Sarah,'' he said quietly. ''What can anyone do about jealousy? It's in her nature. India didn't get to be top student at school. She didn't go on to collect a medical degree. I've noticed that tendency in India. I don't particularly like it. Mitch couldn't be more different.''

Thinking of their friend Mitchell Claydon, Sarah's face relaxed into a smile. ''Mitch spent almost as much time with Christine as you and I did together. We seemed to team up very early. You and I. Mitch and Chris. I know Christine cares about Mitchell Claydon to this day, only the struggle to be free of your mother's domination took her away from him. Just like me. Both of us outcasts.''

''You'll both return,'' Kyall answered somberly. ''Would you consider Joe's proposition? It would bring you back to me.''

Sarah wondered yet again what Ruth McQueen would make of that. ''It's too weighty a decision to be made quickly. It would bring me back to you, certainly. It would also bring me a lot of stress.''

''As in work?'' He picked up on that swiftly. ''If you accepted, I'd do everything in my power to find another doctor, although as you'd know, it's not easy when we're so remote.''

Part of her wanted to answer now. Part of her couldn't. ''I can't say just yet, Kyall. I'm feeling far more vulnerable than I'd like. Going it alone—being separated from my mother—I had to develop a whole set of barriers or be overwhelmed. Can you understand that?''

He answered decisively. ''I understand that, Sarah. What *isn't* clear to me is why you were ever separated in the first place.''

CHAPTER FIVE

KYALL HAD DECIDED at some point in the evening to raise the subject of Sarah's taking over from Joe Randall. He expected outright, bitter hostility from his grandmother and mother, a quiet, reasoned response from his father. He loved his father. He only regretted that his father had married into this family. Of course, he wouldn't have been born otherwise, but his father had missed out on a chance at happiness. Or was he finding it with the delicately beautiful Carol Lu, the artist? Kyall didn't have a lot to go on, except the magnetic current he sensed passing between them whenever they met. The last time was at a concert given by the Matheson String Quartet at the Endeavour theater. No mediocre affair. Alex Matheson, strangely afflicted with periods of near-blindness, was a brilliant violinist, who under better circumstances could have had a career on the international concert platform. Three other gifted people of the town made up the quartet. The redoubtable Harriet Crompton, a woman of many talents, on viola; Lottie Harris, dressmaker extraordinaire, second violin; the newcomer, Evan Thompson, a dark horse if ever there was one, on cello.

Kyall had found it a deeply moving occasion. No one in the immediate family was musical or loved music outside of him and his father. Of course they *had* played the sort of music with wide appeal: Dvořák, Tchaikovsky, Borodin. The "love" music in the Borodin, so captivating and lyrical inevitably put him in mind of Sarah, piercing him to the heart. Afterward he and his father (his mother hadn't come, labeling such an evening a "dead bore") had run into Carol in the foyer. The townspeople reveled in these evenings that so enriched their lives; consequently the theater had been packed. Carol, an exotic mix of European and Asian blood, had been delighted to see them, smiling eagerly, holding out her pretty hands, first to his father, then to him.

God, poor Dad! At this point in his life Kyall didn't blame the man one bit for going after some happiness and comfort. He had often thought his father's best way out of his predicament was divorce, but McQueens didn't countenance divorce even when a marriage was hardly more than in name only. His parents occupied separate quarters. Not something all that unusual in this family. The only thing was, Kyall was fairly certain neither of them went "visiting." Not that he would really know. He had the whole west wing to himself.

Now he looked around the dining table. Not circular. No way. Too democratic. That would mean his grandmother couldn't sit at the head. His allotted chair was at the opposite end. His father had never taken it, despite his protests. Nothing more he could do. If this was an informal dining room and what they were eating was an informal meal, most people's minds would boggle at what formal might be. The table was elaborately set with the best china, sterling silverware and crystal goblets for the red wine they were drinking from their well-stocked cellar. A mass of yellow roses in a large silver bowl stood in the center, flanked by Regency silver candelabra. He counted the tapering candles. Seven. Thank God it was a quiet family gathering, otherwise he might've been expected to wear black tie. As it was, they were all dressed a whole lot more smartly than most people would be for an ordinary evening dinner. Not that he minded. He was prepared to keep up with tradition. Within limits.

His grandmother, as usual, was impeccably groomed. He didn't think anyone had ever seen her less. Not even a dawn raid would have caught her without her makeup on and her copious silver-black hair brushed and styled. Around her neck she wore a single strand of pearls so large the average person might think them costume jewelry, but his grand-mother had never worn costume jewelry in her life. Neither had his mother, for that matter, but Enid lacked both Ruth's style and extraordinary presence. For good or bad, his grandmother was a *personage*. And those eyes! A lot of girls had told him they'd remember him for his eyes alone. But his eyes couldn't compare with his grandmother's for impact. His eyes mirrored his feelings. His grandmother's were obsidian. Completely opaque.

Full of secrets? He was determined to find out.

"I don't know if you've noticed, but Joe Randall looks far from well," he announced to the table.

His mother frowned. "I've asked him, you know, dar-ling. I have a responsibility as mayor. I see him every fort-night. All he says is, he's growing old, or some such thing."

"Must we discuss Joe Randall at the table?" Ruth McQueen interjected, regarding her grandson with what would have been, in anyone else, a look of appeal.

"I'm sorry, Gran, we must. Joe is the town's doctor. He's been a good one. We must do something to show our respect and appreciation—Joe's days are numbered."

"Has he spoken to you, Kyall?" his father asked, folding his napkin.

"Not to me, to Sarah Dempsey."

As expected, all movement at the table stopped.

"To what purpose?" his grandmother asked sharply, black eyes glittering.

"It appears he thinks Sarah, if she's prepared to take the job on, would be an excellent choice as his successor."

"Oh, Kyall!" his mother wailed. "We simply can't have that wretched girl here."

"What wretched girl?" Kyall poured a little more wine into his goblet, his face taut.

"You know what I mean." Enid backed off. "Sarah's done wonderfully well and I wish her the very best but she caused a lot of trouble for this family."

"What on earth are you talking about, Enid?" Ruth snapped.

"Mother, you know very well." Enid's face worked. "She was never an ordinary girl. For one thing, she was much too beautiful. God knows how. Her parents weren't all that good-looking. Poor Muriel, at any rate."

"Jock Dempsey was an extremely handsome man, dear," Max said. "Have you forgotten? When the men tried to rile him they called him 'Golden Boy.'" Max twisted his own handsome head toward his wife.

"Good grief, Max, I never took the slightest notice of his appearance!"

"Then you were the only woman for hundreds of miles around who didn't."

"Oh, for God's sake, Max!" Enid said in exasperation.

"Maybe we can get back to Sarah," Kyall intervened.

Ruth's eyes were veiled quickly. "Kyall, darling, I don't see Sarah Dempsey as having a future here. I can't imagine she'd want to bury herself in an outback town."

"She wouldn't exactly be burying herself, Gran," he said smoothly. "Joe Randall's gained wide experience here. There's plenty of challenge for a good doctor. You know that."

"Not a woman," Ruth answered in a resolute tone.

"You're a woman, Gran. You ran a huge sheep station—with my parents' help."

To everyone's utter surprise Max began laughing. "It's not often I get credit."

Enid stared at her husband. "Of course you do, dear. You've always been very much involved."

"Thank you, Enid. I hadn't thought you'd noticed."

Ruth was very still now, a slight but regal figure in her carver chair. "It's true I did a man's job, but there would be a great deal of opposition in the town to a woman's taking over Joe's position. Joe can deal with anyone, the roughest stockman. I don't think a woman doctor would work at all in Koomera Crossing."

"Joe seems to think so." Kyall looked down the length of the gleaming table at his grandmother. "Why don't we put it to the town?"

"Do you mean to tell me Sarah Dempsey actually *wants* the job?" Ruth's eyes narrowed.

"I don't know." Kyall gave a sardonic smile.

"What does that mean?" His mother's voice was keen.

"It means, dearest Mother, that Sarah's going to think long and hard about it."

"She'd come back in a flash if it meant landing you."

"Landing me? She's taken a lot of years if that's what she's after. Sarah's become practically a stranger to me."

"Then what's changed, Kyall?" his father asked quietly.

"There was something very wrong about the way Sarah was shunted off. I know what I was told. I know what she told me. Same story virtually. The thing is, I've never quite been able to believe it. Whenever I tried to speak to her mother, Muriel wouldn't meet my eyes. She never looked happy. She died young."

"My God, you're not going to blame us for *that*," Ruth said.

"Let me give it some thought and I'll let you know." Kyall stared at his grandmother, holding her gaze. "I want Sarah back."

That visibly upset his mother. "But, darling, what for?"

"I want Sarah," Kyall said. "I've always wanted Sarah. No one else."

"Don't be a fool, Kyall," Ruth said contemptuously. "What hold has this woman got over you?"

"Some people call it love, Gran."

Ruth frowned. "I'll never believe that. She'll hurt you, not help you. She's hurt you already. Equally important, I can tell you that she won't make a suitable wife. There's too big a social divide."

"Gran, why don't you come into the twenty-first century?" Kyall's blue eyes remained fixed on her. His tone was smooth and calm, but there was tension in his body. "And give up on India Claydon while you're at it, instead of fueling her ambitions. I don't want to marry India. She'll find someone who'll suit her better."

"No other young man exists for her," his grandmother answered curtly. "She's madly in love with you."

"With your help. You've encouraged her endlessly. That's cruel." Kyall tried hard to stifle his anger, but there was a decided edge to his voice.

"All I want is your happiness," Ruth said. "You and the town are far better off without Sarah Dempsey. I want you to know I'll do everything I can to oppose it. And I mean exactly that. *Everything*."

Kyall shook his head. "Don't waste your threats on me, Gran. I expected your hostility, but it still astonishes me. If Sarah decides she wants to return to Koomera Crossing, I'm going to make sure her path is smooth."

"I'm the mayor," his mother said. "I'll oppose her."

Kyall's tone, though quiet, was acidic. "No, you won't, Mother. What about you, Dad?"

"As far as I'm concerned, Kyall, it's up to Sarah. But I am concerned for her, given the strong opposition around this table."

"Wisely said, Max," Ruth murmured with sarcasm.

"Oh, darling, how can this be?" Enid shifted in her chair to look at her son. "You're so clever about everything. Except Sarah."

"What have you really got against her, Mum?" Kyall gazed at this mother with hard inquiry. "The way you go on, you'd think she was the town tart, instead of a beautiful, intelligent, well-respected doctor. Your attitude really puzzles me. I don't understand your burning need to have Sarah not only out of town but out of my life. *Why,* in God's name?"

Enid shrank before her son's gaze. "I don't think she could possibly make you happy," she answered at last.

Kyall threw down his napkin and rose from the table. "Which means you won't tell me the truth. Nothing has ever felt right about this."

"Show some sense, Kyall," Ruth compressed her lips. "We did everything to give Sarah Dempsey a real chance at making something of herself. Well and good. She succeeded. What's wrong with her, anyway? Why isn't she married?"

"What's wrong with *me?*" Kyall challenged.

"It was an adolescent fantasy," Ruth said.

"Whatever the truth is," Kyall said, voice soft, blue eyes burning, "I'm going to find out. Muriel's death brought Sarah back to town. I was with her today and I think she's as much mine as she ever was. Which doesn't mean she's ready to fall into my arms. Rather the reverse. There's a reason for that. I hope for all our sakes that what I find out isn't a whole lot different from what I've been told.''

THAT SAME EVENING, Sarah had dinner with Harriet, a bracing yet comforting presence. Sarah waited until they'd finished the meal—an assortment of Thai dishes. Harriet was the most amazing cook, her thirst for knowledge leading her into exhaustive research and experimentation with the cuisines of Southeast Asia. These last recipes she'd brought back from Bangkok.

Sarah, who had thought herself incapable of eating a bite, found her taste buds responding. ''This is delicious, Harriet. And light. Just what I need. What's the noodle dish called?''

Harriet rattled off something in Thai. ''Got it from a local, an elderly matriarch. Apparently she'd once cooked for the royal family.''

''How did you meet her?''

''Ah, on my travels. I talk to everyone, as you know. One comes to a better understanding and appreciation of cultures along the way. I haven't quite perfected this dish, but I'm getting there.''

''It tastes wonderful to me. I don't get a lot of time to cook. Maybe you can help me if I ever come back here.''

Harriet, with her keen mind and razor-sharp intuition, immediately pounced on that. ''Will you ever do that, my dear? It sounds to me you've rediscovered you might want to.''

Sarah drew a breath, set down her fork, emotion in her eyes. Softly she said, ''I'd like to discuss it with you.''

''Hang on, hang on.'' Harriet, ever sprightly, jumped up, going to the refrigerator and withdrawing what was left of their chilled white wine. ''Let me refill that glass for you.''

''No, you have it, Harriet.'' Sarah gave her a fleeting

smile. Harriet, far from being an alcoholic, was known to indulge her taste for fine wine. She watched Harriet, dressed in a flowing kaftan in a wonderful shade of deep purple embellished with gold, pour the excellent Riesling into her glass, lift it and swirl the golden-green contents around, then sniff the bouquet.

"Proceed." She might have been a High Court judge.

Sarah sat back, smiling. Whoever said "proceed" anymore? She enjoyed Harriet's little formalities, the way she said "phwish" when she disagreed with something, even the way she corrected her ex-pupils' grammar, even when those pupils were all grown up. Today at the wake, Sarah had overheard her say, "Not if I *was*, Michael. If I *were*. Remember your subjunctives." This in a quiet aside. Michael Hammond was the deputy mayor.

"Your arthritis a little worse?" Sarah asked as Harriet resumed her seat. "What has Joe prescribed?"

Harriet told her. Sarah nodded. "Try Grandma's old remedy, as well. Cod-liver oil. It'll relieve the inflammation."

Harriet held up her hands, all her fingers knotted, with the exception of the ring finger of her right hand, which was perfectly normal. "I'm ready to try anything. Even snake oil."

"In fact, snake oil could help. There's evidence that snake venom has something to offer. I've never seen an Aborigine with arthritis."

"Neither have I, now that you mention it," Harriet said in some wonderment, trying to curl up her fingers. "Someone has to learn their secrets before it's too late. As I recall, you were quite a one for doing your own investigations when you were a child."

"I must've wanted to study medicine even then. That or science."

"You could have done anything you wanted to," Harriet said.

"Spoken by my great supporter." Sarah's eyes fell to Harriet's hands again. "Curious that ring finger is perfectly straight. Could it possibly be because you've always worn your mother's rings on that finger? Gold and diamonds? The ancients believed gold and precious stones had great curative powers."

"Good gracious!" Harriet hooted. "I've never thought of that. I have my dear father's broad gold wedding band. I'll pop that on a finger to see if it gets results. Another medical breakthrough. I want to keep playing my viola for as long as I can. I love it. Love it. You should come to our concerts. That man, Evan Thompson! Goodness, he's interesting. I play much better when he's around."

Sarah laughed. "I don't think I've met him. Is he a big man, dark, with a handsome, sculpted head?"

"Beethoven in a frenzy!" Harriet rolled her eyes.

"Kyall waved to a man who looked like that when we were driving out of town this afternoon."

"That would be Evan." There was a sparkle in Harriet's gray eyes. "All the eligible young women in town are feeling the need to offer him comfort. Some of them are acting downright silly about it, too. The little Renshaw girl presses her nose to the glass when the poor man goes in to have his hair cut."

"He's not married?"

Harriet paused. "He *was* married, I'm sure, but he says nothing about himself. When he came here, he told us he felt drained and in need of peace. That was the extent of any personal revelation. He has a great desire for privacy. I'm amazed Alex was able to persuade him to join our group."

"How did he know this Evan played the cello?"

"I'm going to take the credit for that," Harriet said. "Actually, he met up with me late one afternoon. He carried my viola home. Isn't that lovely? The truth is, I still get a kick out of an attractive man. Anyway, we got to talking about music. He's so knowledgeable that I asked him straight out if he played an instrument, and he said as a matter of fact he'd studied the cello for many years, though he'd never intended it as a profession. I could've asked him what work he did, but I sensed he didn't want to confide further. Some deep despair there." Again Harriet rolled her eyes, slightly magnified by her stylish spectacles. "Despair cloaked by a standoffish, brooding manner. A damaged man, if you want my opinion."

"You'd be the woman to recognize that," Sarah said soberly.

"So, what are you going to tell me, Sarah?" Harriet looked across the table at her favorite ex-pupil. Sadness lent an ethereal quality to Sarah's beauty, which normally wasn't there. She was too thin, but her body was so graceful, her skin so good, it masked the fact to a degree. "Of course it's about Kyall," she prompted as Sarah seemed to have difficulty starting.

Sarah's voice was low and quiet. "This is about Joe."

"He's dying, isn't he?" Harriet sighed deeply. "Hell to get old. Nothing to recommend it."

Sarah stared at her. "He told you?"

Harriet snorted. "He didn't have to. I've got eyes. I've got ears. I hear how he's been talking—as though he'll be going away on a journey."

"Poor Joe," Sarah said mournfully. "When he told me, it was like another little twist of the knife."

There was a steeliness in Harriet's gaze. "How in the world he succumbed to Ruth McQueen, I'll never know. That woman is evil. Lord, she's even scared the hell out of me, but that was in the early days when I thought she could order me out of town. Joe's so good.'' She shook her head. ''It was sex of course.''

''It must have been brilliant.''

''Brilliant sex will do it every time.''

Sarah couldn't help agreeing. ''Joe asked me if I'd take over from him at the hospital,'' she said. ''Begged me, really. He apparently believes I'd be able to step into his shoes.

Harriet seemed totally unsurprised. ''Well, then... How do you feel yourself?''

Sarah glanced at a wooden statue of Tangaroa, supreme god of Polynesia who was missing a leg, then back at Harriet. ''I realize part of me wants, even needs, to do it. I was uprooted from this town where I'd spent all my life.''

''You were under pressure, Sarah.'' Harriet hesitated to say more. Sarah was looking quite fragile in the wake of her mother's death.

''I knew I'd never be able to face Kyall again without falling back under his spell. I thought I'd learned my lesson.''

''What lesson? Gracious me, Sarah! I feel such an empathy for you both. You're not adolescents any longer. Both of you are free to make big decisions. You love him, don't you?''

''Do you have to ask?'' Sarah said wryly.

''Then Kyall is the only person you have to care about,'' Harriet said strongly. ''If it comes to choosing between you and the women of his family, Kyall will choose you. Isn't that sufficient?''

''It should be, but I'm very worried what might happen if I settle here. You know, and I know, that Ruth McQueen is capable of just about anything. She has many people in her employ. People prepared to do all sorts of jobs for her.''

Harriet barked a laugh. "One wonders what sort of job Molly Fairweather did for her. There was definitely some connection. Ruth owned the house Miss Fairweather supposedly bought, though how the deal was negotiated no one knows. After Miss Fairweather died, the house went back to Ruth. Curious, isn't it?" Harriet asked with some irony.

Despite everything that weighed on her, Sarah had to laugh. "According to Joe, Ruth had her killed. I know she's bad, but not that bad."

"She's pretty damn bad, in my opinion. I shouldn't say this, but I will. What if Mad Molly blackmailed Ruth?"

Sarah lost what little color she had. "About what?"

Harriet saw her expression and tried to inject humor. "I've been reading too many murder mysteries. Ruth Rendell and P.D. James. It was a very odd business, all the same." Harriet was aware that Sarah was listening closely. "Joe told you she died of snakebite. Joe arrived too late to administer the antivenin."

"I know. And I know the house. Old colonial set on high stumps. Desert taipans don't normally climb steps, though I'm sure they could make their way up if they were after prey."

"The prey, as it turned out, was poor Molly." Harriet's eyebrows executed a little dance. "Mad Molly. She was reclusive, but according to a whole gang of children, she used to hold long conversations with herself in the garden. Apparently it would go on for hours until she petered out or she heard them and ran at them wild-eyed and pelting gravel. Needless to say, the children thought she was insane."

"Maybe they were right. She certainly was deeply disturbed."

"Who isn't these days?" Harriet demanded. "It's my

view, and I'm sure it's yours, too, that something was weighing on her mind.''

''Did you ever talk with her?''

Harriet nodded. ''Once. As I recall, it was all about biology. She didn't sound mad when she was speaking to me. It was an intelligent conversation. Her voice remained composed.''

''Was she an attractive woman?''

Harriet considered, then offered drolly. ''Her size was a problem. Big woman. A serial overeater. Let herself go, although she was supposed to have a bad back. Personally I don't think she did.'' Harriet paused, eyes narrowed. ''And I suppose we'll have to forget the face. Yes, let's forget the face. For the strangest reason, and I don't mean to be unkind here—after all, poor Molly is dead—she put me in mind of a vulture.''

''God, Harriet!'' Sarah shivered.

''Something about the stoop of the head and the forward thrust of the shoulders.''

Nothing for a moment. Then Sarah recalled, a long time back, waking dazedly to see a big spooky bird hovering over her. A bird that ever so slowly turned into a woman. The white cap on her head was illuminated by the low light. She bit her lip hard, tasting copper in her mouth. Thank God Harriet was staring at the ceiling, still absorbed in her reflections.

''Curious thing, imagination,'' Harriet murmured, returning her gaze to Sarah. ''You're very pale, my dear,'' she said in concern. ''And why wouldn't you be, with everything's that's happened,'' she chided herself. ''Would you like coffee? Blast!'' Harriet shot up. Her cat, Clara—black-and-white and named after Clara Schumann, brilliant pianist and wife of the famous German composer—was sinking her claws into Harriet's flowing kaftan and hence into her leg. "Get down, Clara!" she ordered sternly. "You've been fed." Harriet looked at Sarah. "If we're talking mad I'll have to put Clara in a cat asylum. It's almost come to that. She's taken to hiding behind the curtains and jumping out at me the minute I walk in. I have to wrench her off. And the leaps! Nijinski would have killed for them. Now, coffee. I've whipped up an interesting passion-fruit tart with toffeed mango. An injection of sugar won't hurt you any."

At the wall of cupboards Harriet turned back, her expression so kind and understanding it lifted Sarah's troubled spirits. "You can't very well make this decision in a hurry, Sarah. I know that. But I think it might help you— and, in fact, the whole town—if you did come back. You're a young woman with a difficult past. One that doesn't seem to be resolved. In a sense, neither you nor Kyall has moved on. Both of you deserve the chance to set things right. Who cares if it's a decision that drives Ruth McQueen into a frenzy?"

Who indeed?

A DAY LATER, after a sleepless night spent trying to confront her problems, Sarah took a drive to the town's outskirts to look at the old colonial once occupied by Molly Fairweather. The house had always intrigued her—the locals claimed it was haunted—but Harriet's talk of Mad Molly and her gruesome end had profoundly unsettled her. For reasons she didn't quite understand, she wanted to visit the place. It had been built in the late 1870s by a colonial architect, Robert Sinclair, part owner of Mygunyah Station, a sheep property on Wunnamurra's northwest border. The Sinclair family had lived there for some years until their eldest daughter, Estelle, a pretty blond girl of twelve, disappeared without trace after disobeying her parents' edict that she not ride unaccompanied in the bush. Like the McQueens' Fiona, young Estelle Sinclair had returned as a ghost. She was said to appear in the small white gazebo erected in the front garden, visible to certain psychically deft passers-by. Just another bit of folklore, Sarah supposed, although the substantial house, its most striking feature a tower section above the entrance hall, had an undeniably melancholy air. Collective wisdom held that the girl had been the victim of someone who knew her, who'd followed her into the bush and then assaulted and murdered her. Whatever the tragic circumstances, the family had packed up and returned to Adelaide, brokenhearted and furious that a local man of low intelligence—very likely innocent—hadn't been lynched.

To Sarah's surprise, the house was open—at least the front door was, as were two of the dark green shuttered French doors giving out onto the wide veranda with its very ornate timber and wrought-iron detailing. Sarah opened the gate and shut it carefully behind her, eyes drawn irresistibly to the old gazebo. The latticework was woven with a hectically blossoming yellow allamanda, which threatened to pull it down.

No sign of the ghostly Estelle. All was quiet. Too quiet. No birdsong, just this eerie air of abandonment even though the grounds were well maintained. Then, as she walked through the garden toward the house, Sarah felt a decided tug on her body and a moment after, a strange surge of vertigo. God! What was that? She shook her head in an effort to clear it. It had to be all the grief she was experiencing, along with the powerful emotions generated by Kyall.

The house almost seemed to be waiting for her. She put one foot in front of the other slowly, as if she was walking into a danger zone. Life was full of unusual experiences one couldn't explain. But in this case, she could. There was absolutely nothing wrong with her except grief. Grief could make one more sensitive to everything. The brain did funny things, sometimes assembling all sorts of variables into… well, ghosts.

Sarah mounted the flight of stone steps, looking toward the open door with its colored fanlight. She stared at the timber boards, wondering how the taipan got access to the house. Taipans, Australia's largest and most-feared venomous snakes, among the deadliest in the world, could be found in a variety of places from the tropical rain forests of North Queensland and Arnhem Land and the Northern Territory to the arid deserts of the interior. Like most people of the town, Sarah had come close to a few in her time. But on every occasion she'd been out in desert country, the snakes all but invisible against the colorations of the desert, coiled up in clumps of golden spinifex or amid rough-textured rocks. As far as she knew, there had never been a fatality in the town from a taipan bite.

Until Mad Molly.

Sarah peered into the entrance hall with its polished timber floor, calling out, "Hello? Anyone there?" Her voice trailed off as a small, wiry woman with a lined, cheery face and hair so dry it looked like rope, emerged from a side room. She was wearing an apron that said Life Is Good and wielding a broom like a weapon.

"Of course! Sarah!" she cried, her expression relaxing. "Dr. Dempsey. So long since I've seen you. You remember me?"

Sarah moved forward, smiling in greeting. "Of course I do, Tilly." Gently she touched the woman's broom-wielding arm. "How are you?"

"Oh, I'm getting there." Tilly pushed a cleaning rag into her pocket, looking at Sarah's face with pleasure. "I work for Mrs. McQueen now. Domestic duties. I get free board and a nice wage. And you? I was so sorry to hear about your mother. Couldn't get to the funeral. I was working.''

"That's all right, Tilly. I'll miss my mother terribly.''

"I understand, dear.'' Tilly's expression was genuinely sympathetic. "Can I help you in some way?''

"Not really.'' Sarah glanced around at the forlorn empty house. "For some reason, I had a compulsion to see this house again.''

"Nothin' good here.'' Tilly swallowed, then shook her head. "I wouldna come for quids, only I had to. Mrs. McQueen wants it kept clean and aired. The bloody place is haunted—excuse the language. I shut the back door and it keeps opening up.'' There was a faint edge of panic to her matter-of-fact voice.

"I expect it's not quite shut, Tilly, and the breeze—''

"Listen, love,'' Tilly interrupted, looking grim. "Would I lie to you? The bloody place is haunted, I tell you, and nothin' ever rattles me. You come with me and I'll show you the back door. I'm positive I shut it.''

The back door was open—obviously no surprise to Tilly—causing her to ditch her broom. "Y'mind havin' a go at shutting it, love?''

Sarah laughed. "There's nothing to fear, Tilly. There's a logical explanation for everything.''

"Not here, there isn't,'' Tilly muttered, scowling darkly. "That poor little soul's hauntin' the place. Me friend, Chrissy Cole—remember her?—swears she's actually seen her. Reckons the little girl's dress is stained with dried blood.''

"Oh, Tilly!'' Sarah said. "You don't believe that. As far as I recall, Chrissy Cole liked to play jokes on people.'' Sarah opened and shut the door a few times, checking it out. No warping. The door opened onto another flight of steps and the rear garden, which had an abandoned air, although the grass had been neatly mown. Fluorescent purple bouganvillea grew so prolifically the back fence couldn't be seen.

"Okay, okay." Tilly shook her head. "But the place gives me the willies all the same. I'm glad to say I'm nearly finished."

"How are you getting back to the station?" There'd been no vehicle out front.

"Someone'll pick me up," Tilly said. "Why do you want to look around? There's a bad feeling in this house."

"Two mysterious deaths might explain it. I suppose there's such a thing as psychological haunting. Did you know Molly Fairweather?"

"Spoke to her a few times. She always acted like she was out of it. Or drunk."

"And was she, do you think? Drunk?"

"She never went into the pub. Afterward no one found any beer bottles or spirits. It was a rum old business, that, forgive the pun."

"She was a nurse, right?"

Tilly nodded. "Never wanted to talk about herself, but once she let something slip. Something about her days at St. Catherine's. You've heard of it?"

"The big maternity hospital in Adelaide." Sarah gazed at the other woman with disturbed eyes.

Tilly was instantly alerted. "What's up, love? Did you know the woman?"

Did I? Sarah thought, desperately trying to contain her muddled feelings, hoping it wasn't true.

"Did you, love?" Tilly persisted, grabbing Sarah's arm. "Are you all right? You've gone very pale."

"Actually, I don't feel too good, Tilly."

"Poor darlin'," Tilly clucked. "It's a sad, sad business

losing a mother. Why don't I make you a cup of tea? I've brought the makings with me.'' Tilly half turned.

"Thank you, Tilly. You're very kind, but I should be getting back to town. I've got many things left to do.''

"When are you leaving, love? I hear you're doing very well at your city clinic. We're all proud of you.''

Sarah smiled her thanks. "I'll probably be here until Friday. It's nice to have spoken to you. Do you enjoy living and working on Wunnamurra?''

Tilly accompanied Sarah to the front door. "Just between the two of us, love, I do and I don't. I think the world of Kyall. He's a wonderful young man. A real doll. His father, Mr. Reardon, is ever the gentleman, no problem at all, but the two ladies, Miss Ruth and Miss Enid—'' here Tilly elbowed Sarah in the ribs "—on a scale of one to ten I give 'em a twelve for treating other humans like they're beneath them. Why do you suppose that is? And Mr. Reardon…I keep asking myself why he doesn't just take off. I expect it's the money. Sometimes too much money can be bad. There was a financial collapse in his family, and Mrs. McQueen is so sarcastic about it, I guess he had to grow another skin—or punch her out.''

"Max is too polite,'' Sarah offered wryly. "Well, I'll be off, Tilly. You take care of yourself.''

"You, too, Dr. Sarah.'' Tilly leaned both arms on the balustrade. "Ever think of comin' back to town? We'd love to have you. Everyone would, in my opinion. Except maybe the good ladies of Wunnamurra.'' Tilly gave a raffish grin. "'Cause I like you so much, Sarah, I'm gonna tell you this. You made a big mistake lettin' Kyall go. I mean, word was you two kids were wild about each other.''

"That's what we were, Tilly. Kids.'' Sarah smiled sadly.

"Ah, well, love, things would have gone a lot better if Mrs. McQueen didn't get between you. No one good enough for her boy. She idolizes Kyall and hates everyone else. Bizarre, eh?''

''Not really, Tilly. It happens. Take care now.''

''You, too, love,'' Tilly called as Sarah walked down the steps. ''Better get your skates on, love. Unless I'm mistaken, that's the bloody Rolls comin'. I better get inside. Mrs. McQ wouldn't thank me for standin' around chattin'. Gotta work till you're bloody exhausted. See ya, love.'' Tilly scuttled off.

CHAPTER SIX

NOT FOR A MINUTE did Sarah expect the Rolls to simply glide by. How Ruth loved all the window dressing, the trappings of money and power. She would have recognized Joe's four-wheel-drive in any case. The pressure was on, Sarah thought. But she was a woman now, not a powerless, vulnerable, near-solitary teenager, living under the so-called protection of the enemy. And Ruth McQueen *was* her enemy. She'd faced up to that a long time ago.

Sarah made her way through the curiously silent garden—curious because birds were an eternal presence in the town—fighting the depression of grief. With the loss of her mother, her life had altered very suddenly and drastically. In short, she didn't have to protect Muriel anymore. She didn't have to live her life according to Ruth McQueen's dictates. Then there was this puzzling business of Molly Fairweather. She knew she wouldn't be able to get it out of her mind. Easy enough to check on the nurse's professional background, which seemed to have become one of her top priorities. Was it possible that Nurse Fairweather had been involved? Had she delivered her child? There'd been no male doctor; of that she was certain. The midwife had delivered her little Rose, with Ruth, extraordinarily enough, present in the room. But then, wasn't that terrible woman her child's great-grandmother? A blood relative. She supposed that, unwelcome as Ruth's presence had been, she'd had a right to be there. Her own mother, the mother she'd loved and lost, had not been there to see her through the most momentous event of her life. She had felt so alone, so sick with disappointment, but Ruth had insisted concealment was crucial. Sarah had been told on a daily basis what was required of her.

Then her baby had died. Tears. Always tears. She hadn't even kissed her tiny Rose goodbye.

Oddly Sarah felt that stir again. That tug. What if Ruth had been lying? No. No. No. She had to reject that. Not even Ruth McQueen was capable of such evil. At the same time, many questions were raised. She prayed she'd get the answers. Ruth claimed the baby had been cremated. Sarah had been unable to give words to her grief, her lack of comprehension. But now she was back to fight Ruth McQueen.

Sarah stood on the pavement as the Rolls slid onto the grassy verge. The window in the rear lowered and there was Ruth, glaring at her, obviously sizzling with anger.

Sarah spoke first. "Good morning, Ruth." She gave an ironic smile.

"Good morning, Sarah." The thinnest veneer of civility. "Would you kindly tell me what you're doing here?"

"I'm just satisfying my curiosity," Sarah answered calmly, turning back to glance at the melancholy house. "You don't mind, do you? I wasn't breaking in."

"You'd be in trouble if you were." Ruth recovered enough to address her driver. "Give me a few minutes, Jensen. I'd like to speak to Dr. Dempsey in private."

"Certainly, ma'am." Jensen was most respectful, opening the driver's door and stepping onto the grass. However with his face half-hidden from Ruth, he winked at Sarah, then moved off to take a stroll in the countryside. The Sinclair house was situated in splendid isolation on the outskirts of town.

"Get in, Sarah." Ruth's voice cracked. "I want to find out where I stand with you."

"Where you stand?" Sarah echoed, making no attempt to obey. "You stand exactly where you've always been. I hate you, Ruth. You took every possible advantage of me and my poor mother. My only comfort is that I never did sign your piece of paper."

That brushed too close. "Which piece of paper are you referring to?" Ruth stared back fixedly.

"You know very well. There were other pieces of paper, too. Papers my mother signed. I wouldn't have touched them."

"Ah, so proud!" Ruth didn't trouble to hide her sneer. "Are you going to get in or aren't you? Or do you like being out in the scorching sun?"

"It's preferable to sitting with you."

Ruth lifted her thin shoulders. "Obviously you're in a disturbed state of mind."

"There's nothing wrong with my state of mind," Sarah answered as calmly as before. "I should've guessed about Molly Fairweather."

"Guessed what?" Ruth drew the words out contemptuously.

"She was the midwife, wasn't she. She delivered my little Rose."

A tiny light leaped in those unfathomable eyes, and then they half closed. "Where on earth did you get that idea?"

"Are you afraid to answer?"

"Me, afraid? Of you?" Ruth laughed as though she couldn't envision the day. "Let's talk about you, Sarah. My loyalty first and foremost is to my grandson. You talk about taking advantage! You certainly took advantage of him, getting yourself pregnant. Wouldn't the town like to know about that?" She gave another low, derisive laugh.

Sarah stood her ground. "Yes, and your part in what happened afterward."

Ruth's face beneath the expert makeup looked white and masklike. "You choose your words badly. I protected you. If it weren't for me, you and your mother would have finished up God knows where. As it is, the fact that you have a profession you owe to me."

"That's true. That's how you try to justify your actions. It wasn't an immaculate conception, Ruth. Kyall was my baby's father. You prevented me from telling him. I *should* have told him. We both should've faced the consequences, but it's been deception, deception, deception."

"Exactly." Ruth clenched her fist and struck it against the plush window frame. "How do you think Kyall would feel if he knew the whole story?" she said fiercely, spitting out the words. "He'd despise you."

"I no longer care." Sarah only half lied. "Secrets have a way of festering. I can't live with the stench anymore. I wouldn't have hidden anything from Kyall, but our child died and that changed everything. It also meant I had to go through all the inner devastation alone. Kyall was spared."

"Why do you speak of this now?" Ruth demanded furiously. "It was over long ago."

"Not to me, it isn't over. The past is never really past, Ruth. Even you know that. I lost a child, the worst blow in life for a woman."

"Anyone would think you were the only one," Ruth said without pity.

"Isn't Kyall the only one in the world for you? The only one you've allowed into what passes for your heart? If anything happened to him, it would leave a great chasm that could never be filled. The same with me. I lost my Rose."

"Your Rose. Your Rose." Ruth spoke with great force. "God, you're pathetic. If you were a real woman like me, you'd get on with your life. Find a man. Have other children. Or aren't you capable of that?''

"I still love Kyall, you know."

An unreadable expression swept Ruth's face. "You won't live happily ever after," she warned. "You know that, don't you? Kyall's passion would soon wither if he ever found out you were prepared to give away his child. No, you're going back to where you belong. The only question is when."

"My plans are my own." Sarah looked at her steadily. "It was your little great-granddaughter who died. Did you grieve?"

"Are you mad?" Ruth reacted violently, the veins standing out in her neck. "I grieved for the whole sorry business, but I had to be vigilant. You were with Kyall yesterday, weren't you? He told me all about it. How that fool Joe Randall suggested you take over from him at the hospital. Don't do it," Ruth said harshly between her teeth. "Don't even think of it. You will not come back to this town."

"How many people are going to stop me?" Sarah's whole manner was controlled.

Ruth gave her thin, malignant smile. "Believe me, my dear, one's enough."

Sarah paused to glance back at the house. "What was Molly Fairweather to you? I understand she was a nurse. It'll be easy enough for me to check out her credentials and where she worked. What did you have on her, Ruth? Or what did she have on you?"

For an instant Ruth flinched, then rallied. "So you're prepared to delve into things that are none of your business and of no possible interest to you. Miss Fairweather is dead. Gone."

"She had to go?" Sarah asked with a bitter urgency.

Ruth McQueen's face suddenly froze. "Get in that vehicle now and drive back to town," she ordered harshly. "I'll follow you. You're no match for me, my girl. You never were and you never will be. If you know what's good for you, you'll go on with your life. There's no place for you here. If you can't see that, you're a fool."

"What an arrogant woman you are," Sarah breathed. "What makes you think you can threaten me?"

"Because I can." Ruth raised her chin. The stretching of her lips signified what she thought of that question.

"No. You can't. I have Kyall on my side."

Ruth thrust her hand out of the window to signal her driver. "That can't happen—*ever*," she said, her voice thick with anger and hate. "I'll make sure of it."

"Keep me posted," Sarah replied. "I'm not running scared of you anymore or your psychological warfare."

"To hell with you, Sarah Dempsey." Ruth sank back into the plush upholstery.

"I know you're a woman who'll stop at nothing," Sarah said calmly, glancing at Jensen as he approached. "You've been protected by your money. I have no doubt that you'll try to turn Kyall against me. I'll just have to live with that, because if I'm the town's choice as doctor, I'm coming back to Koomera Crossing. And no one, not even you, Mrs. McQueen, will stop me."

SHE'D BROUGHT OUT all her mother's things. Not much to show for a life. Now she'd packed them away. Everything except her mother's wedding dress, veil and the string of pearls her father had given her to wear on that very special day. Very good pearls, she thought. Her father had spent time in Broome in far Northwestern Australia, the pearl capital of the country and source of the finest South Sea pearls. She could imagine her father as a young man, carefully looking over the loose pearls, selecting the very finest. Probably well beyond his budget.

Sarah crossed to the dressing table and sat down on the padded seat. She clasped the pearls around her throat. They had a lovely luster that complemented her skin. The pearls had been her mother's prize possession. It had taken her father years to buy her mother a proper engagement ring. A small diamond cluster. Sarah wore it on her right hand. She decided it could stay there until she died.

Father and mother gone. Rose. Her private torment. She had patients with worse griefs. The ghastly, gut-wrenching days when a young cancer patient died. Those deaths were always devastating, no matter how expected. Yet she'd learned to maintain a sense of objectivity, a professional calm. It was either that or go mad.

Sarah stared into the faintly spotty mirror, seeing through and beyond it to the past. The past was Kyall. In a way she'd been reliving it since she arrived in Koomera Crossing. She couldn't see into the future. Much as memories of Kyall had dominated her life, she couldn't picture herself marrying him. Not then. And not now.

Sarah stood up. She went to the bed, picking up her mother's pretty wedding dress. How slender and petite Muriel had been. She herself was taller, longer-limbed. The dress was simple, youthful, with a scooped neck, tulle sleeves bound with satin, a skirt with bands of tulle and satin. Although packed very carefully, the materials had yellowed with age. As had the flower-wreathed veil.

You didn't have much time to be happy, Mum, she thought as she repacked it with fresh tissue paper. *Dad even less. Maybe there's a curse on us all.* Yet she could imagine her mother on her wedding day, floating toward her bridegroom, face radiant with love. Jock Dempsey, from all accounts, had been a prize. It hadn't been unusual to hear her mother ask repeatedly and with some wonder, "Jock, why did you marry me? I'm so ordinary."

"That's ridiculous! You're lovely, inside and out," her father had always replied tenderly. "My lovely loyal wife."

Her parents had been very happy together in the short time they had. Always touching each other, sharing words of love. Maybe it was genetic, this one-man, one-woman thing.

It was well after eleven o'clock, as she was preparing for bed, that she heard footsteps, one after the other, on the rear stairs leading to the store's small flat. Her stomach contracted with apprehension. Who could it be at this time of night? As she listened in some dismay, she heard a knock. And she recognized his voice.

"SARAH? PLEASE OPEN the door. I can see your light."

Kyall. Ruth hadn't taken long. Sarah picked up her robe and slipped it on, tying the silk cord at the waist. No point trying to send him away. Kyall had come looking for her. Probably without pity.

"You finally made it," he said. There was no duplicity in his smile. No anger.

She nearly buckled with relief. Ruth hadn't told him, if only for one reason—that she'd be exposing herself. "Kyall, this isn't a good idea," she protested as if the sleeping town was all ears. "Do you know what time it is?"

"Thirty minutes past the hour of eleven." Laconically he consulted his watch, then looked back at her, his eyes so ablaze they practically blinded her. "Are you going to let me in?"

His voice didn't suggest he'd been drinking. Neither did his appearance. The light from inside revealed the strong planes and angles of his face, the blue-black gloss of his hair.

"This will be all over town before morning." She stood aside to let him enter, the door so narrow and he so tall and wide-shouldered, she had to ease back.

"Why should we care?" His smile sparkled with mockery. "We're admired by just about everyone in town, aren't we? Hell, Sarah, we're not kids who need supervision. We're both over thirty. And getting older every day. I have no woman. You have no man. Neither of us has a child. The fact of the matter is that we're stuck in a time warp." He moved across the small living room to slump into an armchair, yanking free the top button of his shirt. He looked up, studying her. "What happened to us, Sarah? Why the hell are we marooned like this?"

She felt herself flush. "Conflict of interests." *My interests conflicted with your grandmother's. She was determined to erase me from your life.*

"'I do believe her, though I know she lies,'" he quoted from Shakespeare. His eyes moved over her with hunger. Over her graceful body in the pink satin robe, lingering on the lilac-shadowed cleft of her breasts. "I'd swear you had a light beneath your skin," he whispered. "It actually glows."

"It's the pink satin," she offered shakily, glancing around, not knowing what to do when she was assailed by an answering desire. Throughout her pregnancy, she'd dreamed of Kyall charging in like a knight of old to rescue her, vanquishing his grandmother. If only he had been there to share in her experience. If only she'd had his support. At least he'd been spared her terrible grief, although she knew in her heart he mightn't see it that way. She realized now that Kyall wouldn't have minded being "stuck with a baby." Considering that neither of them had progressed to finding other partners, they might just as well have waited a few years, then got married. She still couldn't work out how her baby had come to die, although she'd seen the death certificate. She'd done all the right things. She was young and healthy. Her baby had looked perfect. She couldn't understand it. And she couldn't get over it. There was no burial place to visit. Not even the baby's ashes to keep or to scatter. Ruth McQueen had taken charge of everything.

Ruth McQueen and Nurse Fairweather? Oh, yes, she had a lot of unfinished business in this town.

"Sarah, where are you?" Kyall asked. "Some far place where I can't reach you?"

"I was thinking. A bad habit of mine."

"Don't drive me away. Don't, Sarah," he begged. "I made one big mistake in my life. I don't want to make another. Come here to me."

She went slowly, standing before him. He took one of her hands, kissed it. "What's made you the way you are, Sarah? I know you wanted to be a doctor. I know you're a good one. But don't you want a full life? Doesn't that mean family?"

"What do you want from me, Kyall? What do you expect from me?" Her body was trembling and singing both at the same time.

"A bloody sight more than I'm getting." Roughly he pulled her down into his arms, hands very firm. "I want you to marry me. I've never wanted anything more in my life."

Her face reflected conflict and the fever that was in her. If he knew about their child, he might hate her. He might attach rightful blame.

"You don't have to answer now," he said, fearful he might lose her all over again. "But let me love you. I'm done with words." His hand clenched her hair. "Far better to make you ache for me." His hand stroked her breast, taking its soft weight, his thumb seeking and finding the already erect nipple while sensation hammered away at him. What was romantic love? A sickness with no cure?

She moaned, unable not to. Still he didn't kiss her, holding her face away.

Finally, in an agitated flurry just as he intended, she lifted her arms to encircle his neck, a silken rope to bind him to her.

"What I want is you, calling up the magic." There was no tenderness in his tone. More an edge of sexual hostility for the humiliations she had caused him.

Then, before she could say a word, he brought down his mouth to silence her, tasting the honey and lemon of her breath. How this woman assaulted his every sense! He wanted to do things to her he'd never thought to do with any other woman. He was desperate for her, straining her to him. His hand slid from her breast over the firm flesh of her stomach, moved lower…lower… He knew she wanted it because she didn't stop him. It was ravishing to know her body, but he wanted more, much more. He wanted it to be absolutely his. He wanted her heart and her soul.

Passion raged through him. He found and freed the single satin button that held the low V of her nightgown together. Then he peeled the fabric down, so that it pooled around her waist. "How beautiful you are." He abandoned himself to the sheer erotic pleasure of looking at her. The flowering buds of her nipples were tight with arousal, pink at the edge, rose at the center. They demanded to be suckled. He lowered his head, his mouth eager and hungry.

She gripped his head, as his every nerve end twitched and sizzled. He could feel her body shaking convulsively at his ministrations. He could hear her utter his name on one long-drawn-out moan. It was a powerful incitement to finish what he'd started. With a single move, he lifted himself out of the chair with her in his arms, carrying her off to the small bedroom. The bed had belonged to her mother. Even that thought couldn't distract him. Desire held him in its thrall.

His Sarah. His bright and shining light. His torment.

He knew he ought to ask her if her time was right, and he did, tension in his voice and a sheer, frightening drive.

Her "Yes!" burst out in a wrenching sob.

He stripped her gown from her. She lay perfectly quiescent as he did so. Possessively he trailed a hand up and down her gleaming skin—difficult to imagine a woman's body more beautiful—before stepping back to remove his own clothes and throw them on a chair.

Sarah in turn could only watch him, her own body burning with a fiery need that matched his. He was tanned all over. No band of pale skin. In the outback heat the male station workers thought nothing of skinny-dipping in the creek. It had been years and years since she'd seen his naked body. He'd been little more than a boy then. Now he was a man. Taller, broader of shoulder, with wonderful muscle density. His arousal was thrilling. Promise of what was to come.

Then he was beside her, turning her body toward him, flesh on flesh, enveloping her in his arms as if he were holding the most precious woman in the world.

"Sarah! My darling. Darling. Darling."

She couldn't answer. The force of her hunger was holding her mute. He was where she desperately wanted him to be. Fused to her naked body. Her blood ran like wine. Soon he would be inside her.

She had no doubts of her love for him.

How have I lived without this?
"Come inside me," she crooned.

FOR LONG MINUTES AFTERWARD neither of them spoke. Kyall lay on his back with Sarah's head resting on his shoulder, one arm like the lightest, most welcome pinion across his chest.

Finally he managed a few words. "I needed that to convince me you still want me."

"Well, now you know." She reached out to stroke his cheek. "My chosen one. My only love. I gave my heart to you so many years ago. Now it's impossible to take it back." She bestowed on him her old secret smile.

"Then there's no question of your going away." His hand grasped a handful of golden curls. "You have to stay with me and take over from Joe."

"If the town wants me."

"*Wants* you?" His voice lifted with elation. "Of course they want you. You're their favorite child grown up. I'm not asking you to stay at the hospital forever, Sarah. I know you have ambitions. Hell, I have them myself. I've been approached to go into politics."

"Really?" She lifted herself on an elbow to stare at him. His eyes in the glow from the single lamp glittered like sapphires. "Politics have always mattered to you—the direction our country's taking."

"Sounds all right to you?"

"Of course it does!" She looked at him proudly. "You have so much to offer. You can always oversee the McQueen operations. You have your mother and father, not to mention your grandmother. She's in her seventies, but she could go on forever."

"Will you marry me?" He put a lot of determination into his voice. "Say it, Sarah."

She bent forward and slipped the tip of her tongue into

his mouth, let it entwine with his. "You must let me think about it."

"What's there to think about?" He eased her onto her back. "Our life should be full of love and hope. Hope for the future. I want children. I love children. I know you do, too. Let's build a life together. Starting now. Too much time has already got away. I'll never stop you from furthering your career. I'm too proud of you. We can manage. Others do. You have to say yes."

Was it her moment to scatter all the radiance, the gold dust of dreams? Tell him how she'd had their baby but never seen its tiny lifeless body? He would surely blame her, for she had never ceased to blame herself.

"Sarah?" He raised her to him, almost crushing her, forgetting his strength. "What is it? What's haunting you?"

"Grief," she admitted through the hard lump in her throat. "I'm full of grief. I can't seem to shed it."

"I'm sorry. I'm not even giving you a chance, am I?"

"Hush!" The weight of her secret had grown unbearable. "I love you, Kyall. I want to be with you for always, but you must give me a little breathing space."

"You have nothing to fear from my grandmother," he told her as that possibility leaped into his mind. "I know people hate her. Sadly I can see why. But she will never hurt you."

"What are you going to do? Shove her in prison?" For an instant she used the cutting edge of her tongue. "Maximum security?"

"I'll warn her. I think that'll be enough. Her problem is that she's jealous of you, Sarah."

"Indeed she is. She wants to keep you for herself or marry you off to a woman she can control."

"That's sick!" he groaned.

"It is," Sarah quietly agreed, sinking back against the

bed. As always, she was chilled by any mention of that oppressive woman. "Your grandmother has a darkness in her that separates her from the rest of us. You can't even see into her eyes."

Kyall ranged his long body beside hers, thrusting an arm behind his head. "I know that. I've lived with it all my life. Gran can't envision life without being the one in control. You threaten her, and she loathes that. But even if she opposes your taking over from Joe at the hospital, I'll block her. Trust me. I have my own supporters. My mother will present no problem. She will do as I ask."

Sarah considered this wryly. "Are you sure of that? Your mother doesn't hear what she doesn't want to hear."

Who knew that better than his father? His mother had perfected the art of selective hearing. "If you want Joe's job, it's yours," he said with quiet emphasis. "But you can be sure of one thing." He caught her chin, compelling her to look directly into his eyes. "After tonight I'll never let you go."

CHAPTER SEVEN

BACK AT THE CLINIC in Brisbane, Sarah lost no time handing in her resignation. It was received with such dismay, she might have found it gratifying—but she didn't. Despite her confidence in the decision, she felt torn about leaving her patients and colleagues.

Clinic head Peter Crawley, an attractive man with a reassuring face, threw off his glasses and leaned back in his leather chair. "Lord, Sarah! There can't be much for you way out there. It's still the back o' beyond. You'll spend your life treating snake bites and spider bites and the odd tourist with sunstroke. It's enough to make the eyes glaze over." He looked across his desk at her, marveling at her decision. Sarah Dempsey was a valuable member of his team, a dedicated doctor who invested a heartfelt commitment to her work. The clinic would miss her badly on both a professional and personal basis.

"I was born there, Peter," she reminded him. "I'll have plenty of patients with all manner of ills. Patients are the same everywhere. I'll keep up with the literature. Or try to. There's so much of it."

"But, Sarah!" Peter Crawley was still desperate to talk her out of it. "In all honesty, how could you endure it? You'll go crazy! You're too bright to bury yourself in the bush. The patients here love you, especially the mothers and children. I can't imagine what we're going to do without you. Tell me I'm going to wake up and find this is all a nightmare.''

"You're a sweet man, Peter, but you know I'm not indispensable. I'll be very sorry to leave my patients and the clinic. We've all worked so well together. I can recommend a colleague of mine, though, a friend, Jane Kirby. We went through med school together. She's been looking to buy into the right practice. She'd be ideal to take over from me. I'll sound her out first, if you like.''

"Never. We want you.'' Still in a state of shock, Peter Crawley brooded, staring down at the pile of medical files on his desk. "Someone's taken one of my files,'' he announced irritably, flipping through them.

"Not me.'' Sarah knew he'd eventually find it. "Of course you'll make your own choice, but Jane is very good with women and children.''

"Ah, dear!'' Peter sighed painfully. "I'll consider it. We can meet with her and take it from there. When are you going to leave us?''

"When you have my replacement settled in, Peter,'' Sarah assured him. "There'll be nothing left in disarray. I won't leave you in the lurch or abandon my patients overnight.''

"What a mystery woman you are!'' Peter said, suddenly sighting the "lost" file on top of a cabinet where he'd left it. "I wish I could persuade you to change your mind.'' He put his glasses back on to study her.

"There are things I have to do, Peter,'' she explained in a serious voice. "I have to work my way through a whole maze of personal questions that have never really been answered. It's not just taking over at the hospital. It's an opportunity to sort things out. Sort my *life* out. I've learned that we can never escape the past.''

"No, indeed. As someone rightly said, the past is never past. You're not getting married, are you?"

"I have no immediate plans, Peter," Sarah murmured, not looking up.

"There's a problem, isn't there?" Peter asked perceptively.

"Lots of them, actually," Sarah confessed, but stopped there. She had long since got into the habit of keeping private matters to herself.

"I was going to ask, does this have something to do with the sudden death of your mother?" Peter questioned with care.

Mute for a moment, Sarah nodded.

"All right, all right." Peter sighed. "If I can't talk you out of it, Sarah, it goes without saying I wish all the good fortune in the world. You deserve it." Peter stood up regretfully, circling his desk. "We're all going to miss you."

"Maybe. Maybe not," she joked. "But I'll certainly miss you, Peter." Sarah stood to face him.

He patted her shoulder. "You've got to keep in touch. And if you ever want to come back, I'll find a place for you. Now, what do you say to a quick cup of coffee? It seems to be quiet out there for once. And we have to tell Cliff and the rest, let alone the patients." He shook his head. "They'll all be heartbroken."

Sarah was so moved she couldn't speak.

As SWIFTLY AS she'd delivered her resignation, Sarah sought from the national nurses' unions and agencies all information on a Margaret "Molly" Fairweather, now deceased, believed to have worked at St. Catherine's Maternity Hospital in Adelaide in the eighties and probably at a small private maternity hospital called Glen Ross in the town of Rockhampton some fifteen years ago. A day later all the information she required was e-mailed back. It helped that the request had come from a registered medical practitioner.

Finally she knew. Finally she'd learned the identity of the midwife who had delivered her little Rose. The "spooky bird" that had hovered over her when she was fuzzy with dope. Nurse Margaret Fairweather was well regarded, it appeared, within the nursing profession. No blemishes on her professional name, no strikes against her anywhere. For inexplicable reasons Margaret Fairweather had chosen to retire to a remote outback town where she had no roots, no family, no friends (except Ruth McQueen?). A remote outback town where she'd gone quietly mad.

How had such a thing happened to a woman who, for most of her life had been a respected member of the nursing community? One would have to consider the onset of dementia, perhaps due to Alzheimer's, a global loss of intellectual function, the continuing destruction of neurons in the brain. Margaret Fairweather had been fifty-two at the time of her death. Not old. Still, dementia isn't always restricted to the very old.

But Mad Molly Fairweather had not been suffering from dementia. Two reliable witnesses, Harriet and Tilly, had confirmed that Nurse Fairweather had been quite capable of carrying on an intelligent conversation, driving a vehicle and getting herself periodically into town. Was all the raving to herself in the garden a descent into mental illness— or was she just plain lonely? Psychiatry wasn't Sarah's field, but she knew any number of psychiatrists she could talk to. Without question, Molly Fairweather had had something extremely distressing on her mind. Her episodes of disturbance—if the town's children were to be believed— were fairly frequent. In these long monologues, what did

she rant about? Sarah had to find out, although she expected
she'd have to take a lot of the information with a grain of
salt. Children were notorious for making up stories or em-
bellishing their reports. Not only children. Ruby Hall, her
mother's assistant in the store, had a well-deserved reputation for passing on complicated accounts of events that
were half truth, half fantasy.

And what part did Ruth McQueen play in all this? It
didn't take Sarah long to discover, via an Internet search,
that Ruth McQueen had held the title deed for the old Sinclair residence since the death of her husband. Held it without interruption. The McQueens, in fact, had bought the
property and hundreds of acres around it from the Sinclairs
after their sad departure to Adelaide in the late 1800s.

So Nurse Fairweather had never purchased the property.
She'd been Ruth McQueen's tenant all along. Why? What
had brought the woman to Koomera Crossing? Why did
Ruth McQueen allow her to occupy the house? What was
the connection—if not the fact that Nurse Fairweather had
been the midwife at Rose's birth?

And what about the birth itself? God, why hadn't her
mother been with her? Why hadn't her poor little mother
fought to be with her own child? Damn Ruth McQueen to
hell! The baby's death certificate had said respiratory failure. It did happen. But why the unseemly haste to dispose
of the body? Why the shockingly callous treatment of her?
Surely even a woman like Ruth McQueen could pity a
mother's loss. And the baby had been her own family!

There was so much Sarah knew nothing about. She'd
gone into shock. And afterward? It had seemed pointless
to ask any questions. Her little Rose was lost to her. Nothing would bring her back.

Now this important information. Was it possible there'd
been a cover-up? Had Nurse Fairweather failed in her du-

ties in some way? Had she accidently dropped Rose? That, too, happened. And worse. Drastic mistakes, most tragically, happened all the time. She'd seen her share. She'd seen the anger and despair afterward. The legal action. Nurse Fairweather must have had some hold over Ruth McQueen. It was the most logical explanation.

What?

Glen Ross, a private hospital, no longer existed. Sarah found out in a single phone call that the old maternity home had been demolished a dozen years ago and a motel built on the site.

But there had to be records somewhere.

No. Certainly not dating that far back. But Sarah, as a medical doctor, could easily access the registry of births and deaths, she was told.

Of course she could and did. She had the dates emblazoned on her brain. She even remembered a young woman in the room next to her at the hospital. Much older than she was. Mid-twenties. Maybe older. Stella. Like in Tennessee Williams's play *A Streetcar Named Desire*. That was the only reason she'd remembered it. That and the fact that she'd cried so loud and long Stella had confided in a nurse she couldn't bear it. Sarah had no idea of Stella's surname. But she did remember Stella had gone home with her baby, a little girl. Not that she'd actually seen Stella's child. She had literally been out of her mind with desolation.

Lucky Stella to be so blessed! Stella's girl would be exactly the same age as Sarah's Rose had she lived. Fifteen. In early adolescence. At school.

At fifteen she herself had become a mother. It had been no seduction game with Kyall. Not playing at sex, the way many teenagers did. The circumstances, the relationship had been extraordinary. They'd come together as if preordained. As though at that exact juncture in their lives they were to conceive another human being. She might have lost Rose, but Sarah remembered that her baby had been perfect. Perfectly formed. Her first cry was so robust it had been a wonder. What had altered so suddenly? So drastically? Only Ruth McQueen could supply the missing pieces. Nurse Fairweather was dead. Sarah was certain the answers were back at Koomera Crossing. Back with the stop-at-nothing Ruth.

AT THE END of the week, over dinner with Peter and her friend Jane, it was decided that Jane would join the Waverley Medical Centre, buying out Sarah's share. This enabled Sarah to pay off what was left of her initial bank loan, with several thousand left over. A hectic month after that, Sarah was ready to take up her new appointment as doctor in residence at Koomera Crossing Hospital. In all that time, she had spoken to Kyall daily, sensing—although she was never told—that he and his grandmother had been involved in a titanic clash over the town council's decision. Obviously Kyall had worn down his mother's resistance, but Sarah could just imagine how vehement even that might have been. The citizens of the town, on the other hand, had professed themselves thrilled that Sarah would want to come back to them, particularly as the town's doctor.

Joe, more consumed by his cancer with every passing day, breathed a great sigh of relief. Sarah would be taking over from him. He had brought her into the world. She was one of them—never an outsider. She would fit in wonderfully. Except for Ruth. Ruth, his once-passionate lover—he'd always known it was only the sex, for her, anyway—had been distant from him for years now. Still, before he departed this world, he intended to speak to her. He'd always had a dreadfully uncomfortable feeling about that poor woman, Molly Fairweather. Somehow Ruth was mixed up in that. She'd only given him one sign, a mere flash in those brilliant fathomless eyes, like pretenses stripped away, but he'd seen enough. He'd always been acutely receptive to Ruth and her many moods. She offered few surprises. Sometimes he thought Harriet might have known or deduced more than she'd ever said. But then, Harriet was a very shrewd woman, a close observer of human nature. A man would've been far, far happier with a woman like Harriet, not that she'd ever looked sideways at him. All too late, anyway. He didn't have long to live. There was a palpable change in his body, the yellow-white eyes, the agony that periodically shook him, even while he was numbed by morphine. It signaled the end.

Joe wanted above all to stay alive until Sarah had taken over at the hospital. Sarah, from all reports—and he had made many inquiries over the years—would do good things. Kyall, too, was full of confidence in her. And renewed hope. Kyall and Sarah should marry and have children, as Joe was sure the Lord Himself had intended. The only threat to them was and remained...

Ruth.

Ruth walked a fine line between good and evil. Over the years, he'd had to force himself to confront a terrible truth. No one Ruth perceived to be an enemy was safe.

AT SEVEN O'CLOCK the following evening Joe presented himself at Wunnamurra homestead. It was a hard hour's drive out of the town, so he'd had a friend drive him. He was now quite incapable of making the trip himself. Ruth had taken him by surprise, suggesting he stay overnight. She knew perfectly well he was a sick man. "You looked so frail at Muriel Dempsey's funeral, Joe. I was so worried about you!'' He'd have dinner with the family, and Max would drive him back into town the following day.

So it was all arranged…with Sarah due to arrive in two days. Ruth, the accomplished actress concealing her own anger, remarked quietly to the family that she was glad Joe had called her. She certainly gave every appearance of being pleased. It would be good to have her old friend under their roof. Joe had done so much for the town. It would be a very sad day indeed when he left to spend his retirement—and what remained of his life—with a widowed sister. She and Joe had so much shared history.

"You mean you've just discovered how much you care about him, Gran?" asked Kyall, his voice biting.

"Understand that you, more than anyone, have brought Sarah Dempsey to this town, Kyall," Ruth responded, folding her hands. "I'm sorry, my darling, but I can't think she'll ever fill Joe's shoes. Or get anyone to trust her like they trusted Joe."

Sweet Lord! Why didn't the words stick in her throat? For years now, Kyall had hardly believed a word his grandmother said. She was duplicity itself.

Sensing his skepticism, Ruth met her grandson's eyes. "At least try to appreciate my very real concerns. The town won't like discovering that Sarah isn't up to the job."

Kyall's expression turned to one of mild irony. "Sure she is. Most of us, including Joe, think so, at any rate. Sorry, Gran."

Ruth fought back a bitter retort. She and Kyall had quarreled enough. She was unhappy about it, desperate to restore what she thought of as her unassailable place in his heart. But, dressing for dinner in her bedroom, Ruth calmly and deliberately spread a few little dry seeds across the polished surface of a small antique table. So harmless looking. Joe wanted to talk to her about Molly Fairweather, did he? Molly and her untimely, somewhat horrific, demise. Poor old Molly had wanted to speak to her, too. Molly wound up dead. So would Joe. A pity, but she could see right away that the whole issue would lead to trouble. She had the means at hand. Undetectable. Dear Sarah wasn't the only one who'd delved into native remedies. Not that a powerful poison came into that category, exactly. She'd always been interested in native sorcery—both beneficial and destructive. Many people questioned whether Aborigines really performed sorcery as they claimed. As far as Ruth was concerned, it worked. Molly had been talking for days of a strange feeling in her right leg. A sensation much like a burning sting. How did the disbeliever account for that? Still, no one would be any the wiser. Joe's sudden death would be interpreted as the will of God. He was already a dying man. Hastening the awful process could only be an act of compassion. Preferable to a long-drawn-out agony.

Molly Fairweather, on the other hand, deserved everything she got. Molly Fairweather, despite all the help Ruth had given her, had persuaded herself that the only way to save her immortal soul was to go public. It wasn't too late to put things right, she'd insisted.

"I'm positive, Mrs. McQueen," Molly had shrieked, waving like a fool at the sky. "You'll help me, won't you? I have everyone's best interests at heart. You must tell your grandson and that poor girl. Her screams have haunted me all these years. I must've been mad. You asked too much. It was wicked, you know." Here she grabbed Ruth roughly by the arm, staring into Ruth's eyes, letting go in near terror before she burst into tears. "Please, Mrs. McQueen," Molly had begged. "Have pity."

Naturally she'd been able to persuade Molly to wait a few days, explaining that they had to be very careful how they went about putting things right. There was so much to consider.

Molly had agreed at once.

Poor Molly.

AT SOME POINT during the night Joe Randall woke up. He tried to grope for the light, but his limbs seemed paralyzed. He'd become nothing but bone. A skeleton in his pajamas. The night was black and he was drenched in a cold sweat. His heart pounded so violently he thought his rib cage would shatter under the bombardment. He tried to sit up, fell back totally disoriented, not recognizing the room where he lay. His symptoms confused him. Aberrations from the norm. Or the norm of terminal cancer. No nausea. No racking vomiting. But he couldn't seem to swallow and he had a strangely bitter taste in his mouth. Like scorched nuts. Or poison. Oddly, he didn't seem to be in pain. None of the tearing agony he was accustomed to, like the turn and twist of a blade in his guts. But he couldn't swallow. Couldn't breathe. Could barely move. He was obviously close to death and yet he'd been sure he had a little time left.

A familiar perfume reached his nostrils. A shape moved out of the farthest corner of the room. He stared at it, shivering hard. A ghost in a nightgown. It approached the bed. Joe shrank back instinctively, although he could make no sound.

In a dim flash he saw Ruth. Her face, suddenly illuminated, was as cold and severe as any executioner's. It hovered over him. Its fingers touched his face. *Ruth, were you there all the time?*

"I've come to say goodbye, Joe," she whispered.

She sounded sad.

No. This was the woman he had loved, despite her one hellish flaw.

"You made a terrible mistake, Joe," she murmured, leaning against the bed. "How could you have been so stupid? Now you've got to die." Very gently she bent her head to kiss him, and the terrible irony of it gave him a moment's brilliant clarity. "I swear I didn't want this, Joe, but you forced my hand. You'll never make that mistake again."

Of course. It flooded Joe's faltering mind that he'd walked right into her trap. He'd been prepared for any-thing—he knew the wild Ruth of old. But not this. Though there was little or no air left in his frail, exhausted body, so miraculously, wondrously out of pain, Joe Randall man-aged one word: "Murderer!"

"Hush, Joe," she soothed. "Who are you to judge me? How could you prove it? Tomorrow you'll be carried out on a stretcher. I'll walk behind you to the undertaker's van, seemingly unaware of the tears that stream down my face." Her voice fell to a whisper. "Our special relationship, never spoken about except behind my back, will be remembered. Our friendship goes back a long way, Joe. You built your career in this town because of me. I was the one who hand-picked you and supported you in all your efforts. Naturally my emotions are involved. It's only to be expected, even by my family. The truth about your death will never even be suspected. Not provable, anyway. You were obviously dying. The whole town will turn out for your funeral, mourn your passing. I'll see to it that you're given an im-pressive headstone."

Noooooo!

While Ruth stood motionless at the side of the bed, every light in Joe Randall's body went out.

CHAPTER EIGHT

AT THE SAME TIME the residents of Koomera Crossing were attending Joe Randall's funeral, Stella Hazelton came to her first conscious realization of the truth. All through their beloved daughter's childhood—she was their only child—Stella and her husband, Alan, had made jokes about how the two of them, quite ordinary really, could have produced such a ravishingly pretty and intelligent child.

"She's got my coloring!" Alan, fair and blue-eyed, always boasted, "but where did she get those gorgeous little features and that dimple in her chin?"

"Maybe she's a throwback to someone in the family?" Stella with her nondescript brown hair and gentle gray eyes would suggest. "Or she's simply God's great gift to us." This with tears in her eyes.

"That she is, my love." Alan always hugged his wife at this point. Three miscarriages, including one heartbreaking stillbirth, had followed the miracle of Noni's birth. The last one was life-threatening to Stella. Stella's doctor afterward told them that she and Alan should content themselves with their beautiful little girl. Alan had taken Stella's hand, squeezed it supportively. They would do as the doctor ordered. He couldn't bear the thought of losing his dearest Stella, his best mate, though she had cried and cried, saying it was so strange that Noni had come into the world perfectly, if so quietly. She remembered no vigor in her baby's cries.

Always she wanted to stop there, blocking out the memory of the vulnerable youngster in the next room of the maternity hospital. Fourteen, fifteen, it was hard to tell. She'd had an illegitimate child, of course. Not that she'd actually spoken more than a half a dozen words to the girl. The grandmother had been with the poor kid the whole time. A striking woman, obviously well-off with a beautifully modulated voice. Not kind, though. Stella remembered the hard edge.

The two of them had had their babies within an hour of each other, both of them emerging from the experience with unusual fragility. She was a sturdy girl from sturdy stock, but it had taken her quite a while to recover after Noni's birth. Her mother, delirious with joy, had come to her aid. The youngster's baby had died. It had developed respiratory problems, poor little mite. As a new mother herself, she'd been devastated by the girl's cries. No happy event for that poor girl, little more than a child herself.

When Alan had come to take her and their beautiful baby home, the girl had still been there, sedated for her suffering. Stella had wanted to say goodbye, whisper words of deepest sympathy, but the girl had been asleep, pale as a marble statue, her golden curling locks spread over the pillow like a halo. Her profile was as perfect as a painted angel's. The straight nose, the sculpted cheekbones, the lovely molded mouth…

The dimpled chin.

How remarkable she should remember that. Or had she, at the deepest level, been pushing it out of her mind? Noni—short for Fiona, after her mother—was their baby. Hers and Alan's. They had prayed and prayed she would conceive some three years into the marriage. No sign of a child. They'd both been highly emotional at that time. Both on the verge of despair before she finally got pregnant after a peaceful beach holiday.

Such joy! She'd been almost overwhelmed by a sense of failure, but overnight had turned into a woman of confidence. The birth of their darling Noni had called forth the most wonderful maternal instincts. She was a good mother. Alan was a good father. Everyone said that.

"Take the Hazeltons. Such a happy family." Only a few people took note of the fact that Noni resembled neither parent. As well, these same people pointed out, she shone at school, her intelligence clearly a lot higher than her mother's or father's. But these were women who liked to pass the odd spiteful remark.

Noni was *theirs*. Stella was positive until that day, the day of Joe Randall's funeral in a far-distant town. Her eyes red from weeping, sodden tissues balled at her feet, Stella sat holding one of her daughter's school photographs. Not the class photo. The individual portrait. Noni at fifteen. Class Captain. Grade 10. She was smiling, showing her beautiful white teeth. No dentist's bills there. Noni didn't have a single filling, while Stella had a mouthful of them. Noni's curling mane was pulled back into a single thick rope. Long hair, ponytail or braid, was a school requirement. There was such a sparkle in her glorious eyes. Brown, long-lashed velvet. Not her dad's light blue. And that beguiling shallow dimple in her chin…

I can't take this, Stella thought in fear and trembling. *I can't even continue to speculate what might have happened. Noni is ours.* She was the most loved member of their family. Her grandparents on both sides adored her, to the extent that Stella's sister, Debra, with two girls around the same age, often got jealous.

The truth was lost fifteen years ago. This was her subconscious erupting like a volcano, Stella thought, punishing her. Well, given a little time to hurdle the shock, she would suppress all knowledge. Noni was their golden child. Hers and Alan's.

Stella remained in her bedroom for the rest of the day, dozing fitfully or weeping, trying to manage her distress. Finally, when she heard the front door open and her darling Noni call out excitedly, "Mum, Mum, where are you? Guess what? Clemmie's invited me to spend the June holidays with them. Please, please, could I go? I'm dying to see the outback."

Why not? Clemmie Hungerford was a lovely girl, a boarder at Noni's excellent school. The Hungerfords had a big pastoral property way out in Western Queensland. It would be a new experience for Noni. A wonderful experience!

Stella pulled herself together. She rose from the bed, went to the mirror and ran a comb through her hair before going downstairs to hear what else her daughter had to say. After all, she'd reared Noni. She'd done everything for her. She and Alan. That made Noni their daughter. No reasonable person would deny that.

SARAH BEGAN HER TENURE at the hospital under sad circumstances. She hadn't expected Joe to go so quickly—but she consoled herself with the thought he'd been spared months of incredible pain and the terrible nausea that was one of his cancer's manifestations. She had been present at the funeral. The biggest surprise was Ruth McQueen's obvious distress. Joe's dying at the homestead must have come as a dreadful shock. Death was like that, even when expected. Ruth, for once, looked her age, a fragile figure in her elegant black outfit, her body vibrating with distress. Ruth was growing old. It came as almost as big a shock to Sarah as Joe's dying. Sarah continued to stare, watching the tears slide down Ruth's white cheeks. Did this mean Ruth had to be considered human, after all?

"You trust her?" Harriet asked, majestic in a wide-brimmed black hat with a broad silver ribbon. They were walking away from the church service.

"I gather you don't, Harriet?" Sarah's tone was wry.

"I've yet to see Ruth McQueen prove herself human. That, in my opinion, was a total sham, an over-the-top display of crocodile tears. Ruth really cannot be trusted. But for some reason she wants us all to revise our opinion of her."

"She must have a tender side," Sarah suggested dubiously.

Harriet rolled her eyes and shook her head.

"She adores Kyall."

"Ruth is suffering from a personality disorder, which is not to say Kyall isn't a splendid young man who has a wonderful way with women. But there are two kinds of grandmothers. The very good and the very bad. That's my conclusion, anyway."

"But couldn't she be good *some* of the time?"

"She did build the hospital," Harriet conceded.

"She and Joe were lovers at one time. Joe admitted it."

"Poor old Joe!" Harriet said with a gusty sigh. "Proof that even a good man can be seduced into dangerous sex. Testosterone overriding all common sense." She shook her head. "Though I have to admit, Ruth would've been really something when she put on her seductive garments. At any rate, she swept Joe off his feet."

Sarah shivered, readily picturing Ruth in her younger days. But to kiss her would've been to taste poison. "Then she dumped him."

"I fully expected her to swallow him up." Harriet

glanced around at the other mourners. "We shouldn't be talking like this at a funeral, should we?"

"I suppose not, but I can't come up with anything pleasant. I feel awful about Joe."

"None of us would've wanted him to go on suffering," Harriet said quietly. "Not even Ruth, it seems. I suspect Joe would've got a kick out of her tears. But being the cynical old soul that I am, I have to wonder why the display of grief. Ruth worries me." Harriet's expression intensified.

"Actually, she worries everyone."

"How does this scenario sound?" Harriet asked, rubbing the high bridge of her nose. "Joe wants to square his conscience. He decides to tackle Ruth about Molly Fairweather. Molly didn't own that house, you know."

"I do know."

"How?" Harriet's thick dark brows executed their usual dance.

"Like you, Harriet, I did a search."

"Very clever!" Harriet acknowledged. "But back to my scenario. Joe calls Ruth and tells her he wants to discuss Molly's sudden demise. How did the desert taipan fit in? What, pray, attracted it through Miss Fairweather's open doorway? He implies that Ruth was involved in some way. An incredibly foolish move on Joe's part. Ruth invites him to dinner at her very grand homestead. Afterward she offers him a nightcap."

"Into which she's just broken a couple of cyanide capsules?" Sarah prompted dryly.

"Unless…unless…" Harriet snapped her fingers.

"What?"

"No…" Harriet looked at Sarah with an odd expression.

"It couldn't have happened like that if you're suggesting poison." Sarah sounded shocked.

"Certainly it could," Harriet argued. "Hasn't it passed

into folklore that Ruth once sent for a *kaidaitcha* man to learn his secrets?''

''*What?*'' Sarah's mouth fell open.

''All right, Ruby Hall once tried to sell me that story. I almost bought it. Ruth is a singularly strange woman. She needed her husband to keep her in line, and when he died…'' Her words drifted off. ''So why were you investigating ownership of the Sinclair house?''

''That, I'm afraid, opens up another line of inquiry.''

''I'm aware of that.'' Harriet leaned closer, lowering her resonant voice. ''When are you and Kyall going to make up? The sooner the better, my dear. He has all the attributes of a wonderful mate. For all his looks and glamour, he's the kind of man who would take his marriage vows very seriously.''

''But what kind of wife would I make?''

''The best.'' Harriet's tone was both tender and bracing. ''Don't let life pass you by, Sarah. You certainly should get married and have children. It's a far better choice than being on your own. Take it from a woman who knows.''

THEY WERE ALMOST at Harriet's ancient car when Kyall caught up with them.

''Poor old Joe!'' he said. ''We're all going to miss him, but I'm glad he wasn't faced with a painful end.''

''Your grandmother is very upset,'' Harriet didn't hesitate to say.

''Obviously she was a heck of a lot fonder of Joe than we realized. I think it's fairly safe at this point to acknowledge that they once had an affair. Hard to imagine, though.''

Not when Ruth in her prime was a sex-seeking missile, Harriet thought.

''Where are you going now?'' Kyall asked Sarah.

"We were going to have something to eat at my place," Harriet supplied. Until Sarah found somewhere she wanted to live, she was staying with her. "Would you care to join us?"

"I'd be delighted to, Harriet." Kyall gave her his beautiful, open smile. "I can't remember a meal of yours that wasn't memorable."

"Your grandmother wants to talk to you, Kyall, I think." Sarah had resisted glancing in that direction, but now she noticed Ruth looking their way sternly and lifting an imperious hand.

Kyall turned his head. "I'll meet you at the house."

"What in the wide world of odd behavior has Ruth got against you, Sarah?" Harriet asked when they were driving away. "I know having all that money and being the matriarch of the McQueen family has made her the world's worst snob, but she wasn't a McQueen by birth. I've met quite a few of the extended family over the years and they're not a bit like that."

"I think it's got more to do with the fact that Kyall still wants me," Sarah said. "She's a very self-sufficient woman, but Kyall's her blind spot. Mine, too," she added almost immediately.

"To die for, as the young people used to say," Harriet hooted, driving fast enough to be pulled over for speeding. "Except that Ruth's obsession is downright unhealthy. Ruth was a terrible mother to her son, Stewart, and to Enid. Both of them suffered. Enid's loveless upbringing probably explains her manner. She's been trying all her life to live up to her mother or her mother's expectations, but thank God she's failed. There's nothing really wrong with Enid. She would've been a different woman, I believe, had she and Max moved away from Wunnamurra, but Ruth wasn't going to have that. She cracked the whip. Put Enid and

Max to work. What love there was between them seems to have dissipated over the years. Max is an uncommonly nice man, too.''

"Too much the gentleman?" Sarah suggested ruefully. Harriet snorted. "He tried to get away once. Quite a few years ago.''

"Did he really?" Sarah was amazed.

"He's on pretty short emotional rations with Enid," Harriet said. "Unlike her mother, Enid is not a passionate woman. I think Ruth's coldness when Enid was a child dehumanized her somewhat. Enid's the sort of woman who might put him off by saying things like, 'Max, dear, I have a headache. Turn off the light.' Poor Max looked elsewhere, but I think Ruth brought some pressure to bear. Max stayed. More for Kyall than anyone else, although Kyall would've been seventeen or eighteen at the time. I honestly think Max will leave Enid one day, but it'll take up to six months for her to notice.''

"I didn't know any of this," Sarah said, shaking her head. "Mum never mentioned a word, but then both of us kept off the subject of the McQueen family.''

"Fearful of Ruth?" Harriet executed a double clutch.

"Mum was," Sarah said with deep regret, stealing a glance at the speedometer. "It's awful to feel so powerless.''

"Yes, indeed," Harriet agreed, "but *you're* not. That's why you came back.''

As HARRIET AND SARAH drove away from the cemetery, Ruth held a strained conversation with her grandson from the back seat of the Rolls.

"It's not like you to let me down, Kyall. If we're seriously interested in Numinbar Station, we should work out a strategy.''

"I already have, Gran," Kyall replied courteously, acutely aware of her age and the fragility of her diminutive body. "It's a very attractive property, but I think we can get it for a whole lot less than the three million Bart Colston's asking. There's a big opportunity to develop a parallel enterprise like ecotourism along with the cattle— we should go for high-grade Brahman, in my opinion. It's beautiful country, softwood rain forest, lagoons and creeks, wonderful horse trails, but Bart's allowed the station to run down. Many, many improvements have to be made to bring it up to scratch. I have everything in hand."

"Does *everything* include Sarah Dempsey?"

"Sarah is always that bit beyond reach," Kyall observed wryly.

"You could never live with a cold woman."

"No. Absolutely not. But I've never met a sexier woman than Sarah in my whole life."

"What did you say?" Enid, silent until that moment, stared across her mother's rigid body at her son.

"God, Mum, I forgot. You don't know about sex."

"Kyall, darling, don't be coarse. Obviously I do. But sex is…well, messy. Sometimes I think I could do without it in my life."

"So Dad tells me."

It was a response Enid obviously hadn't expected. "You're joking, aren't you?" Enid looked at him with a mixture of shock, hurt and plain disbelief.

"Then why would Dad say such a thing?" Kyall said. Max had once, and Kyall had never forgotten.

"You need help, Enid, you really do," Ruth interrupted, her voice cold with contempt. "Remember Alice Townsend?"

"Gracious, Mother, let's forget about her." Enid shot her an injured look.

"Some things just don't die."

"No need for you to go on about it, Mother. You're not exactly perfect," Enid responded with a new, cool appraisal.

"The proof being that I had you."

"Please, ladies, this isn't the moment to enjoy an argument." Kyall looked at his womenfolk, thinking they *both* needed psychiatric help, but they were his family. Entitled to his love and support. Or as much as he could give under the prevailing circumstances. "Well, I'm off." He straightened decisively, standing back a little from the car.

"May we ask where?" Ruth asked wearily.

"Certainly, though at this stage of my life I don't think I need to check in. Harriet has invited me to a late lunch. She's a very adventurous cook."

"One would've thought it might have landed her a husband," Ruth remarked.

To Enid's newly awakened ears it sounded like gloating. "Surely she's too independent." Enid actually liked Harriet and secretly admired her.

"Harriet is one of those women who is fulfilled teaching other people's children," Ruth scoffed.

"She certainly had notable success with Sarah," Kyall said smoothly. "See you later."

"Bye, darling," Enid called after him. "Bye."

"Shut up, Enid, and let Jensen know we're ready," Ruth snapped.

"Please don't speak to me in that tone, Mother," Enid said with offended dignity. "It obviously hasn't penetrated that I'm the mayor of Koomera Crossing. And a good one." She sat back against the plush upholstery.

"Really?" Ruth turned her regal head to stare down her daughter. "Then why did you allow Sarah Dempsey to take over from Joe?"

"Because I'd rather have my son love me than never speak to me again. We need to get over our aversion to having Sarah Dempsey in our lives. She mightn't have had much to offer years ago—well, actually she did, but we didn't want to see it. Now she's a beautiful, confident young woman with great presence. A good doctor, by all accounts. I think this nonsense should stop. We have to throw out our silly prejudices. Must we *always* act like wretched snobs?"

Ruth sent her daughter a withering glance. "You may be ready to, but I'm not descending to the common masses, Enid, thank you very much. I've been a McQueen of Wunnamurra Station for most of my life. You, on the other hand, seem to be developing independence. It doesn't suit you."

"What are you afraid of?" Enid startled herself by asking. "A flash of intuition? I have them occasionally. You can be cruel and vindictive, Mother."

"I'm a real woman, Enid, not a cold fish like you."

Enid turned away to wave at Jensen through the window. "Sometimes, Mother, I think I hate you," she said quietly.

"Who would care!" Ruth gave a little contemptuous flutter of her hand. "I've done everything for you and your wimp of a husband. You've lived a life of absolute luxury. No, don't give me that stare. So what if you worked? You did it all for Kyall. As far as I'm concerned, the only thing we have in common is our love for him. I will never see Sarah Dempsey admitted to this family for as long as I live."

HARRIET SERVED the food, a *tori shisomaki,* which she translated for them as chicken wrapped in *shiso* leaves with a dash of lemon juice and soya sauce. She brought the dishes to the table, and the three of them began to eat.

"What you should do, Harriet, is open a restaurant,"
Kyall suggested some time later as they all relaxed under
the influence of the delicious food. "All we have is Bron-
wyn's café." He didn't sound as though he was joking or
merely offering flattery.

"And who would teach school?" Harriet didn't sound
as if she was rejecting the idea, either.

"When you retire is your decision, Harriet." Kyall
looked up. "This town owes you a great deal, as it does
Joe, but I wonder if you're not thinking of expanding your
horizons. You'd be a great success in the restaurant business."

"Are you serious, Kyall?" Sarah stopped eating, her fork
midway to her mouth.

"Just thought of it this very moment." Kyall chuckled.
"I'd like Harriet to be able to enjoy her retirement."

"With a restaurant?" Sarah asked. "Is that the answer?
Wouldn't that be a lot of work?"

"It would," Harriet intervened, "but fun. Fancy your
thinking of that, Kyall. You're always coming up with
something new."

"The town needs a good restaurant. You know a lot
about food. You've won over me." He grinned. "And our
fastidious Sarah. You wouldn't have to do it all yourself.
There are plenty of women—good cooks—in the town
who'd love to be in on such a venture. You'd be boss, of
course."

"Of course," seconded Harriet.

"The whole thing would be based on your ideas. I know
you'd have a lot of customers clamoring to get in. It just
seems like a good change of pace. A rest from school. Life
should be full of new ventures."

Harriet, although she was smiling broadly, had a faraway
look in her eyes. "I've found wonderful satisfaction in my

teaching career, but it's true—I've been battling with feelings of wanting a change. A restaurant! My goodness!'' she exclaimed.

"Let Mum find someone to take over at the school,'' Kyall advised, turning to her with his usual authority.

"You speak like it's already happening.'' Harriet gestured with her free hand.

"Say the word and I'll make it happen,'' Kyall promised.

"And you just came up with this, Kyall?'' Sarah marveled, touched by Harriet's excitement.

"I'm not the only one who thinks Harriet is a great cook.'' He shrugged. "If Harriet can get some pleasure and satisfaction out of it, I'm happy to help set things in motion. After all, a good restaurant could only be an advantage to the town.''

"And where would it be located?'' Sarah asked, thinking the main street had full tenancy.

"We'll build the place from scratch,'' Kyall said, moving his hand to close over Sarah's, caressing her fingers.

"That's just one of the things I love about you, Kyall,'' Harriet enthused. "You're a real dynamo.''

"I haven't been up-to-date in my love life.'' Kyall caught Sarah's beautiful brown eyes, such a contrast to the bright gold of her hair, and held them. "But that's going to change.''

"Is it?'' Sarah asked softly.

"And it's about time!'' Harriet hit the table forcefully with the palm of her hand, making the plates jump. "This is quite extraordinary,'' she murmured. "A restaurant? Now I won't be able to get the idea out of my head.''

"What's life without a bit of excitement?'' Kyall said, his gaze moving over Sarah so intimately she felt the familiar jolt of electricity.

"Goodness, you're even making *me* feel young.'' Harriet

leaped up from the table. "Now, I've got a lime-and-ginger mousse I've put together. I'm great at impromptu desserts, if I do say so. It's light and refreshing. Any takers?"

"Two," Kyall answered for both of them.

Harriet turned to beam at him. "Think of it, a restaurant!"

"Well you'd better hurry up, Harriet, and make your decision," urged Kyall. "If we're going to do it, we should get started."

AN HOUR LATER Sarah and Kyall stepped out into the glittering metallic sunlight, the narrow pathway sizzling beneath Sarah's thin-soled shoes. The whole town had closed down for Joe Randall's funeral, but for once, the children who attended the town school didn't delight in the holiday. Dr. Randall had delivered most of them. He'd been much loved.

"Let's go for a drive."

Staring up into Kyall's taut, tanned face, Sarah could see he wasn't going to take no for an answer.

"If you like, but we shouldn't be long. Sue Reed's very good to do standby duty at the hospital."

Kyall gazed off. "We've already started the search for a locum to help you. Joe carried too big a burden on his shoulders."

"I agree. But not too many doctors are drawn to remote places."

"We'll find somebody," Kyall said with certainty. "The scouts are out looking as we speak."

"You don't think I'll fill Joe's shoes?"

"First of all, I do." Kyall opened the passenger door of the Range Rover for her. "Secondly, I don't want you under too much pressure. You have to have time for yourself. And needless to say, for me."

A situation Sarah might have found blissful except for all the deceptions that got in the way.

As they drove past the small general store, Sarah saw the curtains move. "I'm glad Ruby isn't taking over from Mum." She sighed. "I'm fairly certain that's Ruby behind the curtain."

"I'm sure it is," Kyall agreed offhandedly. "Marjorie Preston was by far the best candidate. Ruby can stay on as shop assistant. I don't know that she actually needs a job. Her chief interest is minding everyone else's business. So, where are you going to live? I know you don't want Joe's place."

"Would your grandmother be willing to lease me the Sinclair house?" Sarah turned to look at his strong profile.

Kyall shook his head. "Don't be ridiculous, Sarah."

"She wouldn't consider it?"

"Listen, Sarah." He shot her a burning glance. "You must be aware that my wishes carry a lot of weight. You could have the Sinclair house if you wanted it, but *I* don't want you there. For one thing, it's too isolated. For another it's got such a desolate, abandoned air. I don't believe in ghosts, but…"

"You don't believe in the infinite?" she asked in a ruminative sort of way. "I had a little patient, a cancer victim, who related his near-death experience to me. He wasn't making anything up—he'd gone far beyond telling stories in his short, painful life—just describing it the way it was. It shook me. Another thing that shakes me is that there's no vestige of the living person, absolutely nothing of the spirit, after death. The soul has left the body. It's not the heart stopping. It's the soul departing. Sometimes I've tried not to believe it. But…I have to."

Kyall nodded seriously. "Well, I believe there has to be a system whereby the good are rewarded and the bad are

punished. All the wrongs righted. I guess that means a kind
of heaven and hell, but I don't accept the traditional version
of either. In any event, that doesn't help us with this issue
of the Sinclair house. That woman, Molly Fairweather—
you never met her—died there. As you may have heard, a
desert taipan got into the house. A bit out of the ordinary,
but not impossible.''

"Why did your grandmother create the impression that
she sold the house to Molly Fairweather? What was the
woman doing there, anyway? She knew no one. She had
no family here. No connection of any kind.''

"Hell, Sarah. Have you been checking up?'' Kyall's
voice cracked discordantly. "People find their way to the
outback. Take Evan Thompson, a real mystery man if ever
there was one. It doesn't seem to me that he's just a normal
dropout from the rat race. I've had a number of conversations with him. He's a brilliant man.''

"Maybe he's brokenhearted,'' Sarah said.

"Maybe he is. He has a damned look behind his eyes.
You'll have to meet him.''

"As he's part of Harriet's string quartet, I'm sure I will.
But don't change the subject.''

"I wasn't, actually. I was simply talking about Evan.
He's a wonderful musician—cello—but that wasn't his previous life. He's like a man who's…who's been in a lot of
dangerous places.'' Kyall shrugged. "What about the old
Fielding place? It's been vacant since Miss Fielding had to
go into a nursing home. It's cool and spacious and it's close
to Harriet's.''

"I'm set on the Sinclair house.''

"That doesn't make sense, Sarah, unless the house has
some significance to you. But what? You've become far
too enigmatic.'' He shook his head. "I, on the other hand,
know exactly what I want for the future. I want you. I want

us to get married as soon as possible. It's our destiny. You said you loved me."

There was a fatalistic note in her voice. "Why wouldn't I love you?"

"Why can't you prove it, then?" His eyes glittered with sudden fierce emotion. "Or make that sound a little happier?"

"I can't at the moment." She grew quiet.

"Which makes me very curious. Why so cryptic? What are you hiding?" He threw a quick glance at her profile, hoping to find *something*. Some clue as to what was going on in her head.

"My path through life hasn't been as easy as yours, Kyall."

That wrenched him. "How could you call mine easy?" His retort was almost curt. "God, Sarah, you know better than anyone what a dysfunctional family I've got. My grandmother has a genius for alienating people. She riles everyone in sight. Most people who meet her for the first time think they've bumped smack into Lucretia Borgia at her worst. She's the same with her own daughter and her son-in-law—my father—who I'm sure is secretly waiting for her to die. As far as Gran's concerned, there are only two people in the world worth a damn. Her and me, and she's starting to have second thoughts about me. You call that an easy, civilized existence? I've had a hard ride since I was a kid."

"Poor little rich kid." Sarah's tone changed to teasing and her expression of quiet solemnity broke up.

Her smile was a radiance that lit up her face, he thought, heartened by it. He sent her a droll look. "Which just goes to prove that life isn't any easier for the rich."

"Well, I suppose that's true in some ways," Sarah said.

"The worst of it is, you want to marry me and make me part of all that."

"Not only want to, I'm going to." Kyall reached out to cover one of her hands with his own.

Instantly she sobered again. What happened when he discovered her tragic secret? He might find that impossible to live with. For all her success in school and later as a doctor, losing their child was the central, defining event of her life. Even now, it dominated both past and future.

"Why the poignant expression?" Kyall was dismayed by the abrupt change in her. "You're acting like marrying me might be some sort of tragedy. Why? Surely you know I'll protect you with my life."

She hesitated, uncertain what to say. Finally she spoke. "We got way ahead of ourselves, Kyall. That first time we made love."

"Oh, Lord, Sarah, will you ever let me forget? It was wonderful for me."

"And me." She touched his arm, linked her fingers like a bracelet. "But it separated us for years and years."

"I've got to ask why. Why did you act like you hated me when you didn't hate me at all?"

"For the reasons I told you. Your family didn't want me in your life, Kyall."

"Ah, the hell with that!" The roughness of his tone reflected his frustration and anger. "I'd have married you, no matter what. It's not that unusual, you know. Plenty of people marry without family approval. It happens every day."

"I know that, only, for years your family—your grandmother—was simply too much for me."

"Surely she isn't now, Sarah? You're your own woman, with your own well-respected identity. People love you. You're beautiful, but there's nothing threatening about you.

Only an aura of goodness and integrity, which must serve you well in your profession.''

"I'm nowhere near as good as you think.''

"Yes, you are. You've just been lonely and filled with grief. There's a tremendous kinship between us, Sarah. I haven't found it with any other woman, and I'll admit there have been a few. I did try to forget you, but it didn't work.''

"Not for me, either,'' she admitted without any trace of embarrassment.

"So we're kindred souls?''

"We seem to be.'' She smiled.

"In the old days, I knew everything about you,'' he mused. "I could read you like a book, as you read me. But you've returned a mystery. Or is it just that you're a woman?'' His mouth twisted wryly.

She thought a moment. "I guess you could say I've come to realize that unsolvable problems exist.''

"Well, if they do, Sarah, you don't have to face them alone. I have this idea that your very sick patients, especially little children—I know how much you love them—drain you emotionally. You need me, Sarah. You need my love.''

That was the absolute truth. Sarah couldn't get away from it. She turned her head, staring out the window at the scenery flying by. Kyall wasn't following the line of billabongs, she realized, but heading toward what they all quaintly called "the Hill Country.'' In the flattest continent on earth, the Hill Country was a series of low, eroded mesas colored a magnificent orange-red, relics of an ancient past. The narrow gorges and canyons were a world apart from the surrounding arid spinifex plains. Here there were permanent pools, even when the creeks had dried out, and species of oasislike tropical palms and plants that managed to survive in the enclosed damp environment. Here, too, located beside the permanent water holes, were fascinating Aboriginal rock paintings, executed on the multicolored horizontal bands of the cliff walls and the interiors of small caves. The Hill country's raw-earth ochres were turning to pinks and rose and violets as the sun went down.

For Kyall and Sarah, wild as it was, with its brooding aura of great antiquity, this was the most beautiful environment on earth. It was a shared love that had suffused their relationship and strengthened the unbreakable bond between them. It also illustrated the fact that the great pioneering families and the white settlers of the outback had, over time, absorbed something of the Aboriginal Dreaming with its belief that this ancient land was sacred, created by the Great Spirit Beings.

Eventually they stopped and climbed out of the Range Rover. "You won't be able to walk far in those shoes," Kyall observed, looking down at her stylish black dress shoes. "You might ruin them. I should've thought of that before."

"I'm not worried about it." Sarah tugged with irritation at the few pins that held her hair in a neat upturned roll. Free of restraint, her golden mane tumbled around her face and floated over her shoulders in the way Kyall loved best. She moved on, walking carefully across the sea of smoothly rounded rocks and pebbles while streams of birds rose in formation on the desert wind. In the distance, a whirlwind was dancing across the sweeping plain. A mirage of shimmering blue lakes that simply didn't exist taunted the eye. This was the fascination of the desert country, the savage beauty and the frightening specter of death. At least at the water hole, they could drink deeply of the pure, surprisingly cold, life-giving water.

Kyall caught up with her easily, taking her hand for the sheer pleasure of holding it, not just to lend support.

Clumps of the ubiquitous spinifex speckled the slope, splashes of gold against the orange-red sand. They avoided coming into contact with their spikes, continuing fairly cautiously because of Sarah's shoes, until they came to the first level of caves.

"I'll go in first," Kyall told her briefly. "Make sure there's nothing around. You stay off to one side."

Sarah did what she was told. Little rock wallabies often took shelter in the caves to avoid the heat. The desert's fearsome-looking but harmless lizards sought the shade of the rocks, although the reptiles had perfected the technique of basking out under the powerful sun.

"All clear." Kyall came back out, his tall body almost doubled over to clear the height of the entrance. "You'll have to take off your shoes here or your heels will sink. It's quite extraordinary. Some of the rock paintings are as vivid as if they were painted in our lifetime, instead of thousands of years ago."

They entered the cave and stood hand in hand, the old familiarity returning to them. This was one of the favorite haunts of their childhood. They stared upward, thrilled by what they saw.

The ceiling of the cave soared to some twenty feet, a veritable treasure trove of drawings. There were many circles and spirals incised on the ceiling and walls that they took to signify rock pools and water holes. There were meandering designs that could mean trails of various kinds, billabongs, creeks, even the travels of ancestral beings. Many of the drawings, executed in ochres, were immediately identifiable. They represented hunters with spears about to throw them, with totemic beings and creatures around them, looking on. There were innumerable drawings of animals, trees, plants, what appeared to be showers of rain and most incredible of all, the unmistakable outline of a giant crocodile. It was so accurate in every detail that when they were children they used to jump with excitement every time they saw it.

Imagine crocodiles living in the large inland sea of pre-history! The sea that was now the Dead Heart. Vertical yellow lines flanked the crocodile's body like the sandy banks of a tidal creek. Scarcely an inch wasn't decorated, some drawings faint, others in vivid tones of yellow, red, white and black. There were no drawings of women. These caves, apparently, had only been available to men. Other symbols appeared, ones impossible to understand as any ancient hieroglyphics.

"The fascination doesn't go away, does it?" Sarah whispered, brushing at the curling tendrils that clung to her temples and cheeks.

"No…it doesn't."

She turned, her heart doing cartwheels at the tone of his voice. There was something tumultuous between them now. A flash flood of desire, building to torrents. It expressed itself in the tautness of his expression, the glitter in his eyes.

Sarah heard the whoosh of her own blood in her ears. She couldn't have moved, even if she'd wanted to. He had such power about him. Marvelous male strength, strong bones, rippling muscle. Sexuality. As always, she was reacting to his nearness, the tingle in her breasts, the knife-edged pain, near-ecstasy…

"I want you, Sarah." The backs of his fingers stroked her cheeks, heating her skin. His hand sank lower, weaving through the neckline of her dress, over the supple skin of her shoulder, down to the curve of her breast, its rose tip already flared into life.

Then he found her mouth, his tongue slipping into the slick interior. She opened her mouth fully to him, allowing him to explore at will. It was all so voluptuous, so sensuous, the cause of bodily weakness and a measure of pain. Whatever he wanted, she couldn't resist him.

His hands continued to smooth and caress, down over her back and her buttocks, her muscles contracting at his touch.

They stood together, he taking her mouth, his hand teasing the hemline of her skirt, then lifting it on a muffled exclamation, as though her dress presented an intolerable barrier. The panties she wore were soon off, a silken slide to her feet, until she moved to step out of them, swaying. It was a tyranny of the senses, the wild sweet fever that burned through her veins.

His fingers entered her and she found herself spreading her legs, eyes tightly shut against the ecstasy that was sucking the breath from her lungs. She thought in an erotic frenzy she might come. Or was he commanding her to come?

"Kyall!"

"You want me. Tell me." His voice, little more than a rasp, was as forceful as she'd ever heard it. A demand, not a question.

"Yes. Oh, yes." She bowed her head, struggling against fainting.

"Is that the truth?"

"God, Kyall, I can't bear it. Yes!" She could scarcely cope with her own explosive desires.

While she stood, he fell to his knees, his strong arms twined around her, locking her to him in a kind of exultation. Her body opened to him. To his hands, to his fingers, to his mouth, to his tongue.

"My beautiful Sarah! My most beautiful Sarah!"

She heard her own convulsive intake of breath, then her hands clutched his glossy dark head, cradling it to her body as he began to kiss her.

It was exquisite. Yet it made her writhe as though surely she were in pain. Her heart seemed to have slipped from her breast down the smooth shallow slope of her stomach to her inner core.

She couldn't think. She could only feel, welcoming and trusting in the glorious bonfire of the senses that only he could ignite. Her whole body was flushed with heat, spirals and spirals of descending, licking flames.

She could no longer stand, rendered helpless and in danger of losing all sense of herself. It was then that he lifted her, laying her on the soft sand, watching her face as he removed what garments were left to her.

The brilliant sunlight outside the cave sent a golden play of light across her naked body. He savored it, loverlike. How long had he wanted this woman?

It might have been forever.

CHAPTER NINE

FAR FROM TREATING snake bites, spider bites and the odd tourist with sunstroke as her former boss at Waverley Medical Centre had suggested, Sarah found herself pitched headlong into medical dramas. In Brisbane she'd often diagnosed chest pains, earaches, sore throats, nosebleeds if they hadn't stopped within thirty minutes—on one occasion it was the sinister messenger of leukemia—fractures, simple and compound. But during her very first week in Koomera Crossing, a young woman was rushed into the hospital in agony from what Sarah quickly diagnosed and confirmed as a life-threatening ectopic pregnancy. Surgery was the only means of rescue, in this case leaving the young woman without one of her fallopian tubes. In the afternoon, just as the hospital had settled into routine procedures, she dealt with a bad dingo bite, which necessitated a tetanus booster and a course of antibiotics. There was a boy who'd fallen from a tree, tearing his leg open. Then a man working on an outlying cattle property presented with a long steel pole rammed through his leg, thigh and buttock. When the junior nurse, Cathy Moran, saw the patient with the pole still in him, she let out a piercing scream. Sarah had just admitted a small Aboriginal child who'd been suffering from diarrhea for more than week and badly needed salt and fluid administered intravenously. She had to speak to Cathy quite sharply to restore the young woman to her senses.

But it did look pretty horrifying.

"What on earth happened?" Sarah asked, turning to the emergency worker who'd brought in the impaled man.

"Poor bugger drove straight through a gate," the worker explained, himself in a state of shock. "The pole ripped through the front of the truck and went straight into his leg and his bum. He's been damned brave, I can tell you, Doctor. He's a bit out of it now, but he was conscious and quite calm while we cut him free."

Sarah bent to the patient. "We'll x-ray this, then go straight into surgery." She straightened from her hurried examination, pleased to find an attentive theater sister by her side. "It's a miracle, but the pole appears to have missed all his bones and major arteries. A little more of an angle and it would've pierced his groin."

"Bet he won't drive through a locked gate again," the worker said. "The sight will haunt me until my dying day."

"Thank God he'll live to tell the tale. Thank you for all your efforts." She looked at the worker closely. "You're a bit pale. Why don't you go to the canteen and have a cup of tea?"

"Don't mind if I do, Doctor." The worker fixed her with a grateful smile.

"This man, you know him?" Sarah asked.

"Sure. Bob Duffy."

"He's married?"

"Wife and four kids. Someone let her know. She should be coming to the hospital fairly soon. Bit of a drive."

"Fine."

As it turned out, Mrs. Duffy didn't bother driving all the way in to the hospital. Her husband regularly had accidents. You name it, he'd fallen over it. It seemed terribly uncaring at the time, but as Sarah was to find out, Mrs. Duffy had been under the impression that "the pipe" was about as thick as a little finger and maybe a foot long, not a terrifying two-inch-thick nine-footer. When she did finally arrive the next morning, it was to find her husband sitting cheerfully in bed, holding the souvenir pole like a great didgeridoo.

Mrs. Duffy fainted.

The following day brought a sadder case. A young father, a bush worker, drove his three-month-old son to the hospital only for Sarah to declare the baby dead on arrival. Baby, hitherto healthy, had been found facedown in his crib. The mother had known her child was dead, but the young father had refused to accept it, jumping into his truck and driving to the hospital. Even when Sarah explained to him as gently as possible that, for reasons still not understood, one in a hundred babies stops breathing in the first few months of life, the father appeared to have difficulty taking the tragedy in. Very gradually Sarah was able to calm him, in the end sedating him against his grief. Eventually the young mother, too, was brought in having temporarily lost the power of speech.

And it didn't slow down. On one of the stations a calf kicked a seven-months-pregnant woman, who went into labor. A helicopter was dispatched from Wunnamurra Station to bring the young woman in. She gave birth in the hospital, the first child Sarah delivered there. A pallid, sickly little creature Sarah privately despaired of, but with an extended period spent in hospital and a good deal of expert care, he was destined to turn into a bright, chubby little boy.

Looking back over a month of battling injuries not common in the city but frequent in the bush, Sarah felt secretly thrilled that she'd acquitted herself well. She'd worked long and hard, sometimes to the point of exhaustion. There was no question that the town had accepted her. She need not have worried they wouldn't. She appeared to have every-

one's support and approval, and it meant a great deal to
her. Added to that, she got on well with the staff, who
showed genuine concern for her well-being. Once she'd
been part of this town's life. Now she was back. She loved
the country-hospital atmosphere, immensely grateful that
bush nursing sisters, double-certificated or not, had become
accustomed to doing practically everything, including domestic duties when the paid domestics had a break. Life at
the hospital was all about pitching in.

Six weeks later, Sarah had moved into the Sinclair house,
despite Kyall's objections. Nothing and no one bothered
her. Soon afterward, her assistant arrived. Dr. Morris
Hughes, a fine-looking man in his late sixties, exuded energy, kindness and humor—and showed an understanding
of life that Sarah responded to from the moment they met.
She and Dr. Hughes would get on. A blessing because
"getting on" was extremely important. Dr. Hughes—
"Please call me Morris"—had retired from private practice
in Adelaide, but after eighteen months of missing his working life with its high level of responsibility and commitment, he decided there were still a few years of doctoring
left in him.

Kyall had gone out of his way to fly to Adelaide to
conduct the brief face-to-face interview, other negotiations
having gone well. The next day, he flew Dr. Hughes into
Koomera Crossing and settled him in Joe Randall's com-
fortable bungalow. The following morning, Kyall arrived
by station helicopter to take the doctor to the hospital to
meet Sarah.

"Let me tell you a few things about myself, Sarah,"
Morris Hughes said when they were all seated in her office,
waiting for morning tea. "I'm a widower. I lost my wife,
Anne, to breast cancer when she was only fifty-six. It was
a dreadful blow. I felt that as a doctor, I should've been

able to save her, but in the end I couldn't. I haven't been able to form a relationship since. I loved Anne so much. I have two sons, both doctors. One's a cardiologist, the other a pediatrician.''

"Dr. Patrick Hughes?" Sarah raised a brow. She knew a doctor of that name by his outstanding reputation.

Morris leaned back in his chair and smiled. "My boy Pat!''

"One of the finest pediatricians working today," Sarah said warmly. "I've read all his articles with the closest attention. And you're his dad! Your sons must have inherited their love of medicine from you.''

Morris inclined his gray head. "We both know it's a difficult, daunting and heartbreaking profession. But there are undoubtedly rewards when you can help along the way.''

"Morris himself has an excellent reputation," Kyall said, standing up in response to the soft tap on Sarah's office door. "Many thanks." He took the tea tray from the junior nurse, whose expression of adoration made Sarah smile.

"Here, Kyall." Sarah indicated the cleared space at the side of her desk before turning back to Dr. Hughes. "I'm sure you have, Morris," she said, knowing Kyall had thoroughly checked out the doctor's credentials. "I'm so pleased you're here. You'll take a lot of the pressure off me. It's a long way from the City of the Churches." Adelaide, capital of South Australia, was famous for the large number of its beautiful churches. Sarah smiled and began serving the tea.

"That's fine by me," Morris replied, his sherry-colored eyes quietly relaxed. "My boys live and work in Sydney. They're both so busy I don't get to see much of them or the grandchildren. I'm in excellent health, touch wood, and I find myself wanting to work again. The outback isn't quite a new experience for me. I've done a good deal of travel out here in my time. Uluru, the Olgas, the Alice, Kakadu and the Kimberley.''

''Then welcome aboard, Morris.'' Sarah gestured with one hand. ''Oddly enough, I've found myself with far more doctoring to do here than in my former practice in Brisbane. Your wanting to join me has come as a great relief. I'm very grateful to Kyall and the McQueen family for everything they've done for this hospital.''

Kyall's eyes lit on Sarah with a faintly mocking look. There had been no warming of relations between Sarah and his grandmother. His mother, though, had shown a lot of courage in defying Ruth, calling in on Sarah every time she came to town. ''What we need to do is have a party to introduce you to Koomera Crossing,'' Kyall decided, giving the older man a smile. ''Maybe a week from now. On Wunnamurra. There are some pretty interesting people in this town, even if it is off the beaten track.''

''Good Lord, yes.'' Morris Hughes surprised Sarah and Kyall by responding so enthusiastically. ''Like that quite wonderful woman I met this morning. Miss Crompton, headmistress of the school?''

''Harriet.'' Sarah smiled. It was plain that Morris Hughes had liked what he'd seen. ''Kyall and I adore her. She taught us both until we went away to boarding school. She's touched many people's lives in this town. We couldn't do without our Harriet. She's a woman of culture.''

''And she's a musician? Viola?'' Morris Hughes's eyes rested on Sarah with open interest.

''You did get to talking, didn't you.'' Kyall laughed, thinking there was a start of a friendship there.

''Such a tremendously *alive* woman,'' Morris said happily. ''She was passing the house by chance this morning.

I was on the porch waiting for Kyall, and Miss Crompton stopped to introduce herself. She reminded me a bit of my Anne. Clever, funny, sensitive. I'll be delighted to meet Miss Crompton again.''

And we'll do our best to encourage it, thought Sarah, wondering if Harriet's ears were burning.

Afterward Sarah excused herself for a few moments to see Kyall off. ''Does it need to be at Wunnamurra?'' she asked as they walked down the short flight of stone steps to the pavement.

Kyall held her by the arm. ''I think so, yes.''

''Sweet Lord! This is a setup, isn't it. You want to bring your grandmother and me together.'' Sarah wasn't sure she could handle it.

He met her gaze, fully aware of her insecurities. ''Don't worry about it, Sarah,'' he said briskly. ''Remember that McQueen money built this hospital. And we've got a magnificent homestead that no one seems to visit anymore. That's got to change. But yes, you're right. I do want to try to bring you and Gran together.''

She sent him an ironic look. ''It's hopeless, Kyall. If your grandmother could have me annihilated, she would. Some things one just can't change. It's the same in medicine. You do everything possible to change the outcomes for your patients, but sometimes they never get better.''

For a moment he didn't speak, wanting nothing more than to gather her into his arms. Today her long, golden hair was drawn back into a thick single rope he longed to untwine. ''At least relations between you and my mother have improved.''

''They have,'' Sarah answered. ''Your mother extended her hand. I was happy to meet her halfway. She must get an unpleasant reaction from your grandmother whenever she visits—if your grandmother even knows about the visits.''

''She knows,'' Kyall confirmed. ''My mother, if she ever frees herself of Gran's domination, could be a woman of substance.''

''Odd,'' Sarah mused. ''Your grandmother's whole purpose in life seems to be having all her demands met. I expect she's being unpleasant to you, too.''

''Not really.'' He flashed her a smile, half amused, half wry. ''She lets out the occasional nasty remark, but it's like water off a duck's back. Gran's never been able to dominate me. She's aware of that. She can't cut me out of my inheritance, either. It's all tied up, and Gran is merely the custodian. Wunnamurra will pass to me. If I want to give a party for Morris, who seems a good, generous man, I will. That goes for marrying you, as well. I can take only so much of this situation, Sarah.'' His expression tightened. ''We can't just coast along. I want you with me. Hell, the wanting is making me frantic. Sometimes I wish...''

''That you didn't love me?''

He pulled on her thick plait. ''I've loved you from childhood. But I have no talent for this waiting. When you told me all those years ago that you wanted no part of me anymore, I used the only defense I had. I tried to forget you with other women, but the memory of you never let me alone. Now that terrible period of our lives is over—and you can't close the door on me again. I want to get married and have our child,'' he said with finality.

Sarah's face paled. ''You promised you'd give me six months.''

''Why can't we get engaged in the meantime?'' he demanded.

''How your grandmother would detest that!''

''Are you afraid of her, Sarah?''

"I'm afraid of what she could do."

"Like what? Come on. We've had this conversation before. We go around and around, but there's a mystery here. What could she do to you?"

"The word *attack* comes to mind."

He gave her a searching glance. "God, Sarah, you can't mean a *physical* attack? She's never done anything like that in her life! She's seventy-five years old."

"That doesn't matter." Sarah couldn't help her reaction. Ruth McQueen would be a force to be reckoned with right up to the end. "If your grandmother can find some way to hurt me, she will."

"Then she'll have me to answer to." Kyall's expression was daunting. "Any other man would give up on you, Sarah. You're so contradictory. So self-contained on the surface, always holding yourself in check, but when we're alone you're the most passionate woman a man could ever want. What's going on here?"

"I'm sorry, Kyall. I can't explain. I have to go in now. I need to show Morris around the hospital. All the beds are filled."

"Morris can wait another few minutes." He held her so she couldn't move. "I can't do anything about my grandmother, Sarah. I *can* do something about you. Our love is not a calamity, as you seem to imply. I know it was willful, selfish, reckless, irresponsible, all of those things, to have slept with you when you were so young. But I wasn't much older." He shook his head. "I've had to learn wisdom. And something I've learned is that one mistake can't tarnish our love or rule our lives. Is this actually what your…reluctance is all about?"

Sarah expelled a breath. *Get it out.* The longer she delayed, the worse it would get. Some secrets were even carried to the grave…. "I love you, Kyall," she said finally, looking past his handsome dark head to where a bauhinia blossomed in all its glory. "I'll love you until my last breath."

"Don't make that sound like that could be next week." Kyall couldn't stop himself. He bent his head and kissed her in full view of the street and the people who looked toward them from doorways. It wasn't as if the town didn't know that Kyall McQueen and Sarah Dempsey had picked up where they left off. This was a piece of news that met with near-universal approval. Hadn't Kyall's Range Rover been seen—more than once—parked overnight at the old Sinclair house since Dr. Sarah had moved in some weeks back? The only mystery for most townspeople was why the doctor had chosen that particular house to live in. Obviously Dr. Dempsey didn't believe in ghosts, although lots of people did.

Kyall, who, like Harriet, had been very much against Sarah's moving in, lifted his head with no interest at all in who might be looking their way. His entire attention was on Sarah. "I want us to get engaged. No, stand quietly for a moment," he said persuasively. "I see no reason why we can't do it next week when we give the party for Morris. No big drama. I can announce it at the end of the evening."

"I've got to think." Sarah couldn't pretend she wasn't agitated.

"No, you don't," Kyall answered with quiet force. "Your thinking's kept us separated for far too long. I'll announce our engagement at the party. Okay? It won't come as any big surprise. Even to Gran."

"You really love me? Unconditionally?" She desperately needed that reassurance. "Tell me." She knew it would kill her if he ever turned away.

"Yes, dammit, I do!" He gave her a lopsided smile. "I should tell you I already have the ring."

"What?" Her spontaneous reaction was incredible joy, like a flowering inside her. For a long moment, she stared into his face. "Kyall!" She saw herself floating down the aisle in some glorious bridal creation. Glowing satin. She had no father to give her away. Joe would have done it, but Joe was no longer with them. Why not break with tradition and have Harriet? Harriet in some resplendent garment only she could carry off. Her favorite royal purple or vermilion embroidered in gold, with a matching fantastic headdress. Harriet favored turbans. Her bridesmaids would walk before them, carrying exquisite bouquets of roses. There would be a little flower girl, too, scattering perfumed petals from a gilded basket tied with ivory ribbons. Most of all, she could see the expression on Kyall's face as he first caught sight of her.

Dear Lord, could it really happen? Could they have a future free of the tragic traumas of the past? Could that be?

"Sarah?" His smile was ineffably tender.

"When did you buy it?" Her voice was soft and excited, shocked out of its habitual calm.

"I would have preferred you with me, but I was scared you'd panic," he told her with mock scorn. "I bought it when I went to pick up Morris. No chance thing. It's going on your finger. I'm debating the precise time. It's very beautiful. Like you."

"How do you know it'll fit if I didn't try it on?"

He smiled into her eyes. "You made it easy for me by showing me your mother's rings. I'm pretty sure it'll fit."

The pull of temptation was too enormously strong. Surely she deserved to be happy. Surely Kyall would receive her tragic story with pity for what she had endured alone.

She tilted her head back, thinking they'd always been part of each other. "Very well, Kyall." She stared into his blue, blue eyes. "I can do this. I can do anything for you. We'll announce our engagement toward the end of the party. I just hope we know what we're doing here."

"I do," he said on a sudden surge of emotion, sliding an arm around her waist and pulling her close. "What else matters as long as we're together?"

DR. MORRIS HUGHES had only been home ten minutes. He felt encouraged by his day at the hospital, but his mood became faintly melancholy as it always did when he returned to an empty house. No welcoming lights, no inviting aromas issuing from the kitchen. No Anne. He'd just taken off his jacket when he was surprised to hear the front doorbell.

"Coming," he called. An emergency? Unlikely, since the hospital could easily contact him via his mobile, which never left his side.

His slight depression changed to delight when he found himself looking at his neighbor, Miss Harriet Crompton, quite dramatic in a dark reddish garment. It was more or less a sari, he supposed, and it made her appear tall and regal. A cluster of beads at her throat glinted and winked.

"Miss Crompton, hello." He ran a quick hand through his hair, trying to restore it to order.

"Good evening, Doctor." Harriet's gracious smile drew him in. "I know you won't have a meal prepared, so I've taken it upon myself to invite you to dinner. You can say no, but I warn you that you'll be missing out on a very good meal."

"Miss Crompton, how very kind of you," he answered, feeling as though he was in some sort of Edwardian play. "I wouldn't dream of saying no, but I do have to wash up."

Harriet Crompton's fine gray eyes whisked over him. "How was your day at the hospital?"

"Fine and informative." He swallowed. "I'm sure I made the right decision coming here. I very much like Sarah. Indeed, everyone at the hospital, with the possible exception of one female patient demanding nonstop attention."

"That would be Celia Gray," she told him, sounding sympathetic. "She's neurotic, but no one's supposed to know. Shall we say thirty minutes? You know where I am."

"Yes, indeed." Morris stepped out onto the porch gazing in the direction of Harriet's splendid colonial. "I couldn't help noticing that wonderful Maori totem pole you have guarding the front door. I'd like to take a closer look. I have a great interest in ethnic artifacts."

Harriet laughed, picking a big cream hibiscus flower and pushing it into her abundant hair. "Then you'll have plenty of cultures to choose from. It's an interest of mine, too."

This was far more than he'd hoped. "Thank you, Miss Crompton. You're very thoughtful."

"Harriet, please," she protested, moving down the steps. At the bottom she waved. Morris waved back, then closed the door.

His melancholy was forgotten.

CHAPTER TEN

SARAH KNEW THE MOMENT she stepped into the house—even before she switched on the lights—that someone had been there. This was what the place had done to her. Made her acutely, perhaps unnaturally, aware. Whatever shadowy figures were about, they apparently avoided her, or they had no wish to frighten her. Her intruder—she accepted the fact quite calmly—was alive and human.

She switched on the hall light and looked quickly around. Nothing had been touched there, at any rate. Everything was precisely as she'd left it that morning. Unopened mail on the central library table, yellow daisies in a copper bowl glowing in the splash of light, her open briefcase on a hall chair, two files protruding from it.

She didn't feel fear. Whoever had been here was here no more. She turned on the dining-room light, a surprisingly beautiful chandelier. Nothing out of place.

And so on. Each room in turn. It was in the main bedroom that her feeling she'd had an invader was confirmed. A strong fragrance wafted up from the Persian rug, as though a perfume bottle had been broken and the contents spilled. Not *her* perfume. This was something entirely different from anything she'd wear. Too floral. Too cloying.

She walked into the dressing room, moving her clothes back and forth on their hangers. She had proof this wasn't just her imagination. It would be absurd to think something like this mightn't happen. In fact, she'd been expecting a disturbance from the day she'd moved in. There was no doubt: someone had been in this room. She didn't like it. She was sure the skirt of her yellow silk dress—one of her best—hadn't been sticking out. She rearranged some outfits to give the garment space so the skirt could hang freely, only then noticing that it had been hacked from hip to hem.

Sparks seemed to fly from her heart while her head went cold. She took the dress from the hanger, carried it to the bed and laid it down on the pink-damask coverlet. Who would do such a thing? She bent over the dress to examine the extent of the damage. This was probably the most expensive dress she owned. A write-off. She could never wear it again. Obviously someone wanted her to know that he— or she—could come and go at will. Why hadn't the intruder taken the dress, cut it into little pieces and left it scattered all over the perfumed rug? Why just *that* dress? Why not do more damage?

Sarah went back to the dressing room, rechecking all her clothes, going slowly so she wouldn't miss anything. Everything else was intact. She turned and went to the chest of drawers, pulling the drawers out one by one. In the last drawer—her slips—the nicest and most expensive had received similar treatment.

No one but a woman would do that, surely? Her mind immediately flew to Ruth McQueen, but sheer reason made her discount it. Ruth McQueen always traveled conspicuously in her chauffeur-driven Rolls. Although the house was fairly isolated, her driver, Jensen, would have been witness to her visit. It was hard to believe that Ruth would do this. The damage wasn't serious, more like something done on impulse—or on orders without a great deal of conviction but with malicious intent. If not Ruth, she couldn't guess who that someone might be. It was something a jealous girlfriend might do. Inevitably that led her to thoughts of India Claydon. But India was safely at home on Marjimba Station. Or had she been a guest at Wunnamurra recently? No, Kyall would have told her. Still, in her experience, jealous women did a lot of peculiar things. She'd rather it was India than Ruth, though. Whoever it was had started on the bout of vandalism, then wavered. Ashamed? Perhaps something had frightened him or her off. The little Sinclair girl looking through the window? Sarah saw absolutely nothing wrong with having the resident ghost stand guard. There wasn't much point in telling Kyall about the "break-in." There was no evidence of forced entry, not that it wouldn't be easy to get into the old house if one was determined enough. *I'm here and I'm going to be all right,* Sarah told herself. *I have to be.* She was still feeling buoyant inside. It all had to do with the excitement of Kyall's engagement proposal, which had thrilled her more than it worried her. She knew it was a mistake *not* to be worried, but she was thirty years old, she loved Kyall, and she wanted above all to be married to him. She hadn't forgotten that he wanted children. She wanted a child badly, never to replace Rose, but to bring fulfillment into her traumatized life.

Kyall would arrive soon; they had planned for him to have dinner with her and, of course, finish up in bed. Sarah had a quick shower, then changed into a simple sundress with a pretty floral print. No use tying her hair back against the heat. Kyall would pull it out of its clasp, anyway.

She greeted him in the hallway, lifting her face for his kiss, still amazed that they were together.

"Darling," he groaned, as if offering up a prayer. "Darling, darling Sarah." He moved his mouth to the side of her neck, breathing in the natural fragrance of her skin, loving the way she turned her head to accommodate the caress. "I've been very clever and parked the vehicle in the garage."

She laughed. "Everyone's aware that you stay over, you know."

He held her close awhile longer. "We were an item before," he said lightly, "and we're one now." He kissed her mouth again, just brushing the surface of her lips.

"They must've wondered about all the items in between," Sarah said when she could manage it. "India Claydon comes to mind. It can't be easy to reconcile herself to losing you. Have you seen her lately?"

Sarah disengaged herself slowly from Kyall's arms, walking in the direction of the kitchen while he followed.

Kyall grimaced. "Gran doesn't miss an opportunity to invite her," he confessed. "We're talking about people who don't know how or when to give up."

"So that's why you're moving the engagement forward." She reached for a couple of fresh limes.

"Much more romantic than that, Sarah." He leaned back against a counter, studying her. "It's the first step before I can finally get you to marry me. As for India—can we please forget about her? She's at the house now, as a matter of fact. Which is one of the many reasons I'm here."

So! She thought of the slashed clothing and instinctively put a hand to her breast. "Obviously she can't get you out of her system."

"I'm sure she could if she worked at it," he said with controlled irritation. "Now, what are we having? I haven't eaten since morning tea with Morris. How did everything go with him?"

Sarah paused, her expression revealing her appreciation. "We clicked, just like that. He knows what he's doing, as we expected, and he has a very pleasant manner with the

staff and patients. I know we're going to work well together."

"That's good." Kyall stooped to look in the refrigerator
he'd had delivered and stocked so she'd have plenty of food
on hand after a long day at the hospital. He took out the
wine. An excellent chardonnay from their own vineyards.

"Very good," Sarah echoed, flashing him a smile. "So
now I can have a little time for you."

"Maybe you can even find time to get married before
Christmas?" he challenged. "It hasn't exactly been a whirlwind romance."

"But incredibly memorable," Sarah reminded him in an
emotional whisper.

"Indeed it was. How I longed for you." His gaze slipped
over her face to her throat and then her breasts.

How could she tell him what he wanted to know?

WHILE SARAH ASSEMBLED the ingredients for dinner, Kyall
moved to the deep casement window and looked out. The
way the moonlight, a white radiance at the front of the
house, missed the back seemed unnatural to him. "I'm far
from happy about your being here, Sarah." The words were
torn from him. Yet again. In truth, he couldn't wait for her
to become his wife. He was desperate to protect her from
all harm. "I hope you've got that .22 by your bed."

"I have it handy," she assured him, not fully knowing
herself why she'd chosen to live in the town's haunted
house. "I detest guns these days, but my childhood with
you made me a good shot. Anyway, a .22 wouldn't stop a
ghost," she joked.

"It's not ghosts I'm worried about," he said. "Drifters
find their way into town all the bloody time."

"I'm quite safe, Kyall. Please don't worry about me. The

town has virtually no history of crime. I'm more concerned about one or two of the people I actually know.''

She'd moved away from him, so he spun her around to face him. ''What's that supposed to mean?'' Was she talking about Ruth? Dammit, what wasn't she telling him?

''Just a little joke.''

''I'm not so sure.'' He searched her eyes, dark like his grandmother's but full of sweetness and sensitivity and golden lights. ''You must tell me everything that concerns you. Promise?'' He gave her a little shake.

''I promise.''

''Sarah, look me in the eye when you say that.''

Her masses of golden hair framed her face. ''I'm going to have trouble with you,'' she said, placing both hands against his chest, feeling the thud of his heart.

''You are if you don't tell me the things I need to know,'' he returned with some emphasis.

She shivered at those words and pushed him gently away, waiting a few moments before she spoke. ''I thought we'd have a Thai-noodle salad. It's very colorful and very good for you.''

''As long as it's filling.'' He didn't care what it was. He only wanted to be alone with her.

''It is.'' She smiled, running an appreciative eye over his tall, powerful frame. ''You can open the coconut milk if you would, and the water chestnuts, too, and grate the ginger. I can manage the rest. But before you do anything, open the wine. It should be nicely chilled by now. I'm going to allow myself two glasses by way of celebration.''

''We haven't even begun to celebrate.'' He turned his sapphire eyes on her. ''That's a very pretty dress, but I can't wait to see it fall to the floor.''

THERE WAS NO SIGN of the Range Rover. Probably it was in the detached garage. He'd built the garage himself some twelve years back for Mrs. McQ. He'd done things for Mrs. McQ that he'd never have done for anyone else, but she knew how to reward him—and scare him, for that matter. He hadn't the slightest doubt that if he ever attempted to apply a little blackmail, he'd be neatly disposed of. Probably finish up in some pond on Wunnamurra, where he'd spent all his working life.

He didn't want to do this now. God almighty, if Kyall ever caught him! He was frightened to be here and he didn't mind admitting it to himself. But Mrs. McQ wanted to know what had been kept from her. Kyall McQueen, heir to Wunnamurra and the family fortune, was with Sarah Dempsey. They were here together.

And why the hell not? All the deep-down hatred he felt for Ruth McQueen suddenly surfaced. She had bought him and, by extension, his family, lock, stock and barrel. He was her henchman. Her tool. After the taipan episode—he couldn't bear to think about it; it was supposed to frighten the old girl away—he knew he had to do this, whether he liked it or not. Spy on Kyall and Sarah Dempsey. Were they together? What were they doing? Report back.

He had never felt so exposed, although he was dressed in dark clothing with a balaclava ready to pull down over his head. It was so damned hot he'd hesitated to put it on, but now he covered his head and face. He had the greatest urge to run away. If Kyall caught him… If Kyall caught him… Didn't bear thinking about.

God, what was that? What the bloody hell was that in the trees? He squinted through the mask, thinking this wasn't the first time the old house had frightened the life out of him. It was one creepy place.

You're crazy, he thought. Crazy old coot. There was nothing lurking in the garden but him. He thought he saw the shadowy figure of the girl—the Sinclair girl—but that was insane. The leaves above his head were whispering, chattering to themselves. What these trees had seen!

Get it over with. Sight the Range Rover. That was all.

Creepy place.

He pushed himself to break cover, moving silently across the lawn, bending low, head down.

Nearing the side of the path, he heard murmurings. A man and a woman. That would be them. He wanted to turn around and go, but he had to bloody sight them. God, that Ruth McQueen had become unglued. She adored her grandson; everyone knew that. But she was obviously determined to put an end to his relationship with Sarah Dempsey, whatever the cost. After the Fairweather woman, he'd decided he'd never do anything remotely like that again, no matter how much she paid him.

The woman was moaning gently. He knew what that meant. They were making love. He didn't want to look. This was private, very private. He'd known both of them since they were kids. He only had to risk one glance through the window. Taking all his courage in his hands, he rose up from his crouched position….

Radiance was streaming into the room. It lovingly traced the outline of a young woman's beautiful naked body. She was swaying up and back, in slow, ecstatic rhythm, her movements gradually gaining momentum. A man's hands came up to cup her small perfect breasts. Then Kyall McQueen's distinctive voice groaned, "Sarah. My Sarah."

Shock and shame burned through his veins.

He couldn't remember getting away. He didn't think he drew a breath until he was safely in the Jeep he'd driven into the bush at the side of the road.

Kyall McQueen would kill him if he ever knew about this. Of course, they wouldn't have heard him. They were too far gone. His groin throbbed. What a beautiful woman. That glittering waterfall of hair spilling down her back. The glory of her woman's body. No wonder Kyall was crazy about her.

In a flurry of dust and leaves, he drove out of the scrub, not turning on his headlights until he was well clear of the house.

To hell with Ruth McQueen. He'd tell her they were together—tell her anything—but he'd be damned if he'd tell her he'd caught them making passionate love.

THE LAST TIME Sarah had seen Kathy Plummer had been a month ago. Then she had confirmed Kathy's pregnancy, her first. Kathy was now sixteen weeks along and her baby was coming along nicely, although Kathy's blood pressure was up, something that needed to be monitored. Sarah finished a careful physical examination, then began to discuss what she thought was every aspect of the pregnancy and its management. But Kathy didn't seem to be listening, plunging, instead, into what was happening in her life, trivia for the most part. Still, Sarah paid careful attention. She knew that Kathy and her husband, Darren, lived with Darren's parents on Wunnamurra, the men employed as ringers. She knew the Plummer family from her childhood in the town. Darren was now a man. Not terribly pleasant. Sarah recalled he had something of a reputation for being a bully. A state of affairs Harriet would never have tolerated at school. At their one meeting, when he'd brought Kathy in the month before, his manner had verged on sullen, with a dash of insolence thrown in. It had been fairly obvious that he didn't rate Sarah, a woman doctor, very highly. Or women at all, for that matter. Sarah's heart had gone out to Kathy, experiencing her first pregnancy with such an insensitive lout. He appeared to regard his wife's pregnancy in the same light as he would regard a cow being with calf.

Now Kathy, in the midst of recounting how she had to juggle all the jobs her mother-in-law set for her, suddenly winced and bent over, arms clutched around her body, a deep furrow between her brows.

"Kathy?" Sarah moved swiftly, coming around her desk. "What's up?"

Kathy straightened. "Nothing much, Doctor. Just one of my headaches."

"Headaches?" Sarah heard the anxious note in her own voice. "You never told me about headaches during your examination, Kathy. It's most important you tell me everything, otherwise I can't know what's going on with you. How often do you get these headaches? Bad on awakening, improving as the day goes on? Impaired vision?"

"None of those. They're nothing to worry about, really," Kathy assured her. "Mrs. Plummer—I'm supposed to call her Mother, but I already have a mum and when the baby comes, I want my mum around, not Mrs. Plummer. Anyway, Darren's mum says headaches are nothing. I shouldn't complain. I should expect a few of them. I'm pregnant after all. She had five kids. She should know."

"With all due respect to Mrs. Plummer, Kathy, I'm your doctor. You should have spoken to me about your headaches. How many? What's the duration? Severity? You winced hard just then. I take it the pain's gone away now?"

"Honest, it's nothing." Kathy tried a laugh, looking embarrassed. "Women are a whole lot tougher out here, and I'm a city girl. Anyway, the headaches come and go, and I suppose they're a bit worse than when I first learned I was pregnant. But really, I don't think there's anything to worry about."

"Let me be the judge of that, Kathy." Sarah returned to

her desk. "An occasional headache, maybe, but not what you're describing."

"I'm under some stress, you know." Kathy tried to explain. "There's pressure living with the in-laws. All I seem to do is cook and clean and wash clothes. Since I'm pregnant, I don't have to get up at dawn like Mrs. Plummer. She never stops all day. One day soon, we're going to have our own place. It'll be much better then. Darren doesn't get on all that well with his mum."

"The headaches, Kathy," Sarah prompted. "Tell me about them, please. They shouldn't be progressively worsening. I don't think they're due to stress or excessively taut muscles, either. Your neck and shoulder muscles seem quite relaxed."

For the first time Kathy opened up about herself and her symptoms, not what was happening at her in-laws' house. "I haven't had them all that long. I don't get headaches as a rule, but I've never been pregnant before. I had a talk with Darren's mum about them, like I said, and she told me pregnancy is a woman's lot and I had to struggle through it."

"Did she really?" Sarah's tone was quietly dismayed. Poor little Kathy, the city girl, looked like she was going to have a difficult pregnancy. "Well, I can't ignore this, Kathy. What you're telling me is worrisome. I'd like you to have a CAT scan."

"What's that?" Kathy sounded frightened.

"It's a form of X ray that's revolutionized the detection and diagnosis of any intracerebral problems." Sarah spoke in a matter-of-fact voice, avoiding the word hemorrhage. "We can't do the procedure here. I'll have to call in the Flying Doctor to airlift you to a larger hospital. I'd like it done right away."

Kathy began to shake her head anxiously. "Why right away? What's wrong with me?"

Sarah played down her concerns. To some patients she might've been able to talk about the possibility of blood clots in the brain, burst blood vessels, aneurysms and so forth, but she didn't think it would be particularly helpful with Kathy. "It's routine, Kathy," she said calmly, not wanting to increase Kathy's anxiety. "It's just that I don't like these severe headaches during your pregnancy. I'd like to check things out to be on the safe side. A CAT scan will tell us what's going on in your brain."

That brought forth an emotional response. "I don't want it," Kathy wailed. "What are you worried about, anyway?"

"I'm worried that if I don't act, I could be missing something. There are these headaches, coupled with the rise in your blood pressure. As I said, I can't ignore it, Kathy. These are measures any good doctor would take. You must trust me."

"Well, I do," Kathy answered, but she sounded tremulous and doubtful. "You've been so nice to me. Don't get me wrong. I like you. I bet you're a good doctor, but Darren would rather I saw Dr. Hughes now that he's here. Darren won't want me having any CAT scan, either. He'll be dead against it, I know."

Sarah had already assumed that. "Kathy, Darren knows nothing about medical matters. You have to be guided by me. I am and will remain your doctor. You'll find Dr. Hughes in complete agreement with that. Can you contact Darren?"

"He won't be pleased," Kathy repeated. "He's coming to pick me up in about an hour. I'm going to do some shopping first."

Exactly what Sarah didn't want her to do. "I would advise against that, Kathy. I suggest you rest quietly until your husband arrives.'' She smiled gently. ''As a matter of fact, there's a spare bed now that Mrs. Gray has gone home. You're looking forward to having your baby, aren't you, Kathy?''

''Oh, yes!'' Kathy's plain face shone.

''Well, then, I'm sure you won't mind making a few little sacrifices. You're well, the baby's well, but your BP is up. The shopping can wait or your husband can do it for you. Once he gets here, I'll talk to him.''

''Good luck,'' Kathy breathed.

When Darren Plummer arrived, he was accompanied by his father, Vernon, a heavyset, balding man who eyed Sarah keenly. Both men were wearing work clothes, riding boots, their *akubras* in hand. Hard, tough men, the father known for having been a troubleshooter for Ruth McQueen. Of the two, Sarah preferred Vernon, who was acting with more civility than his boorish son.

''Doctor was wanting to have a word with you, Darren.'' Kathy gave her husband a worried smile.

''About what?'' he asked coldly.

There was a decided risk of confrontation, and Sarah couldn't allow that to happen in the reception area. ''Perhaps you can all join me in my office,'' Sarah suggested, assuming control.

''Why can't we talk here?'' was Darren's demand.

''This is the waiting room.'' Sarah moved off, forcing them to follow, Darren hissing something at his wife.

When they were all seated, Sarah explained her concerns and what she proposed to do, taking care not to alarm them.

''All because of a few headaches?'' Darren fumbled for a cigarette.

''You can't smoke here, Darren,'' Sarah warned. ''I

wouldn't be advising this course of action if I didn't think it should be done.''

Vernon Plummer asked, ''What's it gonna cost?''

''I don't actually know, Mr. Plummer. It is expensive, but Kathy's health could be on the line here. Hers and her baby's. Your grandchild.''

''Makes sense.'' Vernon Plummer nodded.

''Well, I don't think so,'' Darren muttered. ''I want a second opinion. Why don't you call in Dr. Hughes? He's had far more experience than you.''

''Show some respect, Darren,'' Vernon Plummer said, glaring at his son.

''We can call in Dr. Hughes by all means,'' Sarah answered quickly to calm the situation.

But in fact, when Sarah called Morris Hughes away from a patient, Morris seemed a bit taken aback by her decision.

''We do have to be careful selecting patients for a CAT scan,'' he said cautiously. ''It's an expensive resource, as we know. You're quite satisfied it's not unnecessary testing? Perhaps we could run blood and urine tests?''

''Better to overreact than be found negligent, Morris. I've listened carefully to my patient. I'm going on instinct, as well. I know you've had a great deal more experience than I have, but I have a nose for trouble. I believe she's at risk. You could conduct your own examination.''

''Sure,'' Morris agreed instantly. ''I'm sorry if I seem to be questioning your judgment. I'll go see her.''

''If you would. Something tells me Kathy's headaches— it's a miracle I even got to know about them—are a forerunner of something more serious. I don't ever want to be accused of negligent practice. Especially not with a pregnant woman. We can't exclude subdural hemorrhage.''

''Which means surgery. How far along is she?''

"Four months. I should warn you, the husband is totally against this."

"Oh, dear!" Morris said.

In the end he backed Sarah's decision, but her husband refused to let her go immediately. "I can't figure out what the rush is. You have to give us a few days."

Anger sparked in Sarah at his stubborn stupidity, but she kept it under control. "If anything's really wrong, Darren, Kathy needs the CAT scan today. I take full responsibility."

"Why don't you go over her head?" Darren challenged Morris Hughes. "I reckon she's just bein' a female. My mum can fix Kathy's headaches."

Kathy was brave enough to pipe up. "No, she can't, Darren. If Dr. Sarah thinks I should go, then I'd better."

"Listen, I have to tell ya, we're broke." Darren shot back at his wife, who was sitting with her hands draped over her stomach. Darren's arms were folded across his broad chest, his lips pressed into a tight, surly line.

"You leave that to me, son." Vernon Plummer spoke sharply, pushing his chair back. His eyes moved to Sarah. "Make the arrangements, Doc. If you reckon we can't put this off, we won't."

THE CAT SCAN showed that one of Kathy Plummer's arteries had blown up like a balloon. Had the aneurysm burst, profound physical deficits would have appeared immediately. As it was, she was rushed into emergency surgery. When it was over, her surgeon relayed the good news: the outcome would be fine for mother and child. He also passed on his congratulations to Dr. Dempsey for the swift and, as it happened, excellent diagnosis.

CHAPTER ELEVEN

By SEVEN-THIRTY Sarah was ready. This was the evening of the reception for Morris Hughes, to be held at Wunnamurra homestead in the presence of the matriarch, Ruth McQueen. Kyall had insisted on coming for Sarah in the station helicopter, saying the hour-plus drive in her small car was out of the question.

She had many qualms about this evening. Why wouldn't she have? It wasn't as though the family would be thrilled, although the thaw had started with Enid, and Kyall's father had never been the problem. Apart from Ruth, she knew the Claydon clan was coming. She'd always liked all of them, especially Mitch, but these days she was a bit worried about India. Ruth had filled her head with such false hopes. Cruel, really. Nevertheless, the charge of excitement she always felt at being with Kyall was there. And with his plan to announce their engagement, the thrill of anticipation—despite her concerns—increased by the minute.

She had dressed appropriately for the occasion, knowing exactly how Kyall liked her to look. Very feminine. The dress wasn't new, but it was a favorite. Long, asymmetric in design, the chiffon skirt layered, the color the beautiful sapphire blue of Kyall's eyes, with a misty outline print of pink flowers. She wore her hair full and flowing, a pair of very pretty pendant earrings fastened to her ears. She had found them in an antique shop years before and had her

ears pierced specially for them. The vivid blue enamel
picked up the blue of her dress.

Fully dressed, deliciously scented, she walked through
the house, checking every room. Even with the lights on,
they appeared dimly lit. Sometimes, when she was very
tired or feeling emotional, she expected to encounter the
little Sinclair girl. Whatever had happened to the child? No
closure had ever been brought to the case. The girl had
simply disappeared off the face of the earth. For that matter,
what had happened to Nurse Fairweather? Sarah refused to
speculate any further, not wanting to spoil this enchanted
evening. Or so she hoped it would be. The night of her
engagement to the man she'd always loved. She knew she
was coming to the end of the long years of deceit. Kyall
had to be told what had happened to her. What had happened to their baby. His grandmother's part in it. The extraordinary business surrounding Molly Fairweather. She
prayed Kyall would understand. They could put the tragedy
behind them, turn their attention to making a perfect, living
child. How wonderful that would be. She was desperately
afraid a child would be denied her. Never, as long as she
lived, would she forget the child that had been taken from
her.

The house secure, or as secure as Sarah could make it,
she walked onto the wide veranda, staring out at the night.
It was blessedly cooler than the daytime. The sky was
ablaze with stars. As always, she sought out the Southern
Cross, one of the outstanding constellations of the southern
sky. The desert nomads believed it to be the footmark of
the great wedge-tailed eagle, Waluwara, because of its
shape. Wunnamurra homestead boasted a marvelous collection of Aboriginal paintings, several representing the
stars of the Milky Way. On this cloudless night, the Milky
Way sent its diamond stream across the center of the sky,

a river with many landmarks to the Aboriginals. She loved all the Dreamtime stories about the creation of the sun, moon and stars. She and Kyall had once known a very old Aboriginal who could identify nearly every star in the heavens, most with stories attached as to their origins. In the rarified air of the outback, the stars shone with great brilliance, so near, so luminous, Sarah almost felt she could touch them.

Despite the white radiance of the stars, the garden was in deep shadow. Even a blind person would sense a strange atmosphere about the house. Not normally prone to paranormal experiences, she couldn't deny that this particular house was having a strange effect on her. It was almost as if she could *feel* the past.

Even as she thought it, standing there waiting for the helicopter to appear, from out of nowhere floods of images saturated her brain. Terrible images she was powerless to prevent. Estelle Sinclair, drowning, long, blond hair floating like seaweed. Sarah could see slippery moss-covered boulders rising like ruins, tall, light-leafed trees overhanging the water. Someone was standing on the moonlit sand. A man in silhouette.

Stunned, Sarah shook her head to clear it, her pulse throbbing in her ears. She couldn't handle this—being drawn into another reality. She had to cast it off. Incredibly nervous, she hurried back inside, murmuring a prayer as she went. Swiftly she pulled the door shut, closing out the night. She couldn't believe now that she'd seen anything. It was her imagination. The Sinclair house had always frightened the town's children, including her. Even the bravest had never dared go there at night.

She wasn't a child any longer. But the house hadn't lost its mystery, either. Up until now, it had never really bothered her. For long moments she stood still, her eyes closed tightly to block out any further unwelcome visions. But the old haunting question remained. Had Estelle Sinclair drowned or met some even worse fate? The bush was criss-crossed with lagoons and creeks and billabongs. In a flash of perception she believed that if she could have seen that pool more clearly, she'd have been able to identify it. She and Kyall, comrades of childhood, had known this entire area like the backs of their hands.

She was conscious of her laboring heart and lungs. God! The experience, which seemed more and more real, had affected had bodily, making her take deep breaths. Those images had been riveting. Where had they come from? Normally of a calm disposition, reinforced by her training, she felt unnerved and agitated, marveling at the power of the mind but not understanding it.

The loud whir of a helicopter's rotors came as a huge relief. The fears and rumors surrounding this house might just be well-founded, she thought. Why had she taken over the tenancy in the first place? Because of the connection with Molly Fairweather, of course. Absurd to think poor Molly would speak the truth to her, especially since she was now very certain that Ruth McQueen had controlled Nurse Fairweather.

What would she do if she had that vision again? Sarah asked herself with a chill. Reject it or let it come? Was it possible for the mind to cross to another time? The land-scape had looked familiar. The trees, the big slippery rocks, the unusual shapes like ruins. She was a child again, playing adventurous games. Maybe she could will herself to identify that place.

"Sarah?"

Kyall's voice called to her. Then he was there, filling the open doorway with his height and vivid presence. "Why on earth are you standing with your eyes closed?'' His voice was half amused, half perturbed.

She gave a shaky laugh and went to him almost blindly, feeling his strong arms come around her. ''For the first time ever, the house has made me nervous.''

''Darling, didn't I tell you not to stay here?'' he asked, her unease communicated to him.

''I don't think I had a choice. I was meant to stay here.''

''Sarah!'' He tipped up her chin so he could meet her eyes.

''Maybe there are things that need to come out into the open.''

''Like what?'' His hand moved very gently to her breast. ''Your heart is racing.''

''I'm not surprised. My nerves are as taut as strung wire. I was standing on the veranda waiting for you when out of nowhere I saw the little Sinclair girl drowning. I could see all the floating blond hair. I could see the silhouette of a man standing on the sand. The most unnerving part is, I'm sure I know where they were.''

Kyall frowned. ''Didn't I warn you about this house, Sarah? It's had a calamitous history. You're a very sensitive woman. God knows, there are mysteries in the world, and certain people are drawn into them. I don't know what you picked up on, but I can see you're disturbed. Maybe memories of what's happened here have seeped into the atmosphere. I'm not happy about any of this.''

She forced herself to relax. ''The house doesn't mean me any harm, Kyall, I'm certain of that. Maybe it's letting me see things?'' Sarah's eyes clouded with sadness. ''How that mother must have grieved for her child.''

''Sarah, don't do this.'' For a moment she made him afraid.

''I know. I'm sorry. It's all over. I must have allowed

my imagination to run riot, thinking about the house and its history. I should've kept staring at the stars, instead.''

''They're glorious tonight.'' He sought to calm her. ''We can watch them from bed. I'm sure as hell coming back with you tonight.''

''Lovely.'' She stood on tiptoe and kissed him.

''*You're* lovely,'' he said. ''Exquisite. I love the dress. I love everything about you. Magical! You always were,'' he murmured. ''I wonder if you could be a witch. Bewitching, certainly.''

Her face lit up. ''Remember when I made you that love potion?''

''Sure do. I swallowed it.''

''Narnji said it would work.''

He laughed and shook his head. ''It did. On the other hand, you could have poisoned me.''

She paused to think. ''In that case, I would've poisoned myself, as well. I drank some, too. It was only berry juice and something else. Something Narnji wouldn't tell me. But she would never have harmed us.''

Kyall remembered the powerful influence the Aboriginal woman had had on them. ''Well, she did practice sorcery. She taught you a lot.''

''Oh, to have those times again! I miss her. I miss everything about our wonderful childhood. Being with you I...''

''I'm still here.'' He looked at her, wanting to kiss every inch of her creamy skin. ''I have your ring. Want to see it?''

''Oh, yes, yes, yes!'' Sarah cried. ''Could there be any other answer to that question?''

''How much time has passed, Sarah,'' he lamented. ''We should have been engaged—married—years ago. Give me your hand.''

"My heart. My head. My soul." She went to him, waves of pleasure whipping up inside her as he reached into the breast pocket of the blue dress shirt he wore with a blue-navy-and-silver silk tie, and withdrew the ring. "Receive this ring with all my love." He spoke very formally, then added quickly, "No, don't cry. You'll ruin your makeup."

"How can I not cry?" She tried to control herself, but still the tears stabbed. "These long years…"

"Don't cry, darling," he repeated. "Or I will, too. The bad times are finally over, Sarah. We're together. Do you like your ring? If it's not what you want, I'll get you another. We'll go shopping together."

"I adore it." Her dazzled gaze took in the glorious ring.

"You know what the central stone is?"

"Tanzanite, only found at the base of Mount Kilimanjaro. Unique."

He nodded. "That's why I decided on it. You're unique to me. I could love no other woman on earth."

"And it's almost the color of your eyes," she gently teased.

"It is not! That stone's a cross between blue and purple."

"So are your eyes. It's very beautiful, Kyall. I'll treasure it all my life."

"Then you'd better treasure these, as well!" He dipped once more into his pocket. "I bought them to match."

"Oh, Kyall, that's not a bottomless pocket, is it?" She stared at what he had in his hand. "Earrings! How gorgeous!" Like her engagement ring, the central stones were vivid-blue-and-purple-hued tanzanites set with brilliant diamonds.

"Put them on," Kyall urged. "Your own are very pretty, but these will go beautifully with your dress and later with your ring. The ring can either go back in my pocket, or you can keep it in your evening purse until the announcement tonight.''

Sarah held up her left hand. ''I don't think I can bear to take it off. Perhaps it's best if you keep it for the time being.'' Lingeringly she removed the ring and handed it over. ''I hope that's not bad luck.''

''Don't say that!'' His protest came hard and fast.

''I know. It's impudent to tempt fate.'' Sarah turned and moved to the hall mirror to put on her earrings. ''There, how do they look?'' She made a graceful about-face, throwing out her hands.

''Superb.'' In his blue eyes she could see little flames. ''Do you trust me, Sarah?'' He caught and held her by the wrist, pulling back from his overwhelming desires—desires laced with an odd panic.

''With my life.'' It was the simple truth.

''Tell me again that you'll marry me.'' He stood above her, thinking, *My woman, my woman. This is my woman. My Sarah.*

She lifted a tender hand to his face. ''The great Kyall McQueen uncertain?''

''You've made me like that,'' he countered, his face taut. ''You and no one else.''

She, who had trained herself to be a model of calmness, could have burst into tears. ''You're my dream of the future, Kyall,'' she said, standing very still beneath his hand. ''I feared we could never be together. I've borne the weight of it. Now I know only you can make this happen.''

WUNNAMURRA'S SPLENDID homestead was a blaze of lights, like a great liner afloat on a vast, rolling, black ocean. Even as they approached the house, they could hear the sound of music, conversation and ripples of laughter. It was ten past eight. By now, most people should have arrived.

One hundred in all, not a large crowd, but all the people of influence in the town and the owners of the outlying stations, like the Claydons.

Within a minute of stepping into the house, they were surrounded by polite, smiling people, the women expressing admiration for Sarah's dress, sharp eyes not missing the beautiful earrings, telling her how wonderful it was to have her back. If only, if only, she'd taken up her appointment at the hospital before her dear mother died. There was some irony in that. None of these women had made the slightest attempt to befriend her mother, who ran the store.

Kyall remained at her side, his head turned as guests called to him. Kisses on the cheek from the women. "Kyall, darling, how lovely to see you!" Hearty handshakes from the men. Companionable slaps on the back, a few jolly words, a lot of flattery, warm hellos, many expressions signifying interest at seeing Sarah so obviously by Kyall's side. He knew all kinds of rumors had been circulating. Now, suddenly, he'd proved them true.

Then the crowd parted as Ruth McQueen materialized, rather heavily made-up, her dark hair—she continued to have it colored its original sable—drawn back. For a woman her age she looked remarkably glamorous, her slight, imperious figure encased in a silver-brocade sheath. She wore pearls with a magnificent heart-shaped diamond around her neck. Pearls at her ears. Such was her aura that, like her grandson, she quite naturally stood out from the crowd, and this crowd was dressed in its finest. Invitations to Wunnamurra had become increasingly rare. They all wished to look as worthy of the honor as possible.

"Ah, Kyall, you've arrived," said Ruth, her eyes on her beloved grandson's face.

"You look incredible, Gran." Kyall bent his head to kiss her.

"And Sarah. I'm so glad you could come." Unblinking black gaze. No trace of a smile. As if a smile would have killed her.

Ruth didn't wait for Sarah's response but turned her head. "Do come and join us. We must find the guest of honor. I was fascinated to see him arrive with Harriet Crompton."

"Then he'll be sure to enjoy himself." Kyall gave his grandmother a glinting smile.

"The house looks wonderful," Sarah remarked, watching Ruth incline her head coldly.

"Let me show you around." Kyall took hold of Sarah's arm, glancing in his grandmother's direction.

"Surely that can wait until later?" Ruth stalked off, not waiting for a response.

"Nothing like a family party," Kyall murmured. "Well, I think we're over the worst of it."

"There are only two kinds of people," Sarah said, smiling. "Optimists and pessimists. You're the former."

"So tell me, how did you get to be the latter?" he countered, tightening his hold on her arm. "This is going to be a great night."

"Absolutely." Quietly Sarah crossed her fingers.

Kyall's mother, Enid, and his father, Max, both looking very handsome, were sitting with the Claydons. Golden-haired, blue-eyed Mitch, who put everyone in mind of Robert Redford in his youth, lifted a hand in salute, flashing his engaging smile.

"I've always been fond of Mitch. I'll bet he would've liked you for a brother-in-law," Sarah added dryly.

"Mitch knew that wasn't on."

"Did you discuss it?"

"Didn't have to," Kyall answered in a laconic tone. "Mitch always knew how I felt about you. Don't forget we virtually grew up together, although Mitch is a few years younger.''

"And there's India smiling brightly." Sarah felt a sharp stab of pity. "This can't be a good moment for her. I hate hurting anyone."

"I do, too." Kyall's response was a bit terse. "India and I enjoyed a friendship, but I never led her to believe that marriage would be the outcome."

"Then why has she waited all these years?''

"God, I don't know. Am I supposed to feel guilty?'

"I feel guilty all the time.''

"So you should. You went off and left me. The question is why.''

Sarah sidestepped the answer. She had enough to contend with this evening. "Hush, we're nearly there.''

Enid broke off her conversation with Julanne Claydon to greet them, using all the charm she could muster. "Sarah, my dear, you look absolutely beautiful!'' she said. "Those earrings are fabulous.''

"Thank you.'' It wasn't the time to say, "They're a present from Kyall. And that's not all!''

Julanne Claydon smiled coolly, but managed a few words of welcome. "Good to see you again, Sarah.''

"Yes,'' India tacked on, her eyes sparkling as though she was on the verge of tears. She looked very attractive in a short, sequined dress that showed off her long, tanned legs, staring at Kyall with a mixture of pleasure and disillusionment. The men—Kyall's father, Max, and Brad and Mitchell Claydon—made up for any shortcomings, visibly delighted to see Sarah and Kyall together. First Max and then Brad Claydon, the multimillionaire cattleman who, strangely enough, wore a rumpled shirt, took Sarah's hand, smiling at her with warm, paternal eyes. Mitch planted a feathery kiss on her cheek. "It's great to have you back with us, Sarah," he said.

"It's great to be back." For a moment she actually meant it. Would have meant it only for...only for... She knew in her bones that things were not over.

After a few minutes they moved on to find Morris and Harriet, who were holding court at the far end of the resplendent cream-and-gold drawing room, adorned with masses of beautiful flower arrangements that must have been flown in. The fragrance was all around them. Obviously they were having a good time. Both were in animated conversation with a group of guests that included the big impressive man Sarah had once spotted driving through town. Evan Someone. She would be pleased to meet him. The town's mystery man.

As soon as Harriet spotted them, she held up a hand and waved enthusiastically. Harriet, in her own inimitable way, looked every bit as eye-catching as Ruth. She wore a long, black dress, over which she'd thrown a gorgeous hand-painted-silk Chinese jacket in vibrant imperial yellow with darting turquoise birds and sprays of peonies in deepest pink with leaves of jade. As if that wasn't enough, on her head she wore a most unusual little headdress, oriental in flavor. Something the last Chinese empress might have popped on of an evening.

"It's just not fair!" Sarah burst out affectionately. "Harriet always steals the show."

"What I love about her is that she makes me laugh. What *is* that getup?" Kyall asked in an amused undertone. "I just hope it doesn't reek of mothballs like the last time."

"Well, we know one thing for sure. Morris is very taken with her."

"And she with him. They should get married or move

in together. Harriet looks ten years younger since I last saw her.''

Sarah murmured her agreement.

''The big man is Evan Thompson, by the way. I'm glad he decided to come. He strikes me as tremendously lonely, as opposed to simply being a loner, which he undoubtedly is. You might be able to draw him out.''

''He doesn't look like a man content to answer questions,'' Sarah answered, glancing toward the group.

It took time to move through the beaming crowd, stopping here and there, but when they were a few feet away, Harriet swooped. ''You look wonderful, both of you. Love the dress, Sarah.''

''I like your outfit more.'' Sarah smiled.

''I'll leave it to you in my will.'' Harriet grasped her arm. ''We're having such a good time. It's such a nice evening.''

''Going well, is it?'' Kyall asked, an indulgent expression on his face.

''Morris has practically persuaded me to marry him,'' Harriet said, shocking them. ''Only joking,'' she crowed as Sarah and Kyall visibly reacted. ''Come on. We've been waiting for you. You must meet Evan, Sarah. He's an extremely gifted and intelligent man.''

And so it turned out. Sarah went back a long way with nearly all the people who'd been invited, but Evan Thompson was a newcomer. They didn't exactly chat away; he wasn't that kind of man. But he was charming in a Mr. Rochester kind of way, dark, sculpted head inclined to one side, paying keen attention to everything she said. No wonder every single woman in town had done her level best to get acquainted with him. There was something very intriguing about him. A hint of danger.

Across the crowded room, India Claydon remarked

waspishly, "How nice for Sarah! She's actually got Evan
Thompson to talk."

"Where?" Julanne Claydon asked, her face contorting
with the effort to spot him. Sarah Dempsey wasn't exactly
Julanne's favorite person right now. For a long time she'd
thought India had a good chance with Kyall. Now Sarah
was back.

"Over there, look. She's with Miss Crompton and the
new doctor. And Kyall, of course. God, how I hate her!"
Though she whispered, the words came out almost violently.

Julanne was shocked. "That's not very nice, India. You
shouldn't hate anyone."

"Mrs. McQueen promised me Kyall was mine," India
muttered.

"What?" Julanne asked incredulously. She'd never
heard this before.

India flushed. "Mum, can you please stop the *where*s
and *what*s? And keep your voice down, okay? You know
perfectly well that Mrs. McQueen—"

"You're talking about Ruth?" Julanne grabbed hold of
her daughter's arm, making her turn around.

"Of course, Ruth!" India's bright blue eyes glinted like
glass. She picked her mother's fingers off her arm one by
one. "She told me I'm perfect for Kyall."

"She's a cruel bitch!" Julanne erupted, her maternal
hopes falling meteorically.

"Really, Mum." Now it was India's turn to chastise.

Julanne focused on her daughter. "You mean it's thanks
to *Ruth* you thought you had a chance with Kyall? You
told me—"

"I don't care what I told you!" India said rudely, causing her mother to glare at her.

"Please behave, India, or we might as well go home. I brought you up to be a lady. Ladies don't make scenes."

"Too bad, because that's just what I want to do."

"Then I'll get your father," Julanne warned.

"God, he and Mitch acted like seeing Sarah again was the high point of their lives. Don't they realize I love Kyall? He should be *mine*."

"But sweetheart, falling in love with Kyall McQueen is something all the girls do." She frowned. "You told me Kyle admitted to being in love with you."

"You bet he did!" India lied.

"Then, my poor girl, I think he's about to take that back."

"That's why I hate her," India mumbled.

"She's too nice to hate," Julanne suddenly counterattacked. "The one who needs hating around here is Mrs. Ruth Bloody McQueen. If Ruth McQueen was running the world, we'd all be at war."

"You've never liked her, have you, Mum?"

"India, no one likes Ruth McQueen, with the possible exception of you, and that's only because she's been filling your head with false hopes."

"So no one likes her but no one stays away when she issues an invitation?" India said in a challenging voice.

"It's not like that at all," Julanne Claydon retorted sharply. "Our families tend to stick together. We all go back a long way." She shrugged helplessly. "Ruth might want you to marry Kyall, but even she can't make it happen."

"She's going to give it a darn good try."

"How?" Julanne gasped.

"There you go again. How, when, why? I don't *know,* Mum."

"Put poison in the drinking water?" Julanne volunteered

sarcastically. "Then again, maybe she would if she thought she could get away with it."

"What are you saying, Mum?" India eyed her mother critically.

"I'm saying, my girl, don't trust Ruth McQueen. And get a grip on yourself," Julanne snapped. "This isn't the end of the world. It might feel bad now, but there's always tomorrow. You're young, you're beautiful and you're a Claydon."

"What I really want to be is a McQueen," India announced tartly.

That hurt Julanne's feelings. "Let's get this straight, India," she chided. "The Claydons have always been a happy family. The McQueens, believe me, would fit into a pretty grim movie script. And the woman to blame is right over there watching Kyall—whose hand has just slipped around Sarah Dempsey's waist."

"Do you think I can't see it?" India asked, stung.

"We're not alone. The whole room can see it. I don't know how to tell you this, my darling, but Ruth Bloody McQueen has been wasting your time."

God help me she has, India thought, completely revolted by the woman she had once revered.

THE BUFFET SUPPER was sumptuous, served at ten-thirty in the huge garden room at the rear of the house. This was a fairly recent extension to the original homestead, opening up an informal dining room and giving the whole area a view of the rear landscape—the towering trees, the dark-emerald creek that snaked through the home gardens and by day, the cloudless peacock-blue sky. Tonight the gardens had been strategically lit, the illumination of lights and stars shown to advantage through the series of floor-to-ceiling arched doorways.

"I never thought anyone would go to so much trouble for me," Morris remarked in wonderment to Harriet. He gazed around him with dazzled eyes. "The homestead is magnificent. Such a sense of history. And just look at that food! It would feed an army."

Harriet looked toward the laden buffet tables. "You may be amazed to find how little will be left over," she said dryly. "This family has money, my dear. Not flashy new money. Old money that's grown and grown with time. One has to hand it to Ruth. She handled everything extremely well for many years after she lost her husband. Enid and Max helped a great deal, not that they ever got much credit. But it's been Kyall who's built on everything his forebears accomplished. He's the one with the vision, getting into all kinds of new areas as a safety measure against an uncertain future for wool. You should listen to him sometime, Morris. He's a young man with ideas."

"I'd very much like to." Morris was most impressed with Kyall McQueen. Real character there, and a charm of manner he obviously hadn't inherited from his grandmother. Though Morris was very appreciative of the honor accorded him this evening, not fully realizing it had been Kyall's idea, he found Ruth McQueen rather frightening, although he didn't know why. Normally he wasn't a man who felt threatened by powerful women. He'd met quite a few in his time, but no one like the McQueen matriarch, with her chill demeanor. It was a pleasure to turn back to Harriet, who looked the world straight in the eye. He was becoming increasingly fond of her.

Now she was saying, "Yes, Kyall's a young man with the Midas touch, but he has a lot more to offer than the ability to make money."

"Quite obviously he's in love with Sarah. Indeed, I've

never seen such a couple. The way he looks at her. The
way she leans into him. Part of each other.''

"They've been like that since they were very young,"
Harriet said. "You could say they bonded from the moment
they set eyes on each other. It does happen. The classic
love story."

"How come they broke up?" Morris asked with interest.

"The *R* word again." Harriet answered right away.

"And what on earth is that?"

"Ruth. It's no secret in this town that Kyall's grandmother had very different plans for Kyall. Sarah, as exceptional as she is, simply wasn't good enough."

"Good grief! I would've thought who better?" Morris
replied in an amazed tone.

"India Claydon for one," Harriet said with a sympathetic sigh. "India was very highly regarded in the marriage
stakes. Two great pioneering families united, and so forth."

"I see." Morris bent closer as other guests were approaching. "So neither Mrs. McQueen nor Miss Claydon
can be too happy to see Sarah back?"

"You can be sure, my dear Morris, that they loathe it."

OVER SUPPER Ruth McQueen made an elegant little speech
outlining the history of the town hospital, the McQueen
involvement, and then went on to formally welcome Dr.
Morris Hughes to the hospital and to the community. Some
forty minutes after that, Kyall held up his hand in a gesture
for quiet.

What am I afraid of? Sarah wondered. In finding Kyall
again, hadn't she been released from her terrible spell? The
woman who'd placed the spell on her was only a few feet
away, her face masklike as she lifted her head, eyes glittering with subterranean life.

Sarah's heart was pounding hard, but Kyall put a strong arm around her, drawing her close.

"With my family and our friends here, I'd like to make an announcement," he began, his pride and happiness making him look wonderfully vibrant, his blue eyes afire.

HERE IT COMES, thought Ruth, conscious of a terrible tightness in her chest. *The very thing I've fought for years and years—the intolerable thing.* She, the fighter, forever triumphant in her dealings, trounced by a mere girl. It was not to be borne. From a distance she heard Kyall continue, his voice solemn but exultant.

"...Sarah and I would like to announce our engagement."

A terrible anger flooded the autocrat's veins. *This can't happen.* She wanted to climb to the very top of a tall desert dune and howl like a dingo.

"We can't bear to keep it a secret any longer," Kyall concluded to a cascade of clapping and gasps of genuine pleasure. "Most of you know I fell in love with Sarah when I was about eight years old."

"I think it was before that," Mitch Claydon teased, torn between joy for his old friends and pity and discomfort for his sister, who had refused to listen to a single word of advice he had given her.

"I believe it was." Sarah turned up her face to Kyall. "You turned eight two weeks later." *Oh, yes, and I wasn't invited to your party.*

Kyall simply gazed back at her with love, withdrawing his ring from the inside pocket of his cream silk jacket and putting it on her finger to another outbreak of applause.

Kyall's mother and father reached them first. "Oh, my goodness, look at that ring!" Enid cried, taking Sarah by the arms and lightly kissing both cheeks. "I'm sorry your mother isn't alive to share in your happiness, Sarah,'' she said softly. ''Welcome to the family, my dear, welcome.''

Max took Sarah's face in his hands, dropping a kiss on her forehead. ''My son is a very lucky man,'' he said gently, smiling down at her, his expression one of understanding and an undeniable hint of sadness. ''Be happy, both of you. It's my greatest wish.''

''Thank you, Max.'' Sarah knew it would be easy to grow fond of Kyall's father.

''My turn.'' Mitch Claydon presented himself with a rakish grin. ''About time, too, Sarah. As we're old friends, I don't think Kyall will mind if I steal a kiss?''

In fact, it was a graceful salute that landed between her cheek and mouth. ''Kyall has always needed you.''

''And I need him.''

Ruth, conscious that all eyes were now on her, drew herself up to go through an elaborate little charade, kissing her grandson and saying in a mock-censorious tone, ''You might have told me, darling,'' before moving on to Sarah. She took Sarah's hand, staring down at her ring. ''You always were amazing, Sarah,'' she murmured beneath her breath. ''Do you think you can make my grandson happy?'' She glanced up for a split second, but Sarah saw the flash of anger in her eyes.

''I'm going to prove to you I can.''

''And if you don't?'' This was said so quietly only Sarah heard.

''You'll be the reason,'' Sarah responded in a matching undertone, so the people around them, most of them busy trying to congratulate Kyall, thought the two women were finally making up.

''Just as long as you know. If you think you're good enough, Dr. Dempsey—'' she drew the words out ''—you're not.''

Sarah met her look head-on, impressively cool, hoping her act was convincing. "What undermines me undermines you," she pointed out very gently.

Ruth favored her with a malevolent smile. "And how is the ghost at the house? Been at work? I can promise you, Sarah, I'll destroy you however long it takes."

Reveling in having the last word, Ruth released Sarah's hand, moving off with her habitual—and slightly exaggerated—regal poise.

CHAPTER TWELVE

JOE RANDALL had single-handedly run the hospital for more than thirty years, but Sarah was very grateful to have Morris Hughes on board, especially when the hospital had a run of accident victims. One of them tragically resulted in a death. A stockman herding cattle by motorbike lost control of his machine and was thrown off so violently he broke his neck. There were accidents mending fences, one when the wire snapped back into a man's eye, another a goring by a bull, the amount of bleeding suggesting the injury was a lot worse than it was. Then there were the usual accidents with children. A little boy was admitted unconscious, having been given tablets containing codeine for a cough, the drug suppressing the child's breathing, as well as the cough. As Sarah's former boss had predicted, a tourist was rushed to hospital needing urgent medical attention because of sunstroke. The tourist's car had broken down within the boundaries of Marjimba Station, and he'd set off on foot for help, ignoring all the warnings, posted throughout the outback. The man had taken a canteen of water, but it was not enough. Dehydration had rapidly set in.

Mercifully Mitch had been the one to find him, very near collapse but not far from a water hole. Mitch had driven him there, drenching the man's heated body with buckets of water before having him airlifted into town by the station helicopter. Other frequent procedures involved skin cancer caused by the sun, the solar system's greatest uncontrolled nuclear reactor. Patients who for most of their lives had exposed themselves carelessly to the radiation of the sun presented with squamous and basal-cell carcinomas for removal by liquid nitrogen or surgical procedure. A bleeding ulcer that had been too long ignored was confirmed as a melanoma by laboratory inspection. Sarah had dreaded giving the patient, a family man in his mid-forties, the news.

One morning about two weeks after the party for Morris, Sarah encountered Vernon Plummer on the street. His vehicle was parked outside the store she and her mother had lived and worked in. He was stocking up on supplies.

"Good morning, Mr. Plummer," Sarah called when she realized who it was.

He threw a few more bags in the back, then twisted his heavyset frame. "Mornin', Dr. Sarah." Although he spoke gruffly, he sounded pleased that she'd bothered to greet him. He had been so preoccupied she could easily have walked on by.

Sarah expected the man to continue with his loading; instead, he wiped his hands with a rag and approached her. "I've been wanting to thank you for all you've done for Kathy," he said, genuine gratitude in his eyes.

Sarah nodded. "That's my job, Mr. Plummer." She smiled pleasantly.

"You're very good at it. 'Course we all knew you'd amount to something, even when you was a little kid. Congratulations on your engagement, by the way. Kyall is a very lucky man."

"Well, I guess it took long enough, but we love each other," Sarah responded, short of time, but not wishing to appear rude. Vernon Plummer seemed to have something on his mind.

"Saved her life, didn't ya. I won't forget that."

She could feel him studying her with respect. "By the grace of God, yes. Kathy is well on the way to recovery. She and Darren will have their baby, and you and Mrs. Plummer will have another grandchild."

"I owe you one, Doc." His voice and eyes held a degree of commitment Sarah didn't think was warranted.

She shook her head. "No, you don't, Mr. Plummer. It gave me the greatest satisfaction to know I was there for Kathy. Frankly, that's what a doctor lives for. To save lives."

"You know your stuff," he responded. "That other doctor—Hughes?—didn't seem so sure. You're a good woman." He dropped his gaze for a moment, studying the pavement, then lifted his head, his demeanor quite changed. "Do ya get a sense Mrs. McQ might mean you harm?" The words came out so hoarsely, so full of anger, Sarah was numbed.

"I—I'm afraid I don't know what you mean?"

"Yes, you do. Wasn't she the one who chucked you out of town?"

Sarah didn't deny it, although she was astonished the man had spoken out. He was, after all, in Mrs. McQueen's employ. "Should you be saying this?" she questioned.

"You need to know. Yeah, I still work for her. I've been workin' for her, lemme see, damn near forty years. Started as a kid of twelve. Let's say I'm one person who knows Mrs. McQ."

"Am I to understand you're warning me?" Sarah managed, leveling her gaze on him.

"I'm sure you don't need no warning, Dr. Sarah. She really hates you."

"How do you know that for sure?"

"Let's just say I do."

"And why is that?" Sarah felt deeply troubled.

He shook his head almost regretfully. "Nothing I can say."

"I have Kyall to protect me."

"What if Kyall ain't around? He has to take a lot of trips. Go places for business."

In fact, Kyall was in Sydney on McQueen business right now, due back at the end of the week. "I have absolutely no idea why you're telling me this, Mr. Plummer," Sarah said, apprehensive and trying not to let it show.

"You do something for me and mine," he said. "I do something for you. I got things on Mrs. McQ."

Wasn't that Sarah's gut feeling? "Well, then, shouldn't you keep them quiet? What if she found out? You say you know what she's capable of."

"I do. You don't." He shot her a strange look. "You're too innocent, Doc."

The deepening heat of the morning gave Sarah an excuse to move off. She picked up the briefcase she had rested at her feet. "What do we do now, Mr. Plummer?" she asked.

"We watch and wait," he said. "This is one time Mrs. McQ isn't gonna win. I'm your friend, Dr. Sarah. You can count on it."

WASN'T LIFE FULL of odd turns, Sarah thought as her encounter with Vernon Plummer plagued her throughout the day. Would the man even have approached her had she not been instrumental in saving his daughter-in-law's life? Fate worked in mysterious ways.

Plummer had confessed he had a lot on Ruth McQueen. Didn't that place *him* in danger if Ruth ever found out he'd involved himself with Sarah's safety? What could Ruth do? Sack him? Put his whole family out of a job when working on Wunnamurra was all they'd ever known? Engineer an accident?

Preposterous! She couldn't believe that Ruth McQueen, dangerous as she was, would resort to murder. One would have to be beyond all civilized behavior for that. Prepared to risk exposure, arrest, jail. It was unthinkable. The man she loved was the woman's grandson! *She might detest me,* Sarah reminded herself, *but she loves him.*

"Sarah, have you got a minute?" Morris Hughes appeared at her door.

"Yes, of course, Morris." Shaking off her disturbing thoughts, Sarah stood up, coming round her desk.

Morris shut the door. "I have a patient with me at the moment. A Mrs. Costello."

"She hasn't brought her little girl in again?" Sarah asked in what was almost a groan.

"Then you know her?"

"I know she's had her child in fairly frequently. Joe saw her. I've seen her twice. Now you. Is something bothering you?"

"Something I can't answer easily."

"You suspect the mother might be making her child ill," she said bluntly. "What's wrong with the little girl, anyway?"

"On the face of it, the perfectly innocent diagnosis of diarrhea. Could be a virus. Mrs. Costello, I understand, is a widow. A nervous little thing. She needs treatment herself." He shook his head. "I'd be grateful if you'd take a look at the child."

Fifteen minutes later Sarah had made the decision to keep the little girl overnight for observation. Although the child's tongue was dry and her urine output had fallen off, oral salt and fluid replacement could have been done at home, but Sarah's instincts were working overtime. She had concerns about Mrs. Costello, given that the woman appeared overeager for attention. With any of her other mothers, Sarah would've left the medical management to them. With Mrs. Costello, warning bells were starting to ring. The child always presented with acute diarrhea. So what, then, was inflaming the bowel? Something the mother was administering? Laboratory tests might be helpful.

"Strange—so strange," Morris remarked later. "You're thinking Munchausen by proxy?"

"I'd be pleased to be proved wrong," Sarah said, "but I think we might privately monitor the mother's visits. If she *is* giving the child something, the task then becomes psychiatric treatment for Mrs. Costello. The loss of her husband was a stunning blow. She's alone in the world with a child to rear. Her reaction to such emptiness and grief could be seeking attention through that child. She appears bright and desperately concerned for the little one, but underneath I sense intense dysphoria."

"Terribly problematic," Morris agreed, "but treatable. By the way, I ran an EEG on Les Taylor. You might like to take a look at the results. Not good, I'm afraid. Unilateral slow activity—"

"—which might indicate a structural lesion. Oh, dear." Sarah sighed. "If only we could save them all."

"At least we can save them a lot of the pain. Ready if you are, Dr. Dempsey." Morris smiled in empathy.

WHEN SHE RETURNED that evening, all the lights were on. The ghost? She didn't think so. Someone was trying to frighten her, especially with Kyall away. She didn't have to look far. She could make the long, long drive to Wunnamurra homestead and tell Ruth McQueen to stop. Not tell. *Demand.* She knew Ruth hadn't turned on these lights herself, but she'd ordered someone to do it. She needed to reduce Ruth McQueen to normal size, not the monster of her memories.

All the years away from Kyall, she had lived with her memories, good ones and bad. Ruth McQueen figured largely in the terrible memories. Sarah felt her jaw tighten as she went around the house switching off unnecessary lights. No way was she allowing Ruth McQueen into her future! No way would Ruth continue to have power over her. One day soon—not tonight—Sarah would confront her.

She had to place her trust in Kyall. She had to tell him all about the most significant event in her life—the birth and death of their child. She'd backed away from it for far too long, diminished by her fears and griefs. The pain never went away. She didn't imagine it was going to be a good experience telling Kyall about those heartbreaking events. Kyall was a man of very strong emotions. A man of passion. He'd be shocked, ill with anger and suddenly realized grief. He might push her away. Physically? Emotionally? Both were possible. No matter. She couldn't hold this in anymore. She couldn't marry Kyall knowing she carried such a secret. Let Ruth McQueen do what she liked.

THAT NIGHT Sarah slept with her bedroom door locked, a chair propped up beneath the brass knob. Beside her bed was the rifle Kyall had given her for protection. She knew how to use it. Prayed she'd never have to. She hated guns. Nevertheless, its presence gave her a sense of security. She wasn't worried about the house's resident ghost, even though she'd never seen her except in that strange trance. Estelle Sinclair had been murdered. Incredible as it might seem, she, Sarah, had been at the scene watching with Estelle's murderer as she drowned. The girl had been alive when she hit the water but terribly injured, a little girl raped. Estelle wasn't going to hurt her. Estelle wanted help. Justice. Peace.

As for Nurse Fairweather? Her spirit had moved out. Just as all of Sarah's inquiries regarding her had met a dead end. It made Sarah very uncomfortable to recall Joe Randall's concerns over Molly Fairweather's death. Among other things, hadn't Joe as good as accused Ruth McQueen of involvement? But how? Even if Ruth *had* given someone instructions to release the snake in the house, many things could have gone wrong with that plan. The woman could have spotted the snake first. Locked it in. Called for help. The snake could have found its own way outdoors. Who'd do such a thing, anyway? It was horrible. But what had happened between Ruth and Molly? One might have suspected Ruth was being blackmailed. The big question was why. What had turned a normal, competent nurse into Mad Molly? What had so disturbed the tenor of her mind, what trauma had she suffered, that she'd been reduced to full-fledged ranting monologues in the garden during her last years? Sarah had wanted to speak to some of the children, now older, about the sorts of things Nurse Fairweather had said. But she had to be careful; each of them would probably tell a different story.

Sarah tried to settle herself in the bed, lying on her back, palms upturned as she tried to relax. She concentrated on blue, the color blue. The radiant blue of Kyall's eyes. The glorious blue of the sky. The blue of the ocean. The blue of the Madonna's cloak.

Relax... Relax... Think of nothing but the color blue.

Gradually she drifted off.

THE OLD HOUSE was powerfully connected with visions. Tonight they addressed themselves again to the sleeping Sarah.

A child was running. A man was trying to overtake her. The ground they covered was packed with leaves. The track the child was taking led down to the water. She heard the pinched voice of the man, didn't know what he was saying. The child, a girl barely into her teens, half turned, her long, blond hair skeining across her terrified face.

Estelle.

Sarah's fears rose like bile, but she couldn't open her eyes. Her lashes fluttered wildly, eyeballs twitched, but the lids were heavy, too heavy.

And then things turned far worse. The girl slipped, lost her footing, went hurtling down the slope. Sarah heard the scream even though silence drummed in her ears and her own lips were sealed.

Now the man reached the sand where the child was cowering, her knees drawn up. She was crying, sobbing piteously. "Mummy, Mummy."

Sarah's chest heaved in agony. That "Mummy" broke her heart. She didn't give a thought to herself or her own safety. She broke cover, running from where she was hidden in the scrub, weaving through the tall trees to the banks of the water hole.

Now she knew where she was. Despite her shouts of alarm, the man didn't hear her. She couldn't understand. The man twisted the child onto her back, his hands at her clothing.

Nooooo! Sarah cupped her hands and screamed.

Abhorrence at what she was about to witness surged through her. Sarah launched herself at the man, clawing at his back, raging at him to let go. *Let go!*

Blood was coming from the child's nose. She, too, reached for the man's eyes, clawing, clawing, until he hit her hard, shoving her back onto the sand where she lay dazed and panting. There was no hint of remorse or pity in the man's face. Not this man. All these years he'd been pretending loyalty and respect for the girl's family. Always lusting after the blond one, Estelle. Little star.

He was going to rape her. Sarah knew this. Realized she couldn't prevent it. Still she pulled and pulled at the man's head, tasting the sickness in her throat. The three of them were alone. No one to turn to for help. Sarah thought of a rock. She let go of the man's head and hurriedly went in search of one, although the man didn't appear to notice. She might as well have been absent from this terrible scene.

Nooooo! She could see a thin line of blood run down the child's white leg....

SARAH THOUGHT she'd blacked out for a time, or her mind had closed down on such a crime against heaven. Then suddenly her vision cleared. She could see the man carrying the child to the water hole. She saw him swing his body hard before he pitched his small burden into the center of the water. It was deep there. Very deep. Sarah knew. The children of the town had been forbidden to swim there. The Palmer twins had lost their lives in this same water hole. The Aboriginals had always whispered about it. Wirrabilla, a place frequented by devil spirits.

Wirrabilla. She could see the remarkable contours of the rocks. In the wet season, the golden clay that surrounded the water hole turned into a dangerous bog. Cattle got stuck there. It had never been known why the Palmer twins, boys of ten, had ventured in. Wirrabilla was a place of black magic.

As Estelle disappeared under the black water, holding one hand aloft, Sarah burst out of her nightmare into full consciousness. She threw herself sideways so violently she fell off the bed, landing on the rug with a heavy thud. She made an awkward attempt to rise, fell back, her mouth so dry she could barely swallow, her head filled with revulsion from her dream.

Estelle. The child's name hung in the air.

How the poor child had suffered while her defiler had lived on, never for a moment suspected by those around him. She had focused on his face. Didn't recognize it. How could she? This terrible event had taken place more than a century before. Everything had changed. Except for Wirrabilla.

Sarah stumbled to her feet, lowering herself distractedly to the bed. She was stunned such dreams could come to her, but she understood the house had evoked them, drawing her into another reality.

You can't rest, can you, Estelle? Not until your poor little bones are given a Christian burial.

She knew the job fell to her.

FINALLY IT WAS Friday. With Kyall away, the week had seemed endless. Sarah had missed him in her head, her heart and her bed. The rapturous nature of their sexual relationship flowed from their spiritual rapport. But then, that very fact had got her pregnant in the first place. She'd known so little in those days it hadn't even dawned on her that she could get pregnant from her first sexual encounter. She couldn't, wouldn't, dwell on the years of loneliness she had endured because of it.

But today Kyall was coming home. He was due late afternoon. They'd arranged to spend the night together, and she'd bought all the things he liked for dinner. She already had the wine. They would make love. Afterward, entwined in each other's arms, she would speak of what she'd never spoken of before. It would be a monstrous blow to him. She knew that. She had long since begun to rehearse what she would say. She could hardly expect him to take it all in, without withdrawal or rejection, when she had never come to terms with the loss herself. Despite what she'd achieved as a doctor, the loss of her child and the guilt she felt because of it had left her with feelings of inadequacy as a woman. Hadn't she isolated herself from relationships as a result?

She hadn't been able to do what other women did so easily. She hadn't been able to produce a healthy child. As a doctor, she'd treated other women who had suffered in the same way but went about the business of living. Trying again. It wasn't as though her patients hadn't gone on to bring healthy children into the world. She was very good at guiding mothers through their pregnancies, grappling with their problems. Unfortunately she'd never been able to do much about herself.

Until now. There was no safe place to hide with Ruth McQueen. Even now, Ruth was exploiting her silence. She might attempt to blackmail her. She could no longer let Ruth have the upper hand.

After ward rounds were finished, Sarah returned to her office, surprised when a nurse entered with a long silver box. She opened it to find a sheaf of white lilies.

"For me?" Sarah found herself shaking her head at what it could mean.

"Dr. Dempsey," the nurse confirmed, smiling uncertainly at Sarah's expression.

"Is there a card?"

"Yes, there is. It's tucked away amid the greenery."

"Thank you, Helen. You can leave them on the desk."

After she'd gone, Sarah inspected the box's contents more closely. They were very beautiful lilies, perfect in every detail, yet a chill went through her. Sarah opened the white envelope, carefully pulling out the card.

''For Sarah. Best Wishes. You'll need them. There's so much Kyall's going to learn about you.''

She turned the card over. It bore not a name but the initial R, elaborately wrought. Sarah fought back her anger, conscious only of a determination to bring her tragedy—however small compared to others she'd witnessed—into the open. She hated the way Ruth McQueen treated people. Hated the way she treated *her*.

Sarah hurried to the door, calling to the nurse, who'd returned to the nurses' station. ''Who delivered these, do you know, Helen?''

''It looked a lot like Kathy Plummer's husband. I only saw him as he was moving off. He dropped them here and left.''

''Thank you, Helen.''

Sarah went back to her desk, not to slump in her chair and brood, but to take action. She reached for the phone. Put a call through to Wunnamurra homestead. It was highly likely Ruth would refuse to take her call, but Sarah felt she had to try.

''Wunnamurra Station.'' To her surprise, Ruth herself answered. Her body might be increasingly frail, but her voice resonated down the line, clear and mellifluous.

Sarah identified herself to a momentary quiet, then a dark, derisive, ''Ah, Sarah…''

''I received your message,'' Sarah said in a level voice. ''The lilies are perfect—for a funeral.''

''Really? I thought it was a nice idea. They're from my garden. And what's your ghost doing these days?''

It occurred to her that Ruth might be a touch mad. ''You're getting a little tiresome, Mrs. McQueen. You should come up with something better than ripping my clothing and leaving the lights on.''

Another silence, then the expected explosion of outrage.

"As if I'd do such a thing! You're not the only one, my dear, who's had a bad experience in that house."

"Yes—Molly Fairweather. I thought it quite extraordinary, but Joe had the idea you might've been involved there."

White-hot fury this time. "Don't be ridiculous!" Ruth poured on the contempt. "I don't have to listen to this rubbish from you."

"I don't mean you personally. You're too smart for that. But you have people in your employ. People who are prepared to do whatever you want."

"And you are without sin, are you, my dear?"

"I've committed no grave sins, Mrs. McQueen, only sins of omission. But I've had sins committed against me."

"Look ahead, my dear," Ruth warned. "Your sins could be your downfall."

"And yours." Sarah's voice was low, solemn. "God knows why you hate me the way you do."

"Aren't you the one who tried to destroy my grandson? Ruin his life? I wasn't going to let that happen. Why don't you stop whining? You wouldn't be what you are today without my help."

"Blood money."

"The hell with you!"

"I hate to say this, but *you* might be spending quite a bit of time there. How did Joe die? By design or natural causes? There was no autopsy, was there?"

But Ruth McQueen wasn't easily intimidated. "Don't talk like a fool," she snapped. "Joe Randall was a dying man. He told me that as if I needed to be told."

"Dying maybe, but he should've had more time." Sarah was disturbed at her own line of questioning. She hadn't meant to say any of this, but the words kept tumbling out.

"My God, you've got a nerve!" Ruth's fury resounded

down the line. "You mention any of this, even a word, and you'll find yourself in court. Better yet, kicked out of your profession. That might be too much, even for Kyall. Attacking the grandmother he adores."

"Then you stop playing God, Mrs. McQueen," Sarah warned, not caring where it led. "As for Kyall, I intend to tell him everything tonight."

"Go ahead," Ruth invited, sounding totally self-assured. "You'll lose him."

"I'm prepared to take my chances," Sarah answered. "Lord knows what he'll have to say to you once he learns *your* role."

It seemed as though Ruth McQueen would hang up; instead, she muttered, "I wonder if you know what you're doing. Nothing would give me greater pleasure than to expose you—"

"Except that in doing so, you'd expose yourself."

"I would advise you, Sarah Dempsey, for your own safety, not to tell your story." The tone was dark with threat.

Sarah didn't bother to hide the steel in her own voice. "I'm sorry, Mrs. McQueen," she said, "but nothing you can say or do will prevent me."

After she'd put down the phone, Sarah didn't linger, didn't mull over the things that had been said. There was a great deal still to be done at the hospital. Patients were coming in all the time, one she was particularly worried about. He was a town councillor who'd only come to her because his wife was sick to death of his loud snoring. According to the man's wife, it reached such a crescendo she couldn't sleep in the same room. It was a syndrome Sarah was familiar with. Obstructive sleep apnoea. The trouble was, men who produced such loud snoring, followed by episodes of absent breathing, were twelve times more likely to die from a heart attack than men without the disorder. The councillor, even on medication, had high blood pressure. Sarah would try another drug, but the councillor would be helping himself enormously if he lost weight and reduced his alcohol intake. He hadn't so far, preferring not to take her warnings seriously. But strokes and heart attacks were serious. She would have to speak more severely, but in the end it was up to the patient.

She'd had a disturbing time with her Munchausen-by-proxy mother. Using a video camera—something she thought they ought to do for the child's sake—they'd established that the mother was feeding her little girl quantities of a well-known antacid containing magnesium hydroxide and aluminum hydroxide, double strength, inducing the vomiting and diarrhea. Prior to this, when the mother had taken her child in for treatment, she'd covered her tracks pretty well. Now it was all over. The child was staying with her paternal grandmother, who confessed she'd long been concerned about her daughter-in-law's mental health and the safety of her grandchild. When confronted, the mother had denied everything—until she was interviewed by the town constable. She'd consented to be treated at a private psychiatric hospital in Brisbane, which Sarah had recommended. Sarah and the young mother's family could only hope and pray the outcome would be good.

THE MOMENT KYALL walked through the front door of the house, Sarah knew there was something terribly wrong.

So this is when it happens, she thought, her glowing smile of welcome dying at the prospect of confrontation.

He looked at her as if their love was tarnished, ruined somehow, his handsome face drawn.

"God almighty, Sarah!" he said, and went no further, obviously grappling for control of his inner turmoil.

"She's told you." Sarah felt her brave new future go up in flames around her. One tragedy leading to another…

"Sarah!" he groaned, and shook his head. "My God, how could you do this?"

So *she* was to carry the blame. And the shame. "Do this?" she burst out emotionally, then caught herself. "Kyall, come in. Sit down. I don't know what your grandmother has told you, but I beg you to listen to my side of the story."

He was only a hand's breadth away from her, but a whole world apart. "I don't know if I can listen to any more," he said. "I'm too…shocked. But shock doesn't begin to describe it. I'm devastated, nearly out of my mind. And you never said a word. Don't you have any remorse about that? All these years I never knew I had a child. You were the closest person in the world to me. I worshiped at your altar. Now I'm not sure I ever knew you at all. Didn't you think I deserved to be told? I could've helped you through it. You didn't trust me." He paced the hallway floor as if he had no idea where he was going.

Sarah followed. "Please, Kyall, let me tell you about my past."

"It's my past, too!" He rounded on her, a tall, powerful man emanating a terrible anger. "My child, my daughter, gone forever. I didn't hold her. I didn't kiss her. I have nothing of her. Not even a wisp of hair. Nothing! God!" He lifted his arms impotently to the heavens. "And *you* didn't want her. Isn't it a mercy she died! So all these years, Sarah, you've been consumed by guilt."

She could have crumpled but she was fueled by her own anger. "What has that lying bitch told you?" she exclaimed, acutely aware she had forced the issue with Ruth.

"My grandmother," he reminded her.

"Your grandmother the liar. You have a right to know the truth."

"The truth as *you* see it?" Bitterness flooded his voice. "Our child died, Sarah. You went on with your career. It didn't make you any happier, did it? No wonder you hid yourself from me. But you came back. Why? You came back, but it's too goddamn late."

"Perhaps." She winced. "But I was only trying to protect you."

His laugh was totally without humor. "For God's sake, Sarah, don't make me loathe you." His blue eyes flashed.

"For what? Didn't you forsake me?" She swallowed around the hard knot in her throat.

He stared at her mutely for a moment. "I thought I knew you better than anyone in the world. I didn't know you at all, did I? You're an enigma. The whole town emotes when someone mentions your name. Our own brilliant little Sarah Dempsey, back here as head of the hospital. Engaged to Kyle McQueen. Wonderful! A fairy tale. You got to be a doctor and now your mission is to marry me. Why? For the sex?"

She held that burning stare. "And why not? It's important enough to *you*. Now and then. Didn't sex ruin my life? I was fifteen, Kyall! And I had to deal with the consequences. You didn't."

"No, you relieved me of my responsibilities by running off." He spoke tonelessly. "I didn't abandon you, Sarah. You abandoned me."

"Dragged off by your grandmother!"

"She was trying to give you a chance," he said in a hard, condemning voice.

"What chance? She wanted me to have an abortion. Did you know that?"

He looked appalled. "Dammit, Sarah, what sense is there in claiming that? We're talking about her own grandchild. She loves me. Imagine how much more she would've loved our child. Do you think I don't understand your panic? Your fear? I could never blame you for that, but I would have stood beside you. I would have helped you get through. There was nothing I wouldn't have done for you."

"Nothing—except listen to my side of the story." Despite herself, her eyes filled with tears, which she blinked back furiously. "Your awful, awful grandmother, who must communicate with the devil, has a selective memory. I *was* fearful at first. What else did you expect? My mother wasn't a strong person. She was no match for Ruth McQueen. What your grandmother rammed down our throats was that having the baby, keeping the baby, would ruin your life. Your future. After all, you were the McQueen heir."

"Not that again!" He shook his head violently. "I never did give a damn about any of that. I would've protected you with my life. I loved you. I loved you. I continued to love you for years on end."

"So you're saying you don't anymore?" Anger was an expanding force that pressed against her rib cage.

"Don't you think my mind has been circling round and round, looking for an answer? Who are you, Sarah? *What* are you?"

She put her hands to her temples to stop the pounding. "I've tried to be a good person," she said. "Maybe I've failed, but I've had to live with such terrible loss."

"But…you didn't want the baby. You never stopped saying that. You would cry and cry. You never tried to call me. You didn't give me a chance to help you. You didn't look after yourself when it was so important. You had to be forced to eat. At the same time, you were going to make me pay. For what? I expected the world of you. You could've done so much better. All our hopes and dreams, Sarah!''

"You're not interested in what I have to say?'' His words, words put into his mouth by Ruth, pierced her like knives.

"Say it!'' He moved swiftly, compelled to grasp her by the arms.

"Let go!''

He shook his head, gazing into her eyes. "Don't you know anguish when you see it, Sarah?''

She felt a wrenching pity even as she jerked herself away. "I truly believe your grandmother is an evil woman,'' she said in a trembling voice. "I was fifteen years old. Born and bred in a small outback town. I had no father to protect me. A mother who lacked the strength and courage to stand up to your grandmother. I can't describe to you what those months of waiting were like. Farmed out to a couple your grandmother rounded up. I couldn't get hold of you. I knew I'd be prevented. And I couldn't rid myself of the thought that she might be right and I'd ruin your life. The scandal and the shame. Your grandmother wanted above everything to have the pregnancy aborted. I refused.''

He stared at her as if she were an alien. "Why would she lie? You know what she's like about family.''

"What family?'' Sarah's voice was charged with derision. "She doesn't give a damn about anyone in this world but you. What love does she give your mother? What about your uncle Stewart who died? What chance did *he* have? He had to get away from her. He couldn't stand the control. As for me, I was that little upstart Sarah Dempsey who helped her mother in the grocery shop. Whose father had been a shearer in Wunnamurra's sheds. You don't think I

was going to be allowed into your precious family, do you?
Me or my baby.''

"Our baby." He needed that confirmed. "My child."
He felt as though he was permanently damaged. "I really
don't know what you're saying, Sarah."

"That's because you're not listening." She tried to calm
herself, but to no avail. So much for all her rehearsals. This
wasn't going according to plan. "You want to believe your
grandmother has a good side to her, as you always do,
Kyall. I have to accept that. She's never shown you anything but love. But anyone else, anyone who's a threat to
her—look out! What about that poor woman, Molly Fairweather?''

His face turned utterly disbelieving. "What the hell has
she got to do with anything?" He studied Sarah grimly.

"Molly Fairweather—Mad Molly—was the midwife
who brought our child into the world."

His hand descended like a sword. This time he dragged
her into the living room, standing over her while she fell
onto the sofa.

"Why did she come to Koomera Crossing?" Sarah
raised a challenging face. She knew that however angry he
was, he would never hurt her. "Why did she stay in this
house, a house that belongs to your grandmother? What in
God's name happened between them? *Why did she die?*''

"Stop it!" he said. "Are you saying my grandmother
had her killed?"

With equal force Sarah answered with a question of her
own. "Are you saying she's not capable of murder?"

"No, she's not!" A muscle rippled along the side of his
jaw.

Sarah looked away. "Then explain to me the connection
between your grandmother and that poor woman. You must
have heard the rumors?"

"What rumors?" he retorted, on the offensive.

"Joe thought that your grandmother was somehow involved in Molly Fairweather's untimely death."

"Good God!" He actually reeled back. "Sarah, you're demented! What you're saying is an affront to my family. I can't believe any of it!" Kyall tried desperately to call on some inner reserve of control. He loved this woman. Had loved this woman. Could he ever come to terms with her massive deception? At that point he didn't know, his shock was so profound. "You're trying to muddy the waters. Were you ever going to tell me any of this? Or were you planning to live with your secret for the rest of our lives?"

"Believe what you want, Kyall. Your grandmother still dominates your life. She learned early how to amass power, but it's been her undoing."

"Sarah, she can't help the fact that she's a woman to be reckoned with. Money and power go hand in hand."

"Then why don't you act like her?" Sarah challenged. "You've had everything you could possibly want from the minute you were born. Adoration. Every damn thing provided. You understand nothing about struggle. About having no one to turn to or going without because you didn't have enough money. You're used to being filthy bloody rich, with all the confidence that gives you. But it hasn't spoiled you. You're a hero in this town. You're friendly and charming. You speak everyone's language. You're one of the boys, and the girls have been mad about you ever since I can remember. You're nothing like your grandmother. You know why? It's not in your nature. Thank God you've got a dad who's not a McQueen. And you have a conscience to dictate to you. She doesn't."

The lamplight on her hair turned the loose golden masses to sheer glitter. She wore a silk shirt, a lovely shade of aqua, her small, perfectly shaped breasts rising and falling against the material. She seemed filled with conviction, yet tremendously vulnerable. And God help him, utterly desirable. One day he might be free of her hold over him. He couldn't imagine when.

"I suppose she started on you the minute you got home," Sarah said with a brittle laugh. "It was my fault in a way. I warned her."

"How?"

She watched him move abruptly away from her, as though he hated being in such proximity to her. "She sent me white lilies this morning. The sort one drapes over a coffin."

"She couldn't have done such a terrible thing!"

"Are you going to listen or are you afraid to?"

"How can I trust you, Sarah?" he asked. "You've kept too many things hidden. Someday I might forgive you. Not now."

She stared at him with peculiar intensity, her velvet brown eyes darkened with emotion. "I'm not proud of my life, Kyall. Your grandmother warned my mother and me to keep quiet. I know my mother went in fear of her. She drained all Mum's courage."

"Yet you took the money, McQueen money," he retaliated. "It got you where you are today, Dr. Sarah."

"Without it, I would've been nothing," she acknowledged. "Nothing and nowhere. I had lost my child. I descended into purgatory, but I held the view—and I still hold it—that you McQueens owe me. Had I been a lot older or even a few years older I might have put up a battle—although I know, even now, I'm no match for your grandmother."

"You're as adept at defending yourself as she is. Just as convincing. My grandmother did everything she could to help you. She helped you escape this town. Isn't that what you wanted? What your mother wanted for you? Hell, you told me that yourself. You also told me you wanted nothing more to do with me. Isn't that right? You can't deny it. You've had all these years to straighten things out, but you didn't. My grandmother, for all her faults, supported you during your confinement, when we all thought you'd achieved your ambition to attend a prestigious school.''

"Many months later," she said, staring across the room at him, "I was a schoolgirl who'd held her baby to her breast, then lost her. Just like that. She was perfect.''

"Don't!'' The vision was terrible. He groaned.

"I had no one to tell it to,'' Sarah continued, his words filtering through to her from a distance. "My mother wasn't strong enough to carry the burden, as you know. In the end, I think it killed her. There was no escape from grief for her or for me. You can't know what it was like! The depth of despair. So don't go judging me, Kyall McQueen.''

He felt as though he was looking down at the dregs of their love. "You see yourself as the victim?''

"Indeed I was,'' she said. "I was little more than a child crying herself to sleep. Night after night. Empty arms. Empty breasts. Empty womb. All the overwhelming love I had in me, the great joy of motherhood, was stolen away. Literally overnight. For a while I think I was deranged from grief. My Rose.''

"You'd forgotten she had a father,'' he said with a terrible tonelessness.

"I never forgot that, Kyall. I'd come to believe I saved you the grief. It made up for other things, somehow. Your grandmother was lying to you when she said I didn't take care of myself. I did all the right things for my baby.''

"Our baby,'' he corrected her harshly.

"At least you believe that.'' Her voice was bitter. "It's

a wonder your grandmother didn't suggest I was the town whore.''

He looked at her as if she'd undergone some radical change. "Sarah, nothing like that has *ever* been said. By anybody. Do you think I would've allowed it? My God, what's happened to you? My grandmother told me she tried to handle things as best she could. I know she's too much for most people, but she was trying to *help* you. It was her great-grandchild, after all.''

Suddenly Sarah's voice took on a hard edge. "I never thought you were a fool, Kyall. There's no mystery about what your grandmother and your mother thought of me. They joined forces in their disapproval. Don't pretend you've forgotten.''

"I didn't take any notice, did I. I spent all my time with you, no matter what anyone thought. I loved you—always.''

"And I loved you. Ill-fated, ill-advised lovers. That's what we were. I'm desperately sorry for your unhappiness now, Kyall. Your sense of betrayal. I deserve your condemnation. It's what made me fear telling you, knowing you might turn away from me. But I'd decided on confessing everything tonight. I made the mistake of warning your grandmother of my intentions. So she decided to get in first with her version of the past. It goes without saying that she gave her actions a total whitewash.''

"She told me her heart bled for you.'' He looked directly into her eyes. "She, too, was devastated by grief. She'd idolized my grandfather. She was widowed so young.''

"So she began an affair with Joe.'' Despising herself, Sarah still said it.

His blue eyes shone out of his darkly tanned face, brilliant as jewels. "Was she to be condemned because she wanted a sexual relationship? She was still young. That was a phase of her life. It stopped at some point.''

"When she got tired of him?'' Sarah suggested. "Joe wasn't the most exciting man in the world. But he knew how to keep his mouth shut. Or he did, right up to the end.''

He gritted his teeth in anger. "I don't know what you're talking about, Sarah,'' he said wearily, moving a few feet away and sinking into an armchair, head in hands. "I was there at the family dinner the night Joe died. There was absolutely nothing wrong. Joe was the same as usual, although it was obvious his life was ebbing away. I saw my grandmother the next morning. She was weeping unconsolably. That's pretty foreign to her. But she had no control over those tears. She must have cared more deeply about Joe Randall than any of us realized.''

"A more likely explanation is that she bumped him off,'' Sarah said. Although she spoke in sarcasm, it suddenly made sense.

"Why would she do that?'' Kyall raised his head in disgust. "Don't stop there.''

"Maybe Joe wanted to unburden himself of his feelings of guilt before he met his maker? Joe confessed to me that he thought your grandmother was somehow involved in Molly Fairweather's death.''

"Did he really?'' Kyall asked scornfully. "She'd have had to hold the bloody snake to the woman's throat,'' he said, striking the coffee table with the flat of his hand. "Stop this, Sarah! I've had my share of tragedy for today. My grandmother, God help her, is a strange woman. She has this need to win every battle, but if I believed one word of what you've said, everything would fall apart. Everything. The world I knew would no longer exist.''

"You'd rather believe your grandmother than me,''

Sarah said. "I suppose it's not that unusual. She's your flesh and blood. I'm not even the woman you thought I was. That's the harsh reality."

"Where are the flowers she sent you?" he asked, ignoring what she'd said. "Was there a card? How do you know she sent them?"

How could she convince him she was telling the truth? "I tore the card up. The flowers are at the hospital, mixed in with others. Basically the card said she offered me her best wishes. I was going to need them. That there was so much you had to learn about me."

"That part was dead right."

"It was a form of blackmail to keep me quiet. In telling my story, I'd be exposing her. The way she tried to harass me into an abortion. She'd arrange everything. All we had to do was kill our baby. And the way she dealt with my mother and me! I'll never forgive her. I'll never forget. She hates me—but surely you know that. Or have you shut it out? She sees me as being in competition with her for your love. Her obsession is not only bizarre, it's ruining everyone's life, but she can't put it aside. If she could destroy me, she would."

Powerful emotions seared Kyall's blood. "My God, women!" he moaned. "Don't they make a lot of trouble in the world!"

"Especially when you've got a megalomaniac living in your home," Sarah retorted, her own face stricken. "I'm so very, very sorry, Kyall," she said more quietly. "Our baby died. It's my fault. I couldn't succeed in producing a healthy child. It happens. Women have to cope with it every day, sometimes on their own. You're supposed to handle the grief, then try again. You'd have to experience the emotional trauma to get anywhere near understanding it."

"Do you understand how *I* feel or are you thinking only of yourself?" he asked. "This was my child. At least you have your precious memory of her. She was perfect. A little angel. Well, men's hearts break, too, Sarah. Men can be crushed by grief."

"I know!" she cried urgently, wanting to go to him, knowing she didn't dare. "Please forgive me, Kyall. I was so young, and your grandmother persuaded me it was better you didn't know. It was so you could go on with your life, she said."

"She told me that was your choice." He wondered if he could've done anything to avert the tragedy. Or was it meant to be? "Your subsequent actions bear that out."

Tears sprang to her eyes, slid down her cheeks. "I've always had the feeling she's still with me, my little Rose."

He stood up abruptly, as if he could bear no more.

"Are you going?" She watched him turn away from her. *Don't let it happen.*

Don't let her win. It tugged at her heart to see him so terribly distressed. "Kyall?"

He threw back his head like a horse pulling at a tight bit. "I can't take this, Sarah."

"That's a yes. You are going."

"I wanted you to marry me."

"You don't any longer?"

"What I want... What I want..." He turned to stare at her, noticing that her eyes were glittering with tears. "Oh, God, Sarah!"

"I can't keep your engagement ring." She went to pull it off.

"Take it," he said. "I couldn't give it to anyone else."

"Kyall, I'm sorry." She laid the ring on a small table. "I think I'll go lie down. I feel...really strange."

"What's wrong?" he asked immediately.

"Just upset, I think. I've been rehearsing what I'd say to you for days. I should have realized there are some things in life one simply can't forgive." Her slender arms folded around her, she stood up. "Yet in some ways it's a relief that it's over. You know now. You'll cope. You're a man, not a boy. The boy might not have been able to cope."

"I wasn't given a choice," he said bleakly. "Can I get you anything, Sarah? You're very pale."

"I'm all right." She shook her head. "I know where the little Sinclair girl is," she said suddenly. "Estelle."

"Do you?" Of course she was in shock. He moved to her, unable to stop himself from putting a supportive arm around her.

"I saw it in a dream. Perhaps something good has come out of all this. She was raped and murdered. I saw it all. I saw the man's face. I saw him pitch her body into the middle of Wirrabilla."

"Come and lie down," he said gently.

"I know you think I'm raving. I'm not. Get someone to check it out. Divers. They'll find her bones. She'll stop haunting this place after she's buried. Will you do that, Kyall? No one will think *you're* crazy."

"You're not crazy, Sarah. Child and woman, you've been under far too much pressure. Anyway, I'll have it done. No need to say at the outset what I'm looking for."

"Thank you, Kyall. Don't bother to shut the door when you go. Your grandmother and her little helpers—you must know them—can get in, anyway. I could show you my beautiful yellow dress, all slashed, but I don't think I want to anymore."

They had reached her bedroom. She sank onto the bed, not looking up at him, but looking away. Her heart ached and her head was spinning. *Help me,* she thought. *Please, God, help me. Am I always to lose?*

Despite his profound disillusionment and state of shock, the same old sense of protectiveness ran through Kyall. She was Sarah, after all. "You can sleep if you want to," he said. "I'm not going anywhere."

CHAPTER THIRTEEN

HE FOUND HIMSELF watching her as she slept. She was breathing quietly, one hand beneath her cheek. So beautiful. His Sarah. He was stupefied he could keep loving her when she'd denied him the truth. The irony was, he could almost wish he didn't know, for now he'd have to live with it for the rest of his life.

But wasn't that what Sarah had said? Her wish had been to spare him. Why did the two of them, his grandmother and Sarah, think he was the one who'd needed to be protected? That dumbfounded him. He knew enough about himself to realize he could have handled the situation. He could even have made a difference. Sarah wouldn't have had to disappear from his life. He couldn't see any shame attached to having a baby. He loved babies. Little kids. That was what he wanted. A full life. Family. He'd been happy enough, despite his own disturbed family, but he knew there was a better way. He could have made Sarah so happy. He could have loved and protected his child.

But she had elected to go it alone. Not believing in him. The fact that she hadn't turned to him was too painful to bear. Sarah and his own grandmother had sidelined him, as if he was of no importance. The child's father of no importance? Obviously his relationship with both of them had been incomplete. Lacking in certain essential components—like honesty.

Sweetheart, how badly you treated me. He looked down

at the sleeping Sarah, a pounding desire rising above his anger. She looked small. She was, of course, compared to him. He could see the tiny scar on her wrist. He had a matching one. The bloodletting had sealed their friendship. Forever.

I'll always take care of you, Sarah.

What if you're not able to?

His shoulders slumped. And what about her accusations against his grandmother?

No! Mind and heart were shaken. He shied away from the accusations, chilled and somehow fearful.

"I DON'T EXPECT you to forgive me, my darling," his grandmother said, her face suddenly drawn and lined. "Sarah and I both went through a dreadful time. It must be a bitter truth to hear that she didn't want your baby. She desperately wanted an abortion—she made that very clear—so I had to take charge. Even then, her behavior was extremely dangerous to the baby. All of us paid a terrible price. Your child, my great-grandchild—a McQueen—died. I can't begin to tell you of my sorrow."

He had believed her. Ruth was a hard woman; life had made her hard. But she'd always acted in his best interests. The baby would have made her so happy. As it was, he could see she was filled with the deepest, most painful regrets, her beautiful, resonant voice—the voice of an actress—quavery, on the verge of tears.

But what if Sarah's accusations were true? Even some of them. He'd been struck by her anguish. Would she lie? There was no way of knowing. It was one woman's version against another's. In any case, he'd start an investigation of his own, and he had all the resources to take it as far as it would go. If what Sarah said *was* true, he wouldn't be able to look at his grandmother again. Sarah would be revealed as heroic, resisting intense pressure. Sarah as a child had been fearless, particularly when saying things, true things, he didn't want to hear. Kyall felt he'd never known such confusion, such anger, such sorrow in his life. He couldn't deal with it all now. He needed time. A lot of time.

SHE STIRRED A LITTLE, murmuring something he couldn't catch. And that strange story about the Sinclair child? A foray into the paranormal. He didn't go for it himself, but then, what would he know? Plenty of people over the years claimed to have seen the spirits of the first Fiona and the little Sinclair girl. Had the loss of their child maximized Sarah's already sensitive perceptions, or was this blighted house affecting her as it did most other people? Whether she liked it or not, she had to move out for her own protection.

"Kyall?" Her eyelids fluttered.

The ray of light from the hallway cut a dull gold path across her body, so shining in its grace.

"I'm right here."

She exhaled deeply in gratitude. "Don't leave me," she begged. "If you do, my whole life will unravel. I can't take that again."

"No." Although his voice came out curtly, he recognized the long years of trauma she had endured.

"I love you." She turned her face up to him as he stood above her. "I'm so sorry for what I did to you."

"Don't waste your time!" Pity and hostility went together. He moved back abruptly, causing her to make a frantic grab for him.

"Kyall!"

"Go on. Tell me you need me—when I'd have given anything to hear it anytime all these years. Why don't you go to sleep again?'' he added harshly. He knew once he touched her he wouldn't be capable of stopping. Even when waves of sadness and despair were crashing over him, he wanted her. He wanted to tear the clothes off her, cover her body with his, punish her. Only, he wasn't like that. He was still the bloody gentleman. His father's son. He would never be able to hurt a woman. Never be able to hurt Sarah—although she'd put a huge crack in his world.

''Lie down with me for a while.'' She reached out an imploring hand. ''I just want you to hold me. It hurts so much, your not believing me. I keep seeing the face of that poor woman, Nurse Fairweather, hovering over me. I was so hazy, I thought she was a big bird. Isn't that strange? Then the pain started and it didn't stop until she lay Rose on my breast. So sweet, so soft, so small...so lovely.''

''Don't, Sarah,'' he warned, shifting her slender body over so he could take her side of the bed.

''All I thought of was you.'' She dared to touch his cheek. ''Just you, me and Rose. Once I had my baby, nothing was going to stop me from getting back to you. God knows, I understood that was dangerous. She would've done anything to keep me away. There's something... unnatural about Ruth.''

''And you.'' His voice was deliberately wounding. He slid his arm beneath her and pulled her to him, the whole lovely length of her. Soon he would kiss her. What did any of it matter? he asked himself cynically. It was simple, really. *He loved her.* Unconditionally. But it was a real effort to be gentle right now. He wanted to rip the silk shirt apart to reach her breasts. Her soft skirt was already rucked up to her thighs. He wanted to caress between her legs, let his fingers enter her.

Desire for her was the dark whirlpool that forever pulled

him down. There were tears on her cheeks. He started licking them off with his lips and his tongue.

"Please say you forgive me," she whispered.

He swept her hair aside to bare the exquisite shell of her ear. "Isn't it enough that I'm with you?" He held her tightly, hearing the hard edge in his voice, not bothering to change it.

"Only then am I whole. Kiss me." She knew he couldn't hold back.

"No, *you* kiss *me*." His voice reflected the anger in him.

She raised her face to his, touched his lips with hers.

Oh, yes!

THERE WAS A CONSTANT emotional drain on Sarah in the following weeks. She and Kyall were still together, but she was under no illusion that he'd fully accepted her version of past events. As she expected, he'd had a confrontation with his grandmother; Ruth, of course, had refused to back down. She hadn't changed one word of her story, saying it wasn't surprising that Sarah had denied her own unacceptable plea for an abortion. She'd been fifteen, after all, a mere schoolgirl, frightened of the monumental experience of childbirth. undergoing massive hormonal change. To survive afterward, she'd chosen the path of denial. Not so Ruth. Ruth knew better than most people how hard life really was.

His mother, Enid, on hearing both versions of the story from Kyall, had become ill with shock. She'd had nothing to say beyond, "I had no idea. None. My poor boy! And Sarah? How she must have suffered."

That gave Sarah some comfort.

Kyall's father, Max, dropped into the hospital to see Sarah. "If things had gone well, my dear, I'd have been a grandfather," he said, dark brows drawn together in pain.

"I'm so sorry you didn't feel you could confide in us. At heart Enid is a good woman. She'd have been a much better one away from her mother. We both would've been, but there were too many…issues in the way." He gave Sarah a brief, sardonic smile. "Enid is far from being a submissive woman. She has too much of her mother in her for that—yet she has little sense of her own value. Ruth made sure of that." He paused a moment, very serious. "I'll tell you something in confidence, Sarah, since you'll be joining the family. I'd have left Enid long ago if I thought she was emotionally strong enough, but despite what everyone thinks, she needs me."

"And you? What are *your* needs?" Sarah asked, looking across her desk at this handsome man who was Kyall's father. A man who was essentially a stranger.

"I've had to find a few strategies to survive," he said dryly. "My children are the most important people in the world to me, Sarah. And the fact that my son has scarcely noticed anyone else is palpable proof of his love for you. He's going through a lot of mental pain at the moment."

"I'm to blame for it."

Max considered her with open sympathy. "You were a child, Sarah. Had you been older, or had your father been alive, things would have been different. Or if you'd come to me…"

She nodded in recognition. "I deeply regret I didn't. I know Ruth has told Kyall I was desperate for an abortion. I want you and Enid to know that's not true. I may have been overwhelmed by loneliness, but I wanted the baby. If I could turn back the clock, you'd know how much I fought Ruth when she spoke so calmly of an abortion. I didn't care that she was Mrs. Ruth McQueen. I found my voice. I raged at her that it would never happen. I must have forced her to listen. Then, despite everything my baby died.''

They were both quiet for a while.

''What a tragedy,'' Max breathed eventually, his deep voice gentle.

''My life changed from that point. Do you believe me, Max?''

''I want to believe you, Sarah. I'm your friend.''

''And yet?''

''That would make Ruth a monster.'' He was visibly appalled.

''Let me tell you she is,'' Sarah answered bluntly. She sensed that the day of reckoning was at hand.

It was during this emotionally turbulent time that Sarah had a most unexpected visit from a young woman she'd met together with her doctor husband, at several medical functions in the state capital. Laura Morcombe was a long way from home. And using a different name?

It was morning surgery. Sarah walked into the waiting room looking for her next patient. ''Ms. Graham?''

A young woman stood up, pushing back her lustrous fall of dark hair, green eyes as brilliant as the waters of an outback creek.

Sarah maintained her composure until they were inside her room. There she gestured for the young woman to take the chair beside her desk. ''Laura! This is a surprise. What are you doing here? Where's Colin? How is he?'' Sarah studied the lovely face in front of her. Soft, romantic, with an overall quality of gentleness and sensitivity, shadows of fatigue beneath the eyes.

''I'm not with Colin anymore, Sarah,'' the young woman said quietly. ''I'm using my mother's maiden name.''

''Oh!'' Sarah's hand paused on its way to a file. She had a swift vision of Laura and her husband together. Such an attractive couple; they'd seemed very much in love. Colin in particular. "I'm sorry to hear that," Sarah said with genuine sympathy. "You both seemed so happy."

"It wouldn't have done to show my real face in public." Laura's voice wasn't steady.

"You were unhappy?"

"Desperately so."

"I'm very sorry. Are you able to talk about it?"

Laura met Sarah's eyes. "Actually, Sarah, I knew you were here. I rang the clinic. They told me you'd taken over at the Koomera Bush Hospital. I needed to speak to someone I could trust. Someone trained, who might be able to view Colin objectively. That, and a place to hide. I'm deeply ashamed."

"Of what?" Sarah remained still and quiet.

Laura glanced away. "I was an abused wife, Sarah. Physically, sexually, psychologically. I felt…degraded. It's not an uncommon story. Only I couldn't live with it."

"My God, why would you!" Sarah leaned back, hiding her horror as she invited Laura to tell of her obviously traumatic experiences.

There were the usual flashes of violence before marriage. Nothing too much. Next, he began to show classic controlling behavior—the jealousy and paranoia. The Jekyll and Hyde syndrome. By day he was a rising star in openheart surgery—the charming, eminently respectable Dr. Colin Morcombe. By night, the star image was left at the front door as Colin Morcombe vented his rage in private.

"I left him once," Laura confessed, her lovely skin like marble. "He found me. I took refuge with a girlfriend. He convinced her I was having 'problems.' He was so good he almost convinced me."

"You've had a rough time," Sarah said matter-of-factly,

having made her professional assessment. Laura's story rang too true.

"Sometimes I'm so frightened I can't breathe. Colin's a very disturbed man. He relishes his power over me. He said our marriage would never end. I believe he means it." Laura flinched.

"But what about your family, Laura? Didn't you go to them for protection? The police? Did you get an injunction to keep him away?"

"He'd ignore that." Laura gave a short laugh, sounding extremely sure. "My father died some years ago. My mother remarried and lives in New Zealand now. She met Colin two weeks before the wedding. She thought he was wonderful. He'd be so convincing as the desperate, loving husband with the difficult wife. The police would probably feel sorry for him. Anyway, I couldn't ruin his career. And his parents would hate me. They're prominent people and they idolize him. I'm sure they're busy hating me right now. Colin's their only son, and he can do no wrong. They'd rather accuse *me* of being mentally unstable."

"I see. Well, we have to deal with this, Laura." Sarah stared at the other woman intently. "I'll help you in every way I can. I know how isolated you must feel, but I can tell you you're among friends. Abuse in any form is totally unacceptable. Now, where are you staying? Are you sleeping? Eating? I'll check your blood pressure for a start."

"I'm booked into the pub at the moment." Laura extended her arm. "You don't mind my coming to you, Sarah? Bringing you my problems?"

Sarah smiled at her, wrapping the black pad around Laura's arm. "I'm here to help, Laura. The town will protect you. Now try to relax...."

CHAPTER FOURTEEN

MONDAY-MORNING SURGERY started off in routine fashion. No dramas. No abused wives. No life-threatening cases. One or two minor accidents involving children. It was the beginning of the June holidays, characterized by "big adventures" in the bush. Not unexpectedly, adventures resulted in a lot more accidents than school did. Then, shortly after noon, Kyall strode into the hospital with news of a serious accident on a cattle station called Ngarara Downs, situated to the northeast.

"I can get you there faster than the Flying Doctor," he informed Sarah, wondering if they'd get there in time. "Grab what you have to. The guy was pinned between his vehicle and a tree. Apparently he left the hand brake off and the thing rolled back on him. I was in the air. Heard the call. I've put the chopper down at the intersection. Radioed ahead. Bob's cleared the street."

Sarah wasted no precious moments. Even then, it seemed an eternity before they reached Ngarara's borders. Flying over the actual site, they found themselves looking down at a group of people gathered on the open plains country. Here and there were a few native palms, ghost gums and stretches of mulga. It was against a ghost gum that the unfortunate victim had been pinned, screaming out in agony for more than thirty minutes before a couple of his mates, stockmen on horseback, found him.

"I don't much like his chances," Kyall murmured grimly, his glance sweeping around to size up the situation.

"Let's pray we're not too late." Sarah wasn't hopeful, either.

They were on the ground the instant the rotors stopped, losing no time covering the distance from the chopper to where the accident victim was lying prone on a rug someone had spread under him.

"Thank God you're here, Doctor. Terry Hungerford." The station owner introduced himself. A big man, iron-gray hair, firm handshake, deep husky voice. His expression was one of concern overlaid, as he looked at Sarah, with a kind of perplexity he couldn't hide. "Hi, Kyall." He acknowledged Kyall gratefully with another handshake. "Good of you to come. We've got real trouble here."

"I can see that. We help one another, Terry. I'm just glad I picked up the message." Both men watched Sarah go into action, her every movement assured. "What a damned awful thing." Kyall's throat tightened. That chest wound looked mortal. "Freakish, really. The vehicle could just as easily have missed the tree. He should've been aware of the grade."

"'Course he should have." Terry Hungerford shrugged fatalistically. "But some things seem meant to be. Couldn't avoid them if you tried."

For several tense moments, Sarah examined the unconscious young man, realizing what she was seeing, her urgency replaced by sorrow. They all fell silent watching her, until she slowly stood up, shaking her head. "I'm terribly sorry, Mr. Hungerford." She gazed at the other stricken men, one by one. "This poor boy's gone. The internal injuries are massive. I doubt if it would've helped having the hospital close by. It's that bad."

"My God!" Terry Hungerford was almost overwhelmed

by his feelings. "Poor Sean!" he lamented. "He found life so exciting and wonderful. Dead at twenty-six."

"Family?" Sarah asked painfully.

The station owner shook his head. "Employee. A good lad. A real worker. Full of life. Oh, my God!" he groaned, and swept the *akubra* from his head as a mark of respect. "To think he had to end up like this. My kids will shed some tears, I can tell you. They thought the world of him. A Kiwi, you know, having an adventure. I dread calling his parents. It's going to be terrible. We'll get his body back home." He looked toward his men, then hesitated a moment, as though trying to remember his manners. "You'll stay on for a cup of tea, Doctor, Kyall." Terry Hungerford wanted to mention that his daughter had a school friend staying at the homestead, a dead ringer for the doctor, but it seemed inappropriate with Sean's body lying only feet away. Of course, the boy should have known about the slope of the land; it would have saved his life. Terry stared bleakly at the body so recently full of life, then gestured to the silent stockmen who made no effort to cover their extreme distress. How could something so dreadful happen in this beautiful wide-open land?

Mrs. Hungerford, a slim, attractive woman in her early forties, rushed out onto the veranda as the Jeep carrying Kyall and Sarah hurtled up the drive to the front steps.

"Everything all right?" she asked fearfully, as if there could be only one outcome.

"I'm afraid not, Mrs. Hungerford." Kyall addressed her, while nodding a thank-you to their driver. "Your employee has died. We're so terribly sorry. There are no answers when it comes to tragedies like this. His death was caused by a freak accident." He gestured at Sarah. "This is my fiancée, Dr. Sarah Dempsey from the hospital. She has the sad job of writing the death certificate."

"Oh, my God!" Jill Hungerford covered her face with her hands. "I've been praying and praying. So have the children. They'll be so upset. Poor boy. Poor Sean. I can't believe this!"

"It's a tragedy." Sarah moved forward, with Kyall by her side. "I'm so sorry, Mrs. Hungerford. Even if help had been on hand, I don't think he would've made it. That was a very heavy vehicle and he was a slight young man."

"Terrible. Terrible." Jill Hungerford visibly tried to pull herself together. Tears stood in her eyes; she tried to brush them away. "And Terry?"

"He's seeing to things," Kyall said gently.

"Come in. Please come in." Jill Hungerford lowered the hand she'd been using to shade her eyes as they turned for the veranda that wrapped the homestead. Sarah lowered her sunglasses at the same moment. "But, my dear!" Jill Hungerford said in apparent confusion, her voice startled.

Sarah stepped forward, taking the older woman's arm. "Perhaps you should sit down, Mrs. Hungerford."

"No, it's all right," Jill Hungerford assured her, still staring at Sarah as if at an apparition. "You don't have a young relative by the name of Fiona Hazelton, do you?"

"No." Sarah spoke gently, humoring her.

"It's not possible?"

"Anything's possible, Mrs. Hungerford, but not to my knowledge. You know someone of that name?"

"She's right here in the house." Jill Hungerford still sounded incredulous. "A lovely girl. She goes to school with my daughter Clementine. She could be your younger sister. The curly blond hair, big brown eyes, cleft in the chin. Everything! It's quite extraordinary. They do say we all have a double. You'll be meeting yours."

Sarah didn't respond, trying to make sense of it all. She glanced at Kyall. His face had settled into grim, daunting lines. As Jill Hungerford began to lead the way into the house, four youngsters, three girls and a boy of about ten, burst onto the veranda, their faces reflecting their anxiety. "How's Sean?" They all spoke together.

Jill Hungerford couldn't answer. She burst into tears.

"Sean didn't make it, kids." Kyall took charge. "We're so sorry. Your dad will be here soon. Perhaps one of you girls could make your mother a cup of tea. This is Dr. Sarah, by the way. Head of the hospital at Koomera Crossing."

Three of the children responded with a muffled, "Hello." The one who'd remained silent separated herself from the group, staring at Sarah as if she couldn't believe her eyes.

Lord God almighty! Shock drove the breath from Kyall's body. He felt it rip right through him, hammering at his heart. Then in the next instant, he felt a strange certitude that had nothing to do with the known facts. He was aware of Sarah clutching at him, holding on to his arm as though her knees had turned to water and he was the only man in the world who could keep her upright.

The girl was Sarah at fifteen. As Jill had said, she had the same mane of golden curls, big brown eyes, the same sheen of beautiful skin. Even the shallow dimple in her chin. She carried herself like Sarah. Like a princess.

How did anyone make sense of the impossible? Unless he'd been lied to... White-hot emotions enveloped Kyall. Fury at the magnitude and utter inhumanity of the deception, the certainty that he could never forgive Sarah—and grief at what he had missed. All these years of his child's life.

"This is my friend, Fiona," Clementine Hungerford was saying in a startled voice. "Fiona Hazelton. We go to school together."

Sarah couldn't speak. Her blood was ice. Her limbs rigid. There could be no mistake. This was her daughter. This was her Rose.

With an enormous effort Kyall found his voice. "Hello there, Fiona." He was astounded that he sounded so normal. "What part of Queensland are you from?"

Fiona named the coastal town, thinking Kyall McQueen was gorgeous. Clemmie had told her he was another station owner, flying the doctor in. A real outback hero or, at any rate, the way she liked to imagine one. And Dr. Sarah? She *had* to be a relative, yet Fiona couldn't remember her parents ever mentioning a cousin who looked incredibly like her. A girl of imagination, Fiona started to put together a scenario in her mind. She and the doctor were connected. No doubt about that. A long-lost cousin? A secret in the family? And now their paths had crossed. Here in the grand and glorious outback. The place she had dreamed of visiting.

As for Sarah, the drumming in her ears was so loud she almost didn't hear what the girl was saying. She knew in her soul that this was her Rose. The daughter who had died. The daughter who was very much alive. But how? There was only one answer.

"Are you all right?" the girl asked, arrested by the extraordinary expression in Dr. Sarah's eyes, the way she was clinging to Kyall McQueen's arm, as if she was about to cave in.

Sarah tried to take deep breaths. Couldn't. There was such a constriction around her heart. She knew it was quite possible to die from shock. "I'm...I'm..." she began, then everything went black.

SHE RECOVERED from the faint quickly, aware that Kyall was carrying her into the house. A brooding expression on his face, he set her down on a sofa in the living room, and everyone clustered around her, looking on worriedly. One of the children asked, "What's wrong?" Another whispered, "Are you all right?" Jill Hungerford took over, telling them gently to be quiet for a moment. Clearly everyone felt off balance, aware that too many things were happening.

With a great effort Kyall repressed his anger, taking Sarah's wrist. "Okay now?" She didn't look okay. She looked poleaxed. Pretty much the way he felt.

"I'm sorry," she murmured in apology, focusing on his face. "I've never fainted in my life."

"My dear, you're paper-white." Jill Hungerford leaned forward to touch her cheek. "I'll make tea. Lie quietly. We've all had a terrible shock." Jill hurried off, closely followed by her children, who were full of questions.

Fiona remained behind. "Are you feeling a bit better now?" Shyly she approached Sarah. "I didn't know Sean, but I feel sad, too. This is such a strange day. I woke up this morning thinking I could hear a baby crying. Of course I couldn't. There's no baby here. Clemmie told me it must've been a cat. Then I meet you, Dr. Sarah. We look so much alike we have to be related." Fiona's small face was filled with joyful surprise and tenderness. "Mum never told me I had a cousin like you." Fiona didn't know why, but she felt like bending and putting her arms around the doctor who looked so…sad, so haunted around her eyes. Fiona recognized herself in those eyes.

Sarah tried desperately to get through this first stage. "How old are you, Fiona? Fifteen?" Her voice wasn't her own.

The girl nodded. "My birthday's in September."

Of course it was. Sarah felt a wave of something like

relief break over her. A measure of peace. The peace she'd yearned for. "And your mother's name is Stella?"

The girl smiled at her, real delight in her eyes. "Oh, you *must* be a relative to know that."

"Yes, I must be." Sarah sat up with an effort. "Kyall, I need to go back." She appealed to him, enunciating her words very carefully.

"I'll take you."

"Oh, aren't you going to stay for a while?" The acute disappointment in the girl's voice would have persuaded almost anybody to stay.

"Dr. Sarah is due back at the hospital," Kyall explained as gently as he could, given that he wanted to cry out to heaven.

"What a shame!" Fiona's head dropped, then she lifted it with Sarah's characteristic tilt. "I'm so glad I met you, Dr. Sarah. You, too, Mr. McQueen."

Don't let me break down, Sarah thought. *Don't let me frighten and disturb this child. Yet how I yearn to take her in my arms. To pour out the love I've kept dammed up since the day she was born.*

The ice in Sarah's blood had thawed. What she felt was a kind of delirium, as if she might spin out of control. Instead, she put out a hand to her daughter.

But Fiona didn't shake it. At the last minute she leaned forward and kissed Sarah's cheek.

It was too much for Sarah. With Kyall's glittering blue eyes resting on them, she gathered her daughter into her arms for one brief moment.

Rose. She could scarcely understand any of this, but she knew her baby's smell. The sweetness. The freshness. The uniqueness. It had been trapped in her nostrils all these years.

With the grace of God—surely *this* time He would turn His face to her—all would be well.

THEY SAID NOT ONE WORD to each other until Kyall put down, not at the hospital but in a clearing on Wunnamurra, a short distance from their secret place. The blue lotus lagoon with its wonderful iridescent green waters. He didn't help her out. He didn't touch her but strode on ahead.

"Kyall!" She'd felt his dangerous withdrawal. Guessed he thought she'd become entangled in her own machinations. She knew he wanted to talk. She would have to be very careful in what she said. And yet, she knew *she* bore no guilt. Who'd broken the law here? The woman above the law. The woman who conspired to control the lives of others.

He moved down the grassy slope, crushing the native boronia beneath his feet. Corellas nesting in the trees took off, screeching in fright. A few early-winter showers had fallen, bringing pockets of fire-red color to the wild bush. Shafts of golden light penetrated the green, making the small yellow brushes of the mulga glow like lamps.

Kyall trod heavily, purposefully, his hard-muscled body making light work of the descent. Sarah, strengthened by a kind of prophetic serenity, made her way more delicately, drenched in the scent of boronia crushed underfoot.

Nearing the bank, she slipped a little, humbly accepting his hand.

"Oh, Kyall. I feel…I feel as if I've had a visitation from God."

"I'll bet you do," he said harshly, turning her uncovered head deliberately into a blade of brilliant light. "All your lies have found you out."

"I don't have anything to hide, Kyall." She stared up at him fearlessly. "I was told our child was dead. That she died of respiratory failure. It happens. I was fifteen. Don't ever forget that. Fifteen. I knew nothing. I didn't even know I could *have* a baby the very first time I had sex. I was an ignorant child.''

''Sarah, you were always clever.''

''I know you hate to hear this. I understand your grief—''

''Do you?'' He grabbed her, lifting her clear of the ground. ''I'll tell you what. You don't know a bloody thing about the way I feel. You've lived with all your secrets for years. I've had to take it in one almighty blow.'' He fixed her with an intensely burning gaze. ''So you think you've had some sort of divine visitation? Well, *I'm* devastated. To know you did this awful thing. I don't see how I can tolerate being with you. I can't love you. Make love to you. You gave away our child! Who was it to, again? Oh, yes— Stella. Stella Hazelton. Don't think I won't find her! That child is mine. I was denied her all the years of her growing up. That beautiful girl. I never held her. I never watched her take her first steps. Go to school. I never taught her how to ride. How to embrace her heritage. I can never forgive you for that.''

''You don't want to face the truth, Kyall, but you'll have to. There was no adoption. Your grandmother, God forgive her—although I never will—told me our baby had died during the night. Nurse Fairweather confirmed that. The baby who died was Stella Hazelton's child. I can only think the babies were switched. Deliberately. By Nurse Fairweather at your grandmother's instigation. She would've been very persuasive. It was all for the best, she'd have said. And she would've paid well. What's money to a McQueen? But eventually Molly Fairweather must've been worn down by guilt. It turned her mind.''

Kyall looked at Sarah. So beautiful. So familiar. He

didn't recognize her at all. "It all sounds plausible, but that would make my grandmother a truly wicked woman."

"So she is," Sarah flashed back, phoenixlike, rising from the ashes. Her child's kiss had done that. "Ruth broke not just one heart, Kyall, she's broken many. What about Stella Hazelton's heart? She's reared our daughter believing Rose to be her own. But Stella Hazelton won't talk to you about adoption. As far as she knows, she took her own baby home. The young girl in the room next to her lost her baby. Stella will remember. She'll remember the way I wept."

"Oh, God, Sarah!" His anguish and confusion were ferocious. He moaned aloud with it, shifting his body away from her.

Tentatively she slid her arms around him, feeling the powerful tension in his tall frame. His wide back was like an impregnable wall of defense. Yet he didn't cast her off. They stood like that, Sarah swaying slightly, for several moments. Then she laid her face along his back, nestling her head.

"Kyall, I love you. You are my heart. I'll love you until the sun above us stops shining. I could never lie to you about our baby dying. You must know that. I would've brought her home to you, no matter what your grandmother said. I only held her for a heartbeat of time, but I've never forgotten. I've lived with the grief. Please don't add to my punishment."

"But, Sarah, it's a hideous sin!" he railed. "I'll never get over it."

The pain and rage in his voice cut through to her heart. She dropped her arms. "If you refuse to believe me now, that's the end for both of us." Tears welled up in her eyes.

"I do believe you, Sarah." He turned, hands clenched into fists. His expression was one Sarah had never seen. It made him look older. Formidable.

Her lips moved to speak, but she couldn't find the words.

"You've had laid out for you what I never saw—my grandmother's black soul." His voice was heavy with self-contempt. "I expect Joe saw it, too, and that Fairweather woman, not that I can forgive *her*. She did something that has condemned her forever in my eyes."

"And in mine." Sarah nodded. "We'll have to face your grandmother." She injected determination into her voice.

"That inspires no fear in me," he said harshly. "I'm not a cruel man, but I won't allow her to stay on Wunnamurra a day longer."

"Can you do that?" She couldn't keep the shock from her voice.

"Yes."

"Your mother will be heartbroken."

"No, she won't." He tossed that idea aside. "My mother will be heartbroken when she knows what she's missed. What we've all missed. I don't imagine my grandmother will want to stay, anyway. She's rich. She can go where she likes. Paris. Rome. London. New York. Anywhere, as long as it's far away from me." He reached for Sarah, put his arm around her. "The truly difficult thing will be to get our daughter back. Clearly she's been reared by people who love her. I'm sure she loves them."

"Yes." An enormous wave of pity for the Hazeltons spread through Sarah. "We'll have to go to them. Tell our story. They may demand DNA testing. They won't want to give her up."

"We'll work something out." Kyall spoke confidently. "One thing is certain—I want our child back. We've been robbed of the joy of having her. And to think my own grandmother planned it all. Ruth McQueen has no family anymore."

THE INSTANT SHE LAID EYES on them, Ruth knew the moment of truth had come.

How?

She felt a rush of blind panic, but then she calmed. First of all, she wasn't sure exactly what they knew. But they meant business, no question there. She could see the glitter in her grandson's eyes even from a distance. She'd been congratulating herself that she'd sown sufficient doubt in his mind over Sarah's story. Now there were new suspicions to contend with. Something about that fool woman, Molly Fairweather, perhaps? Even if they exhumed Joe's body for an autopsy, it would tell them nothing. The poison could never be traced. Not that they'd ever do it.

She awaited them, like an empress granting an audience, on the broad veranda of Wunnamurra homestead where she had reigned for so long.

"So what brings you here, Sarah?" She smiled. A smile full of duplicity. "Surely you should be ministering to your patients at the hospital?"

"I have one question, if I may?" Kyall cut in, his voice hard and cold. "How did you get that woman to keep quiet? How much did you pay her?"

Looking stunned and hurt, Ruth stared at him. "My darling, I don't know what you're talking about." There was bewilderment but not a trace of apprehension in her tone.

"Nurse Fairweather," Sarah helped out, well versed in Ruth's behavior.

"Good grief!" Ruth expelled a relieved sigh. "What about her? I gave the poor woman a home. Just as I've said. She didn't want anyone to know."

"And she died for what you didn't want anyone to know," Kyall accused her. "What happened? Did she threaten to reveal what you'd both kept hidden?" He stood above his grandmother as she sat in her peacock chair, immaculately dressed and made up as she had been every single day for as long as he could remember. "Except that things can't be kept hidden forever. Soon the whole town, the whole outback—the whole country, for all I care—will know about the terrible secrets you've kept. Things even Sarah didn't know until today."

"Like what?" Ruth cried, black eyes flashing over Sarah as she stood at Kyall's side.

"That we have a living, breathing daughter, when all these years you've allowed me to believe she was dead," Sarah told her.

"You're talking crazily." Slowly Ruth wiped her mouth with a lace-edged handkerchief. "But do tell me more. This sounds like romantic fiction. Never could read it."

Sarah shook her head. "It's real life. She's staying at Ngarara Station to the northeast. Kyall flew me there to attend an accident victim. That poor young man died, but my daughter is mercifully alive. She's staying with her friend Clemmie for the school holidays. She was waiting for us, Ruth. As if it was meant to be. The name they gave her is Fiona Hazelton. Her mother's name is Stella. I've always remembered the woman in the room next to mine at the hospital. Don't you? Stella, like in the Tennessee Williams play."

Ruth laughed quietly. "What story are you concocting now, Sarah?" She scanned Sarah with open contempt.

"That's enough!" Kyall broke in, goaded beyond measure. "My child is the very image of Sarah. We don't need DNA to tell us she's our daughter. It all adds up. I've known all my life you had a dark side, Gran, but I never realized you're truly evil. Even now I can't shake the utter disbelief from my mind."

"You know why? Because it's not true!" Ruth cried. "How can I be evil when I've done everything—*every-*

thing—for you? I didn't plan any of it for myself. It was for you.''

"Then you admit it?" Kyall asked quietly. How sad it sounded.

"Admit it, be damned!" Ruth rose from her chair.

"You took my baby and gave her to another woman," Sarah said. "Who did you think you were? God?"

"Exactly!" Ruth snorted. "And I'll bet the child hasn't suffered for it. The image of you! How could I love a child like that? To me you're ugly. Ugly!"

Kyall held up his hand. "I want you to go away from here, Gran. Today you've shown yourself for what you really are. I can't and won't live with it."

"Go?" Ruth stared at him in shock. "This place is *mine*. Yours and mine."

"Mine, I think you'll find."

"Haven't I kept it in trust for you?" Ruth asked passionately.

"Your custodianship is over. I want you to have your things packed. What you can't take, I'll send on, anywhere you choose to go. I want you out of here by tomorrow. You can arrange for a charter flight."

"I won't do it!"

"Oh, yes, you will!" Kyall stared her down.

Ruth flung out her hand, the many diamond rings sparkling in the sunlight. "Trust me, Kyall," she implored. "I did it all for you. A baby at that stage of your life would have ruined you. The scandal would've been appalling. I couldn't have it. I couldn't have *her*," she threw at Sarah bitterly. "I'm your grandmother."

"I don't have a grandmother. Not anymore." Kyall drew Sarah close. "You robbed us of our child. Handed her over in place of a dead baby. The most terrible thing is that you have no remorse. You've lost me forever. Now you must finish your life on your own.''

''I'm quite finished now.'' Ruth gathered herself up. ''I'll go to my room. I won't leave it until that woman is out of here. I've spent years and years trying to get rid of her.''

''What you don't understand, Gran, because you know nothing about it, is that I love her.''

''Then have her!'' Ruth gave a great shudder and turned away.

CHAPTER FIFTEEN

IT WAS A STRUGGLE that day for Sarah to keep up with everything that was asked of her. She had to restrain the powerful impulse to burst into tears. Not tears of sadness or distress, but of incredible joy. Was the dream that had been shattered about to come true? Her feelings transcended anything she'd ever experienced before. Her beautiful Rose lived and breathed, walked the earth. And still Sarah had to keep it a secret. But not from Harriet. At the end of that life-changing day, Sarah left her wonderful nurses on night duty as she called in on the woman who'd been like an aunt to her. Harriet deserved to be told the full story, though Sarah had always thought Harriet had her suspicions.

She found her taking advantage of the school holidays to immerse herself in her art. No delicate water colors or flower paintings for Harriet. Robust images, intense in color, enamels and acrylics on canvas. They certainly made an impact, but Sarah didn't have the faintest idea what they were meant to represent.

"My only requirement is that I enjoy myself," Harriet said, standing back from her latest canvas to view it critically. It was extremely colorful and bold, with what appeared to be the outline of a horse galloping flat out. Indeed, its feet had left the ground, or so it seemed amid all the arabesques of violet, orange, green, blue and sulfur-yellow. Nonetheless it was interesting, even decorative in the right place.

"What do you think?"

Sarah smiled. "I think it's dynamic and full of energy, Harriet. Just like you. Is that a horse?"

"Of course it's a horse." Harriet sent her a speaking glance. "Now you're starting to get the idea. It's a brumby. I'm going to call the painting *Freedom*. It's for Morris's birthday. That's next Friday. I'm giving a little party Saturday evening. I want you and Kyall to come and that darling girl you had staying with you for a few days. Laura. There's a story *there*. I'd say she's had a bad time of it. She acts as if she wants to disappear. She's like my friend, Evan, in that way. Actually I was thinking of inviting Evan, too. Do you think Laura might come?"

"I'm sure she would if you asked her, Harriet. No good matchmaking, though."

"She's married?" Harriet said, sounding disappointed. "I had her in mind for Evan."

"I realize that, but Laura's married. I trust you more than any other woman in the world, Harriet, so I'll tell you this much. Laura's on the run from an abusive husband."

Harriet looked appalled. "How absolutely dreadful. But surely I'm missing something here…. When a young woman simply disappears, don't people notice? Hasn't she got family? Friends? Anyway, can't she divorce him?"

"She lives in fear of him, Harriet. Of what he might do."

"My goodness, I'd have him arrested," Harriet said fiercely.

"Laura's not you, Harriet. Abusive men pick their marks. Laura is a very gentle person. You know that— you've met her."

"That doesn't preclude taking action!"

"He has her thoroughly intimidated. As for family, she

lost her father. Her mother's remarried and lives in New Zealand. Her husband, believe it or not, is a doctor. A highly regarded heart surgeon. Prominent family. They think he can do no wrong. Laura is really frightened." Sarah shook her head. "I'm sure when she gets to know you a little better, she'll tell you her story."

Harriet's eyebrows were still dancing. "I thought doctors were supposed to *heal* people? Not willingly and brutally cause them harm. He wouldn't come out here, would he?" Harriet exchanged an alarmed glance with Sarah.

"I expect that if he were able to trace her he would. He told her he'd never let her go."

"Bully!" Harriet barked contemptuously, grabbing up a feather duster and flourishing it over a workbench like a rapier. "If she ran over him, she'd only get six months. Possibly a suspended sentence."

"I don't think she'd do it, Harriet."

"Then go see our local witch doctor, Ruth. Have her make up one of her potions."

Sarah's eyes burned. "Is that what happened to Joe?"

"God forbid. Let's stop there. And what about you? You look very stressed—or excited. Is anything wrong?"

"Not wrong, Harriet. For once all's right with my world. I have something quite extraordinary to tell you. It's still a secret, except to a very few. Kyall. Ruth. And by now Kyall will have spoken to his mother and father."

"You've actually tied the knot?" Harriet guessed.

"Not yet, but it'll be sooner than later."

"Tell me," Harriet begged. "I can't stand the suspense."

"You'll know exactly the kind of woman Ruth McQueen really is."

Harriet rolled her eyes. "My dear, I already know. Come into the kitchen—I'll make coffee. And I've made a lovely

chocolate-truffle tart. You can take it with you if you like.
You've lost weight since I last saw you.''

"That was only four days ago, Harriet.''

"Lose any more, and Kyall will have to shake the sheets
to find you.

"Now, what's happened?'' Harriet asked when the coffee was perked and they were seated at the kitchen table.

For perhaps the hundredth time that day, Sarah thought
she might cry, but her training held her in good stead. "I
warn you, this will amaze and shock you.''

"You were pregnant when Ruth McQueen raced you off
all those years ago,'' Harriet suggested briskly.

"It would help if you waited until the end.'' Sarah gave
her a wry glance.

"Sorry, my dear. I was just trying to get the ball rolling.''

"It turns out you're right, anyway.'' Sarah shrugged. "I
was pregnant. I've never told you or anyone—I just
couldn't speak about it—but Ruth told me the morning after the delivery that my baby had died.''

"Oh, my dearest girl!'' Harriet reached out and grasped
Sarah's hand in a rare display of emotion. "Forgive me,
but I thought Ruth had probably forced you to have an
abortion.''

"She tried.'' Sarah's voice thinned. "She tried hard—
you know Ruth—but I wanted my baby. All these years
I've been crippled by a sense of loss and grief. It seems to
have impinged on everything I've done. It kept me alien-
ated from Kyall when I love him with all my heart.''

"This is awful!'' Harriet murmured. "All these years
you've had to live with the pain. And your poor mother!''

"I think it was all too much for her,'' Sarah said. "My
mother was a stranger to deception, but it was forced on

her. Yesterday I was called out to a terrible accident on Ngarara Station…''

"Yes, Morris told me."

"When are you and Morris moving in together, by the way?" Sarah asked flippantly.

"Sarah, I'm surprised at you." Harriet's eyes widened. "Actually, I'm holding out for marriage. Anyway, no more interruptions."

Sarah nodded. "There was a young girl staying at the homestead for the school holidays. She's a friend of Clemmie Hungerford, the daughter of the house. Fifteen, blond, brown-eyed, dimple in her chin. Me at fifteen."

Harriet let out a cry, jumped up from the table, picked up what looked like a birthday card and began fanning herself with great ferocity. "You can't mean you think she's your child?"

"I'm sure of it, Harriet," Sarah said very quietly. "The shock was profound. I'm not over it. I've been functioning in a trance. As it was, I went into a dead faint. It was worse for Kyall, because he never even knew I was pregnant. Ruth persuaded Mum and me that we'd ruin his life. Even Mum seemed to acknowledge this. She was so frightened of Ruth."

"With good reason." Harriet shuddered. "Ruth's the scariest woman in the country. Are you trying to tell me Ruth had the baby adopted without your knowledge or permission? Of course she did," Harriet said, answering her own question. "She told you your baby was dead. My God, how wicked!"

"Oh, yes, it was wicked," Sarah said. "Enormously wicked. There was a woman in the room next to me at the maternity hospital. Probably about ten years older. Her name was Stella. I've always remembered that. Stella is the name of the woman my daughter calls Mother. It wasn't *my* baby who died.'' The tears began to stream down her face.

"Sarah, you must be feeling unreal!'' Harriet jumped up again to find a box of tissues, her own eyes glistening. "Here. Blow your nose. I'll take a couple of tissues, as well. I've often said I'd put nothing past Ruth McQueen, but this beats anything I could think of. What a response from a grandmother! Kyall must've been horrified.''

Sarah nodded, struggling for control. "It's been such an emotional day. A day like no other. Life is never stationary, is it?'' She sighed. "So much upset and suffering all because of one woman. Kyall told his grandmother to go, to pack up and leave. She's rich. At least she can go anywhere she pleases.''

"Oh, I love the sound of that!'' Harriet gave a hard laugh of irony. "And won't we miss her! You're serious?''

"Kyall was deadly serious. He said he can't and won't live with what she'd done.''

"And the child?''

"She thinks I must be a relative. She's so beautiful, Harriet.'' Sarah's voice broke again. "So beautiful and so sweet. A tender, sensitive girl.''

"She would be if she's your daughter,'' Harriet sniffed. "This is what I call a heart-wrenching story. But it's not over, is it, Sarah? What are you going to do about the…other parents? It sounds as though your daughter's being loved and well cared for.''

"She is, and I'm deeply grateful for that. But she's *our* daughter, Harriet. We've lost fifteen years of her life. We can't just say hello and goodbye. We want our child. We don't want to hurt the Hazeltons—that's their name—but it's inevitable. Because of the way Ruth manipulated things, they'll have a hard time believing the babies were switched. They may fight us, but I'm as certain as I can be of anything that the girl I saw today is my daughter. We have to talk to the Hazeltons. Try to work out some sort of arrangement. It would be too cruel to snatch Fiona away. But we want our child.''

A TERRIBLE APPREHENSION gripped Stella Hazelton. She listened to her daughter's excited voice at the other end of the phone.

"I'm the image of her, Mum! She's the image of me. It's absolutely incredible. Clemmie said she couldn't believe her eyes. We must be cousins or something. You never told me."

There was so much she had never told. Stella put down the phone blindly. Dr. Sarah Dempsey. Fiona thought she was about twenty-seven or -eight. Apparently Dr. Sarah was head of a bush hospital. At Koomera Crossing.

Stella was now so upset she was literally shaking. All these years later, wonderful, fulfilling years, and she still remembered. A special young girl with flowing blond hair. She remembered it spread out on the pillow as golden as the sun's rays. The purity of the profile. The shallow dimple in her chin. The screams of agony when she was told her baby had died.

An immense sadness came over Stella. It was all over. Her heart almost stopped in anguish. She had never been able to conceive another child. Her own sickly baby had died probably within twelve hours of delivery. Somehow there'd been a mix-up. She'd been sent home with the wrong baby. She recalled reading about a case like that. It had disturbed her. DNA testing had proved the child in dispute had been given to the wrong family. The court ruled in favor of the biological mother. Why wouldn't it?

I have two options, Stella thought. *I continue to live this lie or I go to my husband with what I believe to be the truth. It will kill him. Take the life from him.* They both adored their Fiona, their Noni. Only, she wasn't theirs.

Her real mother had been destined to find her.

Stella didn't know how long she sat there staring into space. *Nothing will ever be the same again!* She whispered the prophetic words aloud.

"TELL ME this isn't true!" Enid Reardon burst in on her mother, her face blotched with tears, her eyes glittering with rage. "Look at me, Mother! Do you know I could kill you for what you've done?"

Ruth's laugh was uncaring, slightly mad. "Wouldn't you have done the same if you'd had the guts?"

Enid flew for her, mindless of her mother's physical frailty and advanced years. "You did this to my son. You did this to Sarah. You did this to Max and me." She raised her hand as if to strike her mother, standing there so brazenly, the very image of contempt, and knowing she couldn't hit her. "How in God's name did you do it?" she asked, dropping her hand. "You switched the babies. One little one died. Not Sarah's. You took the chance, but you had to have someone inside the hospital to help you. That woman, that Nurse Fairweather. She was the one, wasn't she. Your coconspirator. No wonder she went insane."

"Do shut up, Enid. Your voice is as shrill as a cockatoo's," Ruth admonished. "I did what I thought was right at the time. I saved your precious boy. He was sixteen, remember, and that conniving little bitch was out to get him. You were very much against her back then."

"I can't believe this!" Enid stumbled into an armchair, face blanched, mouth quivering. "For you to have done this to your own flesh and blood. This was my grandchild, Mother! Your great-grandchild. You gave her away. You did that. You gave away Kyall's baby. You know he'll never forgive you.''

"He'll get over it," Ruth said dismissively.

"I'm sorry, Mother. You've lost him forever. He won't get over it. Neither will I. He told you to leave this house."

"That's fine. I'm packing a few things. I'll take a long trip while he gets over his shock."

"Have you no conscience, Mother?" Enid stared up at the woman who had ruled her life.

Ruth gave her silky, shivery laugh. "I'm not a great believer in the afterlife. All we have is the here and now. I've always had to act because you and your brother—"

"Poor Stewart!" Enid heaved a great sigh. Losing her brother was something that should never have happened.

"—were too gutless. I had to run everyone's life. I had to run this historic station. I had to keep it for Kyall."

Enid shook her head. "If, despite your beliefs, there *is* an afterlife, Mother, you'll go straight to hell. Such power you've possessed and you've used it in all the wrong ways."

"Do stop, Enid. Your sanctimonious manner tires me. You knew where the door was. Just like Stewart, who got too big for his boots. You and your husband could've left at any time."

"That's another lie," Enid erupted. "You've always gone on about how you've run this station. Well, Max and I have been an integral part of it. You've never given us any credit. You've never loved me. Or poor Stewart. The only two people in the world as far as you're concerned are you and Kyall. Yet you did this monstrous thing to him."

"I did not mean to hurt him." Ruth's voice was clear and steady.

"You took hurt to its absolute limits. *No one* can do that

and get away with it. And what about that poor demented woman, Molly Fairweather? I suppose you didn't mean to hurt her, either. How did the taipan get into the house? Did you pay Vernon Plummer to plant it there? He'd do anything for a price.''

A ripple of fear brushed Ruth's heart at the mention of Plummer's name. ''Enid, I don't know what you're talking about.''

''Kyall will get it out of him,'' Enid assured her. ''He's probably asking him questions right now.''

Ruth's heart began to race. ''What on earth for?''

''Well done, Mother.'' Enid clapped her hands. ''You're a talented actress, aren't you?'' She suddenly frowned. ''It was a bit strange, too, Joe dying the very night he stayed in this house.''

''You're actually accusing me of something, Enid?'' Ruth's eyes smoldered. ''You always were a fool.''

''No, Mother. I've allowed myself to be blinded to the truth. Now my eyes are open. You've sold your soul to the devil, haven't you. You've sinned against us all. I think you planned everything that's happened, every bad thing. You could even go to jail. Think of it! Mrs. Ruth McQueen locked in a cell! And you're the one who goes on and on about family! Dear heaven! What do you have against Sarah, anyway? She's a beautiful, distinguished woman who—''

''In plain words, my dear Enid, I hate her.''

Enid closed her eyes at the profundity of the venom. She rose, speaking quietly but firmly. ''I'll ask Mrs. McDermott to help you pack your things. Don't come down to dinner. Or breakfast. They can be sent up. Max is making arrangements for your flight out. He's booking you into a suite at the Wentworth in Sydney. You'll be out of here by noon tomorrow. I couldn't care less whether that suits you or not." Enid's voice rose as she pointed one shaking finger at Ruth. "I've been afraid of you all my life, Mother. That's all over. I'm far from perfect, but I've never done anything to be ashamed of. You have."

VERNON PLUMMER, shoved against a wall with all Kyall's might, confessed to his part in Nurse Fairweather's death. He confessed, too, to entering the Sinclair house in Sarah's absence, doing things that were meant to scare her. He hadn't wanted to do any of it, he swore. He respected and admired Dr. Sarah. She'd saved his daughter-in-law's life. He wasn't ever going to do anything for Mrs. McQueen again.

"She owned us, you understand. The thing with the snake was meant to scare Nurse Fairweather off, not—"

"Damn you!" Kyall cried. "You son of a bitch!"

"I knew it was wrong all along, but I swear I've never deliberately harmed anyone in my life. Your grandmother threatened me—said my whole family would be out of a job and without a home."

Kyall let go of the man, watching him collapse to the ground. "I told Dr. Sarah I was her friend. I meant it."

"You wouldn't have tampered with the brakes on her car if you'd been asked?" Kyall looked down at Plummer with contempt.

"My God, no! Kyall, I used to pray your grandmother would leave me alone."

"She will from now on," Kyall told him grimly. "Get up and get back to work. I might want to speak to you further."

HER HEART WAS ROARING in her chest, but Ruth kept on walking.

"Damn you, Sarah Dempsey," she cried to the wild bush.

She thought she saw a flash through the trees. Long hair, white face, white figure. But it was a trick of the darkness. She was afraid of no ghosts. She was afraid of only one man. Her grandson, Kyall.

"Damn you, Plummer!" she cried again, stumbling but walking on doggedly. The leaves of the ghost gums were moving in the breeze. The moon had gone under a cloud. A night bird screeched so loudly the noise went right through her pounding skull. She'd left the homestead way behind. She was heading for the lagoon. The so-called experts said drowning was euphoric. Not that she'd ever trusted experts. She could think of nothing now but oblivion. Of disappearing without a trace like that other poor creature, Fiona, the first McQueen bride.

The girl's name was Fiona, she'd been told. How very, very odd.

And now she thought the first Fiona might be shadowing her. That white figure seemed to be everywhere she looked.

"Go to hell!" she yelled, then started to laugh until her body shook uncontrollably. It was the mist off the swamp. That was all....

The moon sailed out from beneath the clouds and she saw the glitter of the water. She moved toward it without hesitation. "All right, try and find me," she dared her family. "My own daughter to talk about jail. Me! There'd be no bars to hold me."

The long scratches on her arms and legs were bleeding, but she paid them no mind. When she was young she could walk for miles and miles. When she was young she could do anything. She was beautiful with long, jet-black hair. She thought of Ewan, her husband, who couldn't get enough of her body. How disgusted he would be with her. His parting words to her had been, "Love you, Ruthie. See you soon."

I had to do it, Ewan, she mumbled. Her poor lifeless Ewan who went and left her.

She'd been so young and a widow. All alone. Full of unsatisfied passions.

A boulder rose up in front of her. She tripped, tried to find her balance, fell cursing. The boulder loomed over her like a headstone. She lay there for a moment to rest before she moved on once more toward the water.

Her heart was burning in her chest. She forced herself up, tasting blood in her mouth. She must have bitten her tongue. Death held no terror for her. There was nothing to live for anymore. Sarah Dempsey and her child had won. The thing she could not accept had happened. She got clear of the boulders, one of them taller than her, walking, stumbling, toward the silent, shining waters that could easily trap a body.

Ruth!

She wheeled and sent a panicked glance into the trees. At something. Someone. She'd heard her name clearly. The thing, the illusion that had been following her, seemed to float out of the top branches.

For the first time in her life, Ruth knew pure terror. All her strength withered away. Excruciating pain rose into her neck.

"Get away from me!" she screamed, flailing her arms. But the white haze kept coming. "Get!" Ruth McQueen cried. "I'm not afraid of you. Or anyone."

The iron brace around her heart tightened by notches. The white haze seemed to grow brighter and brighter. It dazzled her eyes. A trick of the moonlight? She ground her teeth against the pain that now gripped her back like steely fingers.

How it hurt!

Oddly, she began to have flashes of her childhood in a

place more than a thousand miles away. Her mother and father. Both dead. Then an image of her dead son, Stewart. Ewan, exactly as he was the day she'd met him—the same day she'd decided she was going to be Mrs. Ewan McQueen. She'd wanted Ewan, and all that marriage to Ewan brought with it. An historic station. A magnificent homestead. Wealth and position. A grand pioneering family.

Lastly, Kyall, who would not forgive her for her sins.

"How can I live with that? I will die."

Ruth gave a final shuddering cry, then slowly folded backward onto the sand, coming to rest in a small inert bundle.

After that, nothing. Nothing save the whisperings of the trees and the scuttling of numerous small nocturnal desert creatures that lay concealed in their burrows during the heat of the day.

The lagoon was a setting as old as the world, richly colorful under the sun, by night a study in shades of black and charcoal, darkest purple and gleaming silver. From time to time the primitive landscape was illuminated by the bright rays of the moon as it sailed from behind the night's cloud cover. It was wondrously white, passing over the body of the woman who stared up at it blindly.

CHAPTER SIXTEEN

September (four months later)
Wunnamurra Station

SARAH FELT as though her heart could not contain all the happiness that was in her. It blazed through her veins and sharpened all her senses; everyone who looked at her thought she vibrated with inner light. Ruth McQueen's name had been swept clean the moment she was laid to rest, her casket decked with masses of lilies that even in the cooler weather had wilted quickly. The veil of tension and countless other desperate emotions that for so long had hung over the family had lifted. It was like a liberation after long years of war. Now it almost seemed that there was nothing to mark Ruth McQueen's long tenure except her handsome white marble tombstone in the family cemetery near the fork of the creek.

From the moment Sarah and Kyall had laid eyes on their daughter, the decision had been made to bring her back to her family. To her mother, her father and her doting grandparents, Enid and Max. They had flown more than a thousand miles to meet the Hazeltons, not unnaturally expecting massive resistance, heartbreaking scenes, protests, denials and refusals—but by the time they sat down together, all areas of conflict seemed to have dissipated. All that was left was a deeply sad acceptance. It was obvious to Kyall and Sarah that Stella and her husband had been over and over the dilemma that had invaded their home and their marriage. Although it was never said, Sarah had the intuitive feeling that Stella Hazelton had long suspected Fiona was not her biological child. Both Hazeltons, in fact, had gasped when they laid eyes on Sarah. The resemblance between her and ''their'' daughter was too remarkable to be explained away.

Afterward both women sat quietly, the tears rolling down their cheeks.

''Fiona will always be part of your family, Stella.'' Sarah sought to comfort her, fully conscious of the older woman's pain and mental stress. Both women had achieved an intense two-way connection. ''You'll see her often. I'm so sorry, Stella, but you realize that Kyall and I want our daughter.''

''God willed it,'' Stella heard herself say, never doubting it for a minute. She knew in her heart that she had no real right to hold on to the child who had so graced their lives.

Afterward, when Fiona came home from school, her eyes brilliant with excitement because she'd been told Sarah and Kyall would be visiting, Sarah and her ''mother'' sat with her, telling her all the things she didn't know. It had taken quite a while. Fiona had been alarmed and overwhelmed by their disclosures, looking from one to the other as though she couldn't absorb such stunning revelations all at once.

Several times she put out her hand to Stella for support. Stella grasped it and carried it to her mouth. But Fiona listened until finally both women ceased talking.

''So you're my mother?'' Fiona turned to Sarah, obviously shaken but unafraid.

''The mother who loves you.'' Sarah reached to take Fiona's hand. ''The mother who loved you from the minute she gave birth to you. You would've come home with me, Fiona, except for a terrible stroke of fate.''

"You're so young!" Fiona shyly touched the beautiful face in front of her. "You could be my sister."

"I'm your mother, I promise." Sarah tried to smile. "Your father and I don't wish to take you away immediately from the people who've been so good to you, but we want you to come home."

"And what if I won't go?" Fiona was trying to hold back a torrent of tears.

"We're not going to force you to do anything, Fiona," Sarah said in a gentle voice. "I can only say we desperately want our daughter with us. Please try to understand that we've missed nearly all your childhood."

"Mum?" Fiona turned to Stella for help.

"I want what's best for you, sweetheart. Dad and I will always love you." Already Stella saw her beautiful girl slipping away.

"So all those people were right." Fiona suddenly remembered things she'd pushed to the back of her mind. "Even Aunty Debby calls me a changeling."

Stella suddenly caved in, as if she'd taken a knife through the chest. "Oh, God!" she cried. "Of course it worried me. It always worried me."

Fiona picked up on that right away. "Did you know, Mum?" she asked anxiously.

There was a note of accusation in the girl's tone, causing Sarah to intervene swiftly. "No, Stella didn't know, Fiona. How could she?" Sarah laid a firm but tender hand on the girl's shoulder. "This is a tumultuous time for us all."

"Incredibly painful!" Stella moaned, while Fiona put an arm around her.

"I'm afraid about all this, Mum. I feel like my head is floating. Yet I know inside—" Fiona touched a hand to her heart ''—that Sarah gave birth to me. I was drawn to her the instant I saw her. I recognized that we were…blood. Not merely look-alikes. I thought Mr. McQueen was marvelous, too. And he's my father! He wants me to live with him.''

''If you want to go,'' Sarah said in a soft voice. ''We know how much you'll miss being here, but the last thing any of us want is to upset you. You can visit whenever you like. We're not going to lose touch. Stella and Alan can come to us, too. With the grace of God, we can all make this transition smoothly.''

''Am I supposed to make the decision now?'' Fiona asked fearfully, her slender throat swelling with emotion.

''No, Fiona.'' Sarah longed to take her daughter in her arms. ''That wouldn't be fair to you. We wanted you to listen to our story. Think about it. Make your decision then. Your father and I can't pretend we don't want you as soon as possible. You have grandparents, too. Kyall's mother and father. My own parents are dead. I've been very much alone in the world.''

''But you have…Kyall?'' Fiona blushed at the use of the Christian name.

''Kyall and I were parted for a long time, Fiona,'' Sarah explained. ''Thinking you, my own little baby, had died, changed my life drastically. I've mourned you your entire lifetime. My grief almost ended a wonderful friendship. Kyall and I were inseparable all through our childhood.'' Sarah couldn't help it. She smoothed back her child's beautiful hair with gentle, loving fingers.

Fiona stared into Sarah's eyes as if searching for her soul. ''I'm so sorry,'' she whispered, allowing Sarah to continue stroking her hair. ''It must have been terrible for you.''

"Seeing you so beautiful, so alive, has changed everything," Sarah said in a low voice, thinking she'd been given heaven in exchange for purgatory. "I can almost forget the pain, just as a woman forgets the pain of childbirth when her baby arrives. Losing you set me on the path to becoming a doctor."

"You must be clever!" Fiona managed a tremulous smile. "I'm doing well at school, too. Aren't I, Mum?" she asked Stella, who sat there the very picture of resignation.

"Top of the class," Stella tried to smile back, her eyes red-rimmed.

"Mum's been the best mum in the world!" Fiona proclaimed loyally. "She's done everything for me."

"I know, and I couldn't be more grateful," Sarah said. "Stella and I have opened our hearts to each other. We're going to become good friends."

"Oh, I'd like that!" said Fiona, then without apparent thought, laid her head on Sarah's breast.

It was almost as if she remembered.

THAT SAME NIGHT Sarah and Kyall lay naked in each other's arms, their bodies trembling, breathless in the aftermath of lovemaking so intense, so passionate, so charged, Sarah could recall vividly that night under the brilliantly blossoming desert stars when their daughter had been conceived. They had achieved perfection in their adult sex life, but on this night there was a return to the heart-stopping "unknown," when two lovers first come together. One half of their lovemaking was given over to the past, with its unearthly quality; the other brought into play the fullness of maturity as neither held back from expressing their desires.

Afterward, they didn't withdraw from each other but kissed tenderly, whispering endearments.

She was his. He was hers. And they'd both finally found their daughter.

ON THIS DAY OF DAYS, her wedding day, Sarah stood for a moment staring into the tall pier mirror. She was quite alone. Enid, who'd gained a new lease on life, had retired flushed and excited, telling Sarah she looked "as radiant as an angel!"

Sarah wasn't wearing the traditional bridal regalia—her maid of honor had just turned sixteen—but her dress was exquisite. The palest shade of lustrous gold, reaching almost to her ankles, a lovely combination of silk chiffon, ribbons and lace with the shimmer of tiny sequins and crystals for decoration. On her feet she wore beautiful high-heeled gold sandals. On her head, atop her flowing hair, because that was the way Kyall liked it, a simple garland of yellow and cream roses to match the small bouquet she was to hold. Suspended around her throat from a golden chain was Kyall's gift to her, a diamond heart like a sunburst surmounted by a diamond lover's knot.

I have never, but never, looked like this before, Sarah thought, studying her image. It was perfectly true. A bride did look wonderful on her wedding day.

Sarah turned as she heard a knock at the door. "Come in, it's open."

As she hoped, it was Fiona, enchanting in a beautiful cream dress, silk chiffon, like Sarah's, with a perfect floating skirt. Her pre-Raphaelite hair was caught to one side by two lovely fragrant cream roses. Sarah could smell their perfume from across the room.

"Oh, Sarah, how heavenly you look!" she declared rapturously. "I've never seen anyone more beautiful."

"Well, I have," Sarah said, thinking she'd never get over the miracle of her daughter. "I'm looking at her right now."

Fiona smiled but shook her head. "I'm so happy I feel like I'm dreaming. I wish Stella and Alan could've come."

"They thought it was our day, darling. There'll be plenty of other times."

"Why do I feel so different?" Fiona asked in some wonderment, coming to stand beside Sarah. "I thought I'd have such a hard time adjusting to my new life, but I feel like I've always known this place. Isn't that strange?" She slipped her arm around Sarah's waist, smiling in pleasure at their reflections. "I even feel guilty about enjoying myself when I'm not with Stella and Alan anymore. I miss them, of course I miss them, I love them so much, but—"

"You've found your true home, Fiona. Your real parents. And the grandparents you've never known. No need to feel guilty. Stella and Alan will always be in your life. That's the way your father and I want it, my rose."

Fiona beamed at her. "Oh, say that again!" she begged. "It sounds lovely. My rose."

"You *are* like a flower." Sarah was savoring all the maternal love in her heart. "I'd already named you before you were born. Rosalind, after my grandmother. She was the warmest, kindest person. My own mother, her daughter, was a lot like that. I wish both of them had lived to see you."

"They'd recognize me, wouldn't they?" Fiona asked quietly.

"Yes," Sarah whispered, knowing she couldn't surrender to tears.

"Mother," Fiona said, trying out the word on her tongue. Compulsively she took Sarah's hand. "I'd better start calling you that, I guess.'' Her great velvety eyes sought Sarah's.

Sarah bent and kissed her. ''There's no word that would sound sweeter to my ears.''

EPILOGUE

THE WEDDING WAS at three o'clock in the homestead's beautiful old ballroom, which had been turned into a splendid chapel. Masses and masses of flowers had been flown in. A fantasy of ivory-white orchids, luscious peonies as exquisite as any the Chinese emperors of old had exchanged for dowries, magnificent cream delphiniums, double-cream lisianthus, glorious perfumed pink, white and cream roses, frosted lilies all intermingled with the flowing branches of white-flowering shrubs.

It was all too wonderful, swelling the heart and bringing tears to the eyes at the same time, Harriet thought. She gazed about her with the greatest satisfaction. She might have orchestrated all this, so proud did she feel. Her dear Sarah and Kyall were to be married at last in the presence of the extended McQueen family and the happy couple's many friends. Guests had traveled from all over, she'd been told. They filled the huge room to capacity. Seated in a finely wrought chair, decorated lavishly with cream and gold ribbons, Harriet smiled to herself. What she'd hoped and prayed for was about to happen. She turned to the well-dressed gentleman seated beside her, gently tapping his knee.

"This was destined, you know, Morris."

"I believe it." Morris Hughes smiled back at her with great serenity. Kyall wasn't the only one to have his heart conquered, he thought.

The stately music began. The bridesmaids, four in all, began to move up the carpeted aisle between the long rows of decorated gold chairs. Lovely girls! Harriet gazed at them with pleasure. They all wore cream, ankle-length chiffon dresses, but each dress featured a different design in seed pearls, beads and sequins. Lovely as the bridesmaids were, though, Fiona eclipsed them. She was beyond any question Sarah's child. Harriet knew a momentary sadness as she looked at her. The image of her mother. She'd have recognized Fiona anywhere in the world. The girl was radiant, perfectly at home in Wunnamurra's ballroom. Fiona, the miracle child. After the town's initial shock had subsided, Fiona had been accepted into everyone's heart. Why not? They'd known that face all along.

There was a sudden hush as the bride moved gracefully down the aisle on the arm of her soon-to-be father-in-law. Max had never looked better, Harriet thought. But Sarah stole everyone's breath away. She dazzled as an angel might dazzle, casting her smile all around her as if to say, "This is heaven!"

I'll always remember this day. Harriet blinked tears from her eyes. The last thing she wanted was to smear her mascara.

At last Sarah reached her rightful place by her handsome groom's side. Harriet's tears began again as she witnessed the expression on Kyall's face. His soul shone out of those sapphire-blue eyes.

"God bless you both, always," Harriet whispered beneath her breath, catching Morris's answering, "Amen!"

The bishop, who had not risen to that eminence when he'd christened Kyall years ago, began the traditional words. It was at this point that Harriet slipped her slightly trembling hand into Morris's, charmed and gratified when he held it tenderly and firmly. *Oh, my goodness!* she thought. *I feel like a girl again.*

Solemn minutes passed and then the ceremony was over. Everyone turned to smile at the guests beside and behind them, their hearts opened to the grace that flowed in.

Under the benign eye of the bishop, Kyall took his wife in his arms to bestow upon her the ceremonial kiss.

"I love you, Sarah," he whispered as he sought her lovely mouth.

"I love you, my husband."

"Goodness, how perfectly beautiful!" exclaimed Harriet, her normally confident, self-assured voice surprisingly shaky. "Small wonder people believe love conquers all. It truly does!"

*   *   *   *   *

Turn the page for an excerpt from
Laura's story, in Margaret Way's

KOOMERA CROSSING
series.

Coming from Harlequin Romance
in October 2003.

CHAPTER ONE

THREE WEEKS LATER, when Sarah and Kyall were on their honeymoon in Thailand along with Fiona, the glossy magazine that had featured their wedding landed on the table of a certain doctor's waiting room.

"Why, isn't that Laura?" The voice of Anthea Dickson, head receptionist, voice rose sharply as she stared down at the open pages. "Surely it is."

"Where?" trilled Donna, her second-in-charge, coming to stand beside her unlikable but terribly efficient superior. Everyone knew dear old Anthea imagined herself in love with Dr. Morcombe, although Donna found him surprisingly off-putting for all his cleverness and charm. "All I can see is that gorgeous guy. You don't see guys like that except in the movies. I have to say the bride isn't bad, either." She smiled at her own understatement.

"Not *them*. There. There in the crowd behind them." Anthea stabbed the paper. "Beside the woman in the extraordinary headgear. What is it, a gold turban? Look carefully—that's dear little Laura. It's not all that clear because she has her head turned away, but I'd stake my life on it. Isn't she supposed to be staying with her mother in New Zealand? That was her story, anyway. I must show this to the doctor." Anthea yielded to the powerful impulse to make trouble. "He'll be *so* interested."

Three months earlier

SHE WAS FRIGHTENED. Laura knew all the signs. Emotional and physical exhaustion, trembling limbs, fluttery pulse, sick panic inside her. After Colin's attack on her the previous night, irrational and unprovoked, she knew she had to go somewhere he'd never find her. She had to reclaim herself, her body, her mind, her drastically fractured self-esteem. Reared by wonderful, loving parents, she found Colin's behavior entirely incomprehensible. Since their "dream" marriage almost a year before—how ironic!—reality was a far cry from the public image. Their marriage had become a nightmare. Her dream of happiness, security, children was shattered. Her brilliant young husband, a rising star in open-heart surgery, had turned out to be dangerously unstable.

Colin had taught her not to love him but to fear him. Because of his moods, his demands, his profound jealousies and insecurities, she'd lost most of her friends. She saw far less of everyone. He'd forbidden her to continue with her music. It was his role to "take care" of her. Clever, manipulative Colin. Psychotic Colin. Apparently it had been ordained from on high that he should occupy the central position in her life. He was the only one she'd ever need, ever want. After each terrifying outburst of rage, he insisted he loved her dearly.

"You'll never leave me, Laura. Never!"

Laura knew quite well that it was a warning. He was perfectly capable of uttering protestations of love when he thought nothing of flinging her up against the wall with one violent sweep of his arm. Until last night, he'd always taken great care never to damage her face. She had a sickening image of him standing over her gloating, as she huddled on the floor, her arms wrapped protectively around her body. Colin was a slim man but very fit, an inch under six feet. She was a light-limbed five-three, her body weight constantly dropping as she lost her appetite. She'd learned from her mother how to be a good cook, a good hostess, a good homemaker, but Colin had never been satisfied with her. There was no way she could please him. Not even in bed, although sex seemed very important to him.

"Just as well you're beautiful, Laura, because you're bloody frigid in bed. You don't know the first thing about pleasing a man."

She was frigid now. With him. Mentally and emotionally removing herself from the act. Was this lovemaking or was it rape? She felt demeaned and defiled—humiliated beyond all telling.

They'd met by chance. Overnight the whole tenor of her quiet, studious life had changed. He'd bombarded her with attention, bouquets of roses, chocolates, fine wine, books he wanted her to read—although he never read them himself. He was so charming, so attentive, and their romance flowered. She realized now that it had simply filled the deep void left by the premature death of her father in an accident when she was seventeen.

So the stage was set. She'd been studying classical piano. Very motivated, self-disciplined, a born musician. Her father's death had been a tremendous blow to her and to her mother, grief striking deep into their souls. Laura was an only child, living a privileged, near-idyllic life. She'd grown up overnight.

Strangely her mother adjusted to her new life and their loss much more quickly than Laura did. Her mother confided that she couldn't face life being alone. She'd had one happy marriage, a wonderful partner. She desired another.

Three years after her father died, her mother found a kind, caring man, a fellow guest at a wedding. Six months later, she married her sheep farmer and went to settle with

Craig in the South Island of New Zealand, a beautiful part of the world.

Laura stayed behind, though they both wanted her to join them. She'd already graduated from the conservatory and started on her doctorate of music at the university. She took private pupils, as well, for experience and to supplement her income, although her highly successful businessman father had left her and her mother well provided for.

The first time she'd met Colin was at a concert given by a visiting piano virtuoso. A gifted woman, though Colin had made much of the fact that no woman pianist could ever hope to match a man. In his opinion. As if he'd know. He'd have done better to stick to surgery, where he could play God. Colin, the dyed-in-the-wool chauvinist. She should've been warned then. As chance would have it, or malign fate, they each attended the concert on their own. During the intermission, Colin had shifted in his seat to ask her a question, smiling with open pleasure and admiration into her eyes. He suggested a glass of champagne in the foyer. It was the first time ever she'd allowed herself to be "picked up," as she thought of it, but he seemed eminently respectable, especially when he told her he was a doctor from a well-known medical family. The Morcombes. She'd heard of them.

After the performance, they went on to have coffee at a popular nightspot. There she'd opened up as she'd never done before. She was lonely; that was why. She recognized it all now. She'd been in a very vulnerable situation, badly missing her mother and her father. Colin seemed so sympathetic. Also, he loved music, which she intended to make her profession.

She soon learned that Colin had only pretended to love music. In actual fact, he was tone-deaf. A friend had give him the ticket. At a rare loose end, he'd decided to go. The man of culture, after all, was the image he liked to cultivate.

Their meeting was destiny, he'd told her. She was there waiting for him. He'd fallen in love with her on sight.

"Your long, gleaming, dark hair, your green eyes, your gentle haunting beauty."

She hadn't been ready for a commitment, not just then, but Colin had swept her off her feet. He was already thirty-two, which he perceived as exactly the right age for a man to marry. She was an innocent, nearly ten years his junior. Colin accomplished an engagement within three months. His parents—she tried to hide from herself the fact that she couldn't begin to like them—seemed to realize she was the sort of young woman their son wanted.

Someone he could dominate.

Her mother and new stepfather had journeyed from New Zealand to meet Colin a couple of weeks before the wedding. Her mother had been genuinely delighted with her prospective son-in-law. Colin had gone all out to be charming. Craig hadn't been quite so forthcoming, simply saying it was obvious that Colin was very much in love with his lovely, gifted fiancée.

The wedding had been a big society event. The Morcombes were establishment, very pleased that their adored but scarcely humble Colin had finally found himself a young woman he wished to marry.

The abuse started on their honeymoon, shocking Laura terribly. She mustn't flirt with every man she met, he told her coldly. She mustn't look up at them through her eyelashes. She mustn't smile and tilt her head so. She was being deliberately provocative and he wouldn't have it.

"You're my wife. Mine. I won't put up with coy glances elsewhere."

An hour later, he was cordial, composed, even loving,

wanting to take her to bed. He acted as though nothing disturbing had happened. It was a man's right to chastise his wife. On their honeymoon the marriage had taken a giant leap backward. She didn't know where to turn.

She felt trapped. She *was* trapped.

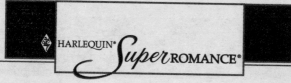

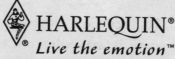

If you enjoyed what you just read,
then we've got an offer you can't resist!

Take 2 bestselling love stories FREE!

Plus get a FREE surprise gift!

Clip this page and mail it to Harlequin Reader Service®

IN U.S.A.	**IN CANADA**
3010 Walden Ave.	P.O. Box 609
P.O. Box 1867	Fort Erie, Ontario
Buffalo, N.Y. 14240-1867	L2A 5X3

YES! Please send me 2 free Harlequin Superromance® novels and my free surprise gift. After receiving them, if I don't wish to receive anymore, I can return the shipping statement marked cancel. If I don't cancel, I will receive 6 brand-new novels every month, before they're available in stores. In the U.S.A., bill me at the bargain price of $4.47 plus 25¢ shipping and handling per book and applicable sales tax, if any*. In Canada, bill me at the bargain price of $4.99 plus 25¢ shipping and handling per book and applicable taxes**. That's the complete price, and a savings of at least 10% off the cover prices—what a great deal! I understand that accepting the 2 free books and gift places me under no obligation ever to buy any books. I can always return a shipment and cancel at any time. Even if I never buy another book from Harlequin, the 2 free books and gift are mine to keep forever.

135 HDN DNT3
336 HDN DNT4

Name	(PLEASE PRINT)	
Address	Apt.#	
City	State/Prov.	Zip/Postal Code

* Terms and prices subject to change without notice. Sales tax applicable in N.Y.
** Canadian residents will be charged applicable provincial taxes and GST.
   All orders subject to approval. Offer limited to one per household and not valid to
   current Harlequin Superromance® subscribers.
® is a registered trademark of Harlequin Enterprises Limited.

SUP02   ©1998 Harlequin Enterprises Limited